NO WAY OUT

NO WAY OUT

JEFFREY MILLER

NEW YORK   LOS ANGELES

Jacket design by Rafido
Jacket Copyright 2023 by Winding Road Stories
Interior book design by A Raven Design

ISBN#: 979-8-9871737-3-2 (pbk)
ISBN#: 979-8-9866043-7-4 (ebook)

Published by Winding Road Stories
www.windingroadstories.com

For Ken Celmer

ONE

On my third day in South Korea, I woke up in bed naked, next to a dead woman.

Someone banging out a headache on a metal door had jerked me awake from my alcohol-induced slumber. I cracked open my eyes and squinted in the bright sunlight slanting into the room. I wasn't in the bed back in my apartment. But the bigger problem was the woman whose bed I shared.

The woman, who was wearing a red negligee, had not moved, not even a murmur.

I propped myself up on an elbow and prepared to roll out of bed on the other side, but stopped when the room started spinning.

"Whoa. That's not good." I squeezed my eyes shut.

When I opened my eyes again, the spinning had stopped. Sitting on the edge of the bed, the room, actually a small apartment, slowly came into focus. One large room served as the dining room, living room, and bedroom. Off to the right was a tiny bathroom, and to the left was a small kitchenette densely populated with dirty pots, pans, and bottles. A dirty off-white refrigerator, the door embellished with what looked like restaurant menus attached to magnets, sagged on the filthy floor. Directly in front of the bed was a small television set and a portable cassette player on a black and red stand next to a vanity cluttered with makeup, cans of hairspray, bottles of perfume, and dried flower bouquets stuck in empty green and brown bottles. A polished black lacquered wardrobe with a mother-of-pearl inlaid design of two cranes in flight on the front completed the room's meager furnishings. A calendar on the wall covered with yellowed, water-stained beige wallpaper showed a photograph of a snowy, craggy mountain peak.

From where I was sitting, I could also see my jeans with one leg turned inside out, sweater, underwear, and socks scattered on the floor between the bed and the bathroom.

Snippets of last night's revelry and the reason for my being here slowly materialized. My new roommate had wanted to show me some of the city's nightlife. We had been drinking in a small bar until he wandered off. When he didn't come back, I went looking for him. Somehow I ended up in another hole-in-the-wall bar, drinking with the woman lying next to me. At least, that's who I thought this mystery woman was. I was pretty wasted when we left.

When we had gotten to wherever I was, she had put on some music and we sat on the bed together. She said that I looked like the TV character MacGyver. We had something to drink. Soju. Korean rice wine. That stuff knocked me for a loop on top of all the other booze I had. We started kissing, and after that—

The banging on the door got louder, more frequent. Whoever was doing it really wanted to get into the apartment, but the woman still hadn't stirred at all.

"Hey, wake up." I tried to work up some saliva in my mouth, but my mouth was not cooperating. I gave the woman a nudge with my elbow. "There's someone at the door."

She didn't move.

"Hey, did you hear me?"

I nudged her again.

As I leaned over her body, her wide, clouded eyes bulging out of their sockets stared back at me with a permanently molded look of agony. Her throat was swollen, and her flesh had turned reddish-purple from a massive bruise spreading around it. Mouth agape, her pink tongue lolled from the side of her mouth. Her body lay awry, her arms bent at an awkward angle, and her head tilted back. Her silk negligee was torn and ripped away in several places in an apparent struggle, exposing her breasts.

"Oh, my God!"

I recoiled off the bed and fell to the floor, trembling.

Did I do this? Could we have had a fight last night, and I—? My heart became louder than the knocking. My breathing, fast and shallow, sped up to keep pace with my heart. "Oh God," I said under my breath. "Oh God, oh God, oh God." It was turning into a mantra.

Wait a minute. Get a grip, Turner. You're having one terrible, fucked-up nightmare, and when you open your eyes, you're going to be back in your room, in your apartment. You had too much to drink last night. Here's what you're going to do. First, you're going to close your eyes and take a deep breath. Good. Then, slowly count to ten. When you reach ten, you're going to open your eyes. Got it?

I closed my eyes and took a deep breath. One, two, three…. When I got to ten, I slowly opened my eyes. The woman was still there. And she was still very dead.

Outside, a woman's shrill voice sent shivers down my spine. She yelled something in Korean, pummeling the door with both fists, wrenching the door knob. Panic punctured my heart. If she got inside and saw me with the dead woman in the bed, she would think that I had killed her, which, at this point, I couldn't deny with conviction.

I gathered my clothes on the floor and quickly dressed. While putting on my jeans, I stumbled and fell, banging my head on the edge of a table. Wincing from the pain, I gritted my teeth to keep from cursing and alerting the person outside of my presence.

In my haste to grab my leather jacket hanging from a wooden coat rack next to several other coats, I pulled the coat rack down, scattering coats across the floor. I froze. Whoever was outside must have heard that. I walked to the door, put my ear against it, and listened. Silence.

I picked up my jacket, cigarettes, lighter, and a pack of chewing gum, which had fallen out of my pockets, and put it on. What the fuck was I going to do? I took several deep breaths. The thoughts, I should get out of here and don't touch anything, competed ferociously with letting in whoever had been outside if they returned.

Staying here would have been the logical thing to do.

The right thing to do.

Leave. An inner voice commanded me. Get the fuck out of here now. Call for help somewhere else.

So, I decided to make a run for it.

I know it was cold and callous to leave the woman like that on the bed, but what could I do? Then I remembered her name. Joo-hee. I liked the sound of it when she told it to me. I smoothed down her negligee around her hips and crossed her arms over her chest. It was the least I could do.

"Sorry, Joo-hee."

Peering out the window through a crack in the curtains, I recognized the circular iron stairwell we climbed to her apartment on the second floor. Below was the courtyard and the gate we had entered last night. Most importantly, I couldn't see the woman who had been banging on the door or anyone else in the courtyard.

I opened the door slowly and eased outside. The bright sunlight momentarily blinded me as I stumbled down the steps. Somewhere in the house below, a door opened and slammed shut. Whoever it was cleared their throat and spat. An elderly Korean woman in baggy gray pants and a dark-colored blouse stood on the steps outside her apartment. She looked in my direction and sneered.

Halfway down the stairwell, I froze. A woman wearing a black miniskirt and leather jacket came up the steps. Could she have been the one banging on the door earlier? We both couldn't pass each other on the narrow stairwell. One of us would have to go back—and it wasn't going to be me. I put my head down and walked down three more steps, forcing the woman back down to the landing below. She reeked of cigarette smoke, liquor, and some sweet-smelling perfume.

In my haste to get out, I stepped on the black high heel adorning her left foot. She let out a yelp and shot me a dirty look.

"Ouch! Hey!"

I hurried toward the gate as the click-clack of the woman's high heels echoed across the courtyard. No sooner had I reached the gate than a blood-curdling scream came from inside the apartment.

TWO

FORTY HOURS EARLIER, AFTER I DISEMBARKED FROM THE Northwest Airlines 747 at Kimpo Airport in Seoul, my biggest worry was clean underwear.

My luggage was somewhere between Seoul and Chicago, where I had left the day before. I had a bad feeling when I checked in at the Northwest counter and the luggage conveyor belt wasn't working. Equally troubling was watching one of the ground staff lugging my suitcases to a door I presumed led to the baggage handling area downstairs. That bad feeling came full circle as I stood at the Seoul airport, watching the empty baggage carousel spin around and around, waiting for my bags to appear. At least I wasn't alone. Three soldiers on their way to military bases in Korea who were on the same flight didn't have their luggage.

I had come to Seoul to teach English at one of the top language institutes in the city. Three months earlier, not happy with my current job, and at the suggestion of a college buddy, I applied for a teaching position with a company based out of Culver City, California, that operated English language school franchises worldwide. A few weeks later, a recruiter called and offered me a job at a language institute in Seoul in early December.

"I know it's right before Christmas and all, but you'll be so excited you won't feel homesick," the recruiter said.

It wasn't a hard sell: a one-year contract, airfare, furnished apartment. Two weeks paid vacation plus all Korean national holidays and medical insurance.

Eight weeks later, minus my luggage, the inauspicious start to my sojourn in the Land of the Morning Calm included an hour sorting out the paperwork with a ground staff member whose English was barely passable. By the time we finished, the arrivals area had cleared out except for a flustered, pudgy man with slicked-back hair holding a sign with my name on it.

"Hi, I'm Robert Turner," I said, holding out my hand.

"Doug Gilbert," the pudgy man replied. His hand was cold and clammy. "What happened?"

I recognized the name immediately. He was the Academic Director of the school. In early November, not long after I had been hired, he had written to send me some basic information about the school and living in Korea.

"I made it. My luggage didn't."

Gilbert sighed in exasperation. "Let's go. It's late, and we're all tired."

Standing behind him were three other teachers who had arrived that night on an earlier flight. By the looks on their faces, they didn't look too happy that I had kept them waiting. I gave them a slight nod and a "sorry about that" expression and slung my carry-on bag over my shoulder.

After spending the last twenty-four hours cooped up in a departure lounge and an overcrowded airplane, it felt refreshing to walk out into the cool night air. I stuck a Marlboro Light in the corner of my mouth and lit it with a disposable lighter. Taking a deep drag, I held the smoke for a moment, then blew it out in a long blue stream. A thirty-foot-high Korean woman, in a flowing pink and green dress, holding a drum that resembled an hourglass at her side, loomed magnificently on a billboard across the street from the airport parking lot welcoming visitors to Korea. I looked up at this towering, ravishing beauty and nodded my approval.

Several other billboards of similar size, emblazoned with Samsung, Lucky-Goldstar, and Hyundai logos, also welcomed arrivals.

Approaching the van that would take us to our new apartments, Gilbert handed each of us a yellow envelope containing three hundred thousand won—a little over three hundred bucks. Relocation money. Sweet. I hadn't even started teaching yet, and I already had money to burn.

It was about a thirty-minute drive to our apartments in the southeastern part of the city. Along the way, Gilbert pointed out several landmarks, including this unassuming square building with columns on all four sides and a dome on top, which reminded me of Old Chicago, an amusement park south of Chicago.

"That's the National Assembly," Gilbert said matter-of-factly. "It's like the Capitol in Washington, DC, but if you ask me, it looks like a hatbox. And up ahead, that's the 63 Building."

"63 Building?" one teacher asked.

"Daehan Insurance Building. It is supposed to have sixty-three floors, but it only has sixty. It was originally called the Daehan 60 building. Later, someone called it the 63 Building because they counted the three basement floors. Go figure, huh?"

As I looked out of the van to my left, a strong feeling of déjà vu suddenly overcame me. When I found out that I was going to Korea, the Korean National Tourism Office in Chicago was gracious enough to share all their literature on Korea. Though most of it had been for the Olympics, I got a pretty good idea of what awaited me in Seoul. On our left was the Han River, which bisected the city. Several bridges spanned the river, which reminded me of the Seine in Paris or the Danube in Budapest. Across the river, lights from towering blocks of apartment buildings reflected off its slow-moving dark waters. In the distance, a brightly lit tower rising from a small mountain seemed to stand guard over the city. This tower, called Seoul Tower, was the highest structure in the city.

The van rounded a curve and crossed a bridge. Out of the darkness on the right appeared the gigantic Olympic rings on the side of the Olympic Stadium. With its sweeping, delicately curved contours, the outline of the stadium resembled a large bowl or vase. Two years earlier, while I was slogging away at my dead-end job in Chicago, I watched most of NBC's coverage of the Seoul Olympics. Who would have thought I would end up here, in South Korea, of all places?

"We're here," Gilbert said, snapping me out of my reverie.

After passing the Olympic Stadium, the van turned down a tree-lined street with blocks of drab, nondescript five-story apartment buildings rising on both sides of the street. Fog weaved its way between the buildings and blanketed the neighborhood with wet gray swirls that clung like ghosts underneath the streetlights and in the headlights of passing cars. If I had been teleported to where I was now, I would have thought that I was on the east side of New York, not Seoul.

I was the last one taken to my apartment, directly across the street from several rows of much taller apartment buildings in the neighborhood. At least I didn't have to lug my suitcase up the four flights of stairs to my apartment.

"You've got a roommate, but I don't know where he is," Gilbert said, handing me the key. His tone suggested that he didn't think too highly of my roommate. "Your mentor, David Kendall, will stop by in the morning to show you around. See you on Monday."

The door slammed shut.

I did a quick tour of the five-room apartment and found my bedroom down a hallway on the right, where I stowed my carry-on bag. Judging from the décor, my roommate had been in Asia for a while. On one of the yellowed walls in the living room was the Korean national flag and a beer poster with a buxom Korean woman in a red bikini hoisting two beer mugs. Two rectangular silk paintings of mountains and pine trees hung from another wall. There was some mismatched furniture, a television, and a throw rug. It felt like my old college apartment, minus the bong and rolling papers.

I helped myself to a can of Coke in the refrigerator, hoping my new roommate wouldn't mind, and stood out on the balcony to smoke. Across the street, barely discernible in the fog, I could see endless rows of the same-looking buildings with huge, black numbers on their side. They reminded me of giant toasters. Yellowish lights shining from the windows of all these apartments cast an eerie pall over the neighborhood. The noir vibes felt perfect for this new adventure, like I was in a Cold War thriller.

I took a long drag off the cigarette and exhaled slowly. Filtering up from the sidewalk and street below, I heard snippets of conversations from residents returning home and the hum of traffic on the expressway just down the street.

I didn't feel like a stranger in a strange land, but I felt humbled just the same.

After finishing my cigarette, I went back to my room. I flopped down onto the bed, a lumpy, unforgiving mattress that smelled of old sweat. Thirty-six hours after leaving home and flying halfway around the world into the next day, I was out like a light as soon as my head rested on the pillow.

At some point during the night, a loud crash and a woman screaming startled me awake. I thought it was outside on the sidewalk below until I saw the band of light underneath my door.

"Look what you did," a man's drunken voice said down the hall from my room. "I'm not going to clean it up."

"Fuck you," the woman said with a thick, slurred voice.

"And that's the last one!"

I hoped the man's voice belonged to my roommate, but I was too tired to get up and find out. There was no need. The door flew open, and the light was turned on.

"Shit!" A short Korean woman in a black miniskirt and white go-go boots stood in the doorway, staring at me. "Sorry, wrong room."

A tall man with a sharp nose and shaggy blonde hair, wearing a black leather trench coat, came up behind her and moved her out of the way.

"Sorry, man. My lady friend here dropped a bottle of beer. Hope we didn't startle you or anything."

"Whatever," I said. "No problem."

"I'm Keith. You must be Robert."

I sat up in bed and nodded.

"Nice to meet you." Keith walked over to my bed and stuck out his hand. "And this is So-young."

"Yeah, nice to meet you," I said.

"You said no roommate," she said, crossing her arms over her chest.

"Oops. Busted," Keith said with a sheepish grin.

"Not funny," she said, glaring at him.

"He just got in tonight, okay?" Keith put an arm around the woman, but she backed away.

"Fuck you," she said, turning and walking into Keith's room across the hallway.

"What a firecracker, huh? I just met her tonight."

"That's nice," I said, yawning.

"Sorry I wasn't here when you arrived. You find everything, okay?"

I nodded again. "Yeah. Just a little bushed, you know?"

"I hear you. Anyway, welcome to Korea. I'll let you get back to sleep."

"Thanks."

"See you tomorrow."

Keith shut the door, and I closed my eyes. I heard music coming from his room, some Michael Bolton tune, followed by my roommate's girlfriend shouting in Korean, which, by the tone of her voice, didn't bode well for my roommate before I finally drifted off to sleep.

THREE

THE FOLLOWING DAY, MY MENTOR, A MIDDLE-AGED CANADIAN teacher, gave me the lay of the land, taking me around the neighborhood, showing me where to catch the subway, and visiting this mammoth shopping and entertainment complex, Lotte World, which had opened shortly after the Seoul Olympics.

We rode the subway downtown and walked around Insa-dong, a traditional market in the heart of the city. Tiny traditional shops selling scroll paintings, pottery, and antiques lined the main street through the center of the market. I felt I had stepped back in time, judging from the weatherworn stone and wood façades with cracked and faded wooden signs written in Chinese characters. The air was delightfully seasoned with exotic sandalwood, pine, and cinnamon incense fragrances wafting from shops selling Buddhist merchandise and the warm, sweet smells of roasted chestnuts and small cakes—in the shape of fish—frying on small grills.

I cut our whirlwind tour of the city short as jet lag started catching up. When I got back to my apartment later that afternoon, I thought I'd take a nap for an hour or two. Instead, four hours later, someone banging on the door to my room woke me. Before I could say anything, the door flew open, and my roommate stuck his head inside. He had a bottle of Budweiser in one hand and a cigarette in the other.

"Hey, Bro. You're not in for the evening, are you?"

"What? Oh, no. I just crashed." I sat up in bed and looked for my smokes. "What time is it?"

"It's almost eight."

"Shit."

"Jet lag is a bitch, huh?"

"You're telling me."

Keith took a hearty swig of his beer. "Hungry?"

"Yeah, I am."

"Come on, then. Let's grab a bite to eat. I know a good place."

After splashing water on my face, Keith and I caught a taxi outside our building. I thought we would get something to eat nearby; instead, a few minutes later, we were speeding along the Olympic Expressway toward the city's center. On my left was the Olympic Stadium, and on my right was the Han River.

"Where exactly are we going?" I said.

"It's not too far."

I kept my eye on Seoul Tower, the brightly lit tower I had seen last night as if it were some beacon guiding us to our destination, with red, blue, and yellow lights encircling it at the top, blinking in the clear night. One minute it was to our right; the next minute, it seemed right in front of us as the highway meandered along the river.

"Sorry, I couldn't have been a better roomie and showed you around town today," Keith said after a while. "Saturday is my day for privates."

"Privates?"

"Private English classes. I make just as much teaching private classes on a couple of Saturdays as I do all month at ELS."

"Is it legal?"

Keith laughed. "Everybody teaches them. There's this woman, Kim Young-ju, who sets teachers up with the classes. It's really sweet. You go to the student's apartments. They're just a few subway stops from school. She makes sure the parents pay on time, which, of course, they always do, and she gets her cut. Everybody's happy. If you'd like, I can hook you up with her."

"That would be amazing." The contract I signed last month stipulated around a million won a month, which came out to around twelve hundred dollars. Not too bad when you threw in the apartment and medical insurance. But a little extra money was always welcome.

"No prob," Keith said.

Soon, we were crossing the river, and the tower was directly above, staring down at us. The taxi traveled along an elevated highway for about a mile. Clustered below, along narrow streets choked with traffic, were nondescript brick and stone buildings of various sizes and heights. Red crosses appeared to float in the sky above several of these buildings.

"What's with all these red crosses?" I must have counted at least a dozen.

"Churches."

"You're kidding?"

"They're mostly storefront churches. There's practically one on every block. You'll see."

The driver drove down an off-ramp and turned down a busy, noisy street lined with brightly lit restaurants, clubs, and shops. Much of the signage was in English, advertising tailors, Korean antiques, souvenirs, and BBQ beef. Sidewalk vendors hawked socks, gloves, NFL and NBA stocking caps, cassette tapes, and kitschy Korean souvenirs under strands of lightbulbs swaying in the frosty night air. There were also a few reminders of home—a Wendy's, a Pizza Hut, and in the distance, the golden arches of McDonald's.

"Welcome to Itaewon," Keith said, paying the taxi driver. "Now, your real orientation begins."

We got out of the taxi and darted across the busy street, barely avoiding a taxi running a red light. Swirls of steam escaping from manhole covers and sewer grates cast a diaphanous veil over the street. Noxious car and bus fumes weighed down the air.

Overhead, the hum and buzz of garish pink, red, and blue neon signage in Korean and English shimmered and spangled like a carnival midway. Grimy, sooty, pink and yellow rectangular tiles covered the exteriors of most buildings, which made me think of the tiles in my grandparents' bathroom.

As we headed up a narrow side street, a medley of pungent aromas seasoned the air as we passed several wooden food carts on the side of the street. From a metal pan on one of these carts, a vendor bundled up in a frumpy brown wool coat ladled cylindrical rice cakes, about the size of a piece of chalk, bubbling in a thick red sauce, into paper cups. Wooden skewers, attached to brown fishcakes simmering in a pan of brown broth, stood at attention, waiting to be plucked free from the depths of the churning liquid. Several young Korean women, shivering in miniskirts and thin jackets, stood around the food cart, spearing the rice cakes with toothpicks and popping them into their dainty mouths, careful not to smear their perfectly applied red lipstick with the red sauce dripping from the cakes.

Further up the street, steam billowed from a stack of metal pans ladened with thick, puffy white dumplings at a food stall. Seated in front of the stall on plastic stools, customers slurped bowls of noodles or munched on deep-fried tempura veggies dipped in soy sauce. The owner, a short, frizzy-haired woman with ruddy cheeks, beckoned us to stop and eat, but Keith waved her off.

"Next time, ajumoni," Keith said, grinning.

"Aju—what?" I asked.

"Ajumoni. It means aunt, but it's used for addressing middle-aged women."

Another Korean word learned. I smiled at the ajumoni and nodded my head as we passed.

Roving packs of boisterous GIs weaved and shouldered their way up the same street. I caught snatches of barked raunchy conversations among some of these GIs about which clubs had the hottest women and their sexual prowess. It felt like I had stepped back in time to my Air Force days cruising J Street in Panama

City as a wide-eyed, bushy-tailed eighteen-year-old as yet uncorrupted by sexual debauchery.

At the end of the block, Keith stopped in front of a four-story building.

"We're here."

"Where?"

"The Twilight Zone." Keith pointed to a sign at the top of the building.

"That's an odd name for a bar."

"Wait until you get inside," Keith said, grinning.

We rode an elevator to the top floor and entered a large, dimly lit room where we encountered a haze of dense smoke and the odor of stale beer and cheap perfume. The room, which took up the entire top floor, was packed with American GIs and Korean women. I couldn't see any Korean males in the club other than the three bartenders scurrying back and forth behind the bar. Looking for a place to sit down, we weaved through a labyrinth of tables and cushioned chairs until we found a table in the middle of the room. Above the din, the thumping beat of Vanilla Ice's "Ice, Ice Baby" filled the room.

"What do you recommend?" I said.

"The kimchi fried rice here is pretty good," Keith said, getting the attention of a server moving through the crowd. "The burgers aren't bad, either. You have tried kimchi, haven't you?"

I thought about the side dish of kimchi I had with my lunch when my mentor showed me around our neighborhood. It wasn't as spicy as I thought it would be, but its pungent smell would take some getting used to. "What do you think? That I just got off the boat?"

Keith laughed. "Fair enough."

"Let's give that kimchi fried rice a whirl."

"You got it, Bro."

When the server arrived, Keith, speaking Korean, ordered kimchi fried rice and Jungle Juice for us.

"Jungle Juice? What the hell is that?" I asked.

"It's a popular drink here."

I nodded, shook a Marlboro from a pack I had in my shirt pocket, stuck it in my mouth, and looked around the room, which took up the top floor of the building. On two sides of the room, huge plate-glass windows looked out on the smaller buildings and the street below. Neon signage pulsing outside reflected off the glass in a swirling kaleidoscope of red, yellow, and pink.

"So, how did you end up in Korea?"

"I was knocking around in Southeast Asia on the old hippie backpacker trail, doing a little of this and a little of that, when I ran into this one dude on the island of Koh Samui who told me about teaching in South Korea. I had been working as a food and beverage manager at a hotel in Karachi, but I wanted a change of scenery. It was right after the Olympics, and everyone was talking about how South Korea was a happening place. So I sent off my résumé to a couple of language schools in Seoul, hopped on a plane, and the rest is history."

"Cool, man."

"What's your excuse?"

I blew a stream of smoke out of the side of my mouth. "Not as exotic as yours. I was working this dead-end job as a copyeditor for a medical supply company in Chicago, editing trade catalogs. Talk about putting my MA in English to good use. There are just so many ways you can describe rectal thermometers, bedpans, and catheters without sounding redundant. Do you know what I mean?"

Keith laughed.

"Either I found myself a new job, or I was going to lose my mind. And then, one day, out of the blue, one of my college buddies told me about teaching opportunities in South Korea. He had come over here for a year to teach, save a little money, and pay off his student loans. So I figured, what the hell, you know? What have I got to lose? And on top of that, my girlfriend and I had just broken off our engagement, so nothing was holding me back. I sent off my résumé to a recruiter, and the next thing I know, like you, I'm on a plane bound for Korea."

"Dig it."

"What's it like living here and all?" I said, taking a long draw from my cigarette.

"This place has been hopping since the Olympics. Koreans are letting down their hair after years of military dictatorships. Sure, there's still North Korea to contend with, but what the hell, if it were truly dangerous, do you think the two of us would be sitting here in the Twilight Zone?"

I grinned, digging the obvious ironic underpinnings. "What about our school? What's that like?"

"It's a sweet gig, though some teachers are only here because they want some kind of Asian experience or some crap like that."

I lifted an eyebrow. "What do you mean?"

"You know the type. Ones who've got this romanticized notion of what Asia should be like and think Korea will be something right out of a Pearl Buck novel. That's okay by me, just as long as their interests and mine don't collide. There's this one old gal, Betty. She's a trip. She came here thinking Koreans still lived in thatched-roof huts and used oxen to plow the paddies. Can you believe that?"

I shrugged and smiled to be polite. "What about our students?"

"They're pretty good, actually. All you have to do is follow the curriculum. It's pretty straightforward. Just stick with the program, and you'll do fine. It's not like Robin Williams in Good Morning, Vietnam. You just can't walk into the classroom and wing it."

"Of course not," I said, smiling. "By the way, what's Gilbert like?"

"He's a bit of a tight ass."

"Really?"

"He used to be the academic director of an ELS school in Thailand before he came here. From what I heard, he was a real prick with the staff, so they sent him here as some kind of punishment. How that could be a punishment, I have no idea. Just take a look around you. This is the land of milk and honey." Keith outstretched his arms to emphasize his point. "So anyway, along he comes with this chip on his shoulder the size of Texas and proceeds to take it out on the staff."

"That sucks."

Keith grunted. "It takes all types."

"Sounds like you two don't get along."

"That's putting it mildly."

"What happened, if you don't mind me asking?"

"Another teacher, Mike, and I were trying to get home one night from this college area in the western part of the city when we had an incident with a taxi driver. Granted, we were pretty tanked, but we should have known better."

"What do you mean?"

"The taxi driver wouldn't take us."

"I don't understand."

"Sometimes, when you're trying to catch a taxi late at night, the drivers don't want to take you because it's too far or they're worried that they won't get a return fare. So you have to stand on the side of the road and yell your destination, and if they're headed in that direction, they might stop and pick you up."

"Might?"

"Sometimes they'll try to charge you double or even triple to take you. Well, this driver at first didn't want to take us, but then he agreed and demanded a double fare. Mike pleaded with the driver to no avail. We should have just walked away, but Mike didn't like to take no for an answer. Then it got ugly. All Mike did was bang the roof of the taxi because he was angry and accidentally broke the blue taxi 'in service' light on top. The next thing I know, the taxi driver gets out of the car and starts yelling at Mike, who was not about to back down. This, in turn, gets the attention of several Korean bystanders, who thought Mike had assaulted the driver. Then, this mob materializes out of nowhere and carts off Mike to a police box. All the while, I had been standing on the sidewalk watching this drama unfold, but the mob left me alone."

"Shit, that's intense."

"Tell me about it. Gilbert, the managing director, and even the

Chairman of the publishing company that owns our school had to go to the police station. It got really ugly after that. Some bystanders claimed Mike had hit them and wanted to squeeze money out of him for getting injured or some shit like that. It was really messed up. Mike spent two days in jail and was deported right after that."

Before he could finish the story, our server returned with our Jungle Juice, served in tall beer mugs. I took one drink and winced from all the alcohol inside. "Damn, what the hell is in this?"

Keith laughed. "I don't know for sure. Whiskey, rum, soju, Kool-Aid, or Hawaiian Punch, maybe. It goes down a little rough at first, but you'll get used to it."

"What's soju?"

"It's the local firewater here made from rice. It's cheap and effective. The hangovers from it can be a little wicked, though."

The second sip went down smoother than the first, leaving a nice, warm trail to my stomach. The drink reminded me of another drink, "The Motherfucker" that I often bought at the Paris Bar in Panama City. Loaded with three or four different kinds of alcohol, it also went down rough at first. A couple of those, and you were legally brain-dead. I could see the same thing happening with a couple of mugs of Jungle Juice. I took another drink, a deeper one, and could feel the alcohol coursing through my body like a stream of fire.

"See, what did I tell you?" Keith said, chugging his drink. "Smooth."

He was right. I was hooked. "So, what happened to you after your buddy was arrested?"

"Nothing, really. Gilbert gave me a dressing down the next day. You know, shape up or ship out. I've been on his shit list ever since."

Our kimchi fried rice came, which was fried rice mixed with fiery kimchi pieces and topped with a fried egg. It probably would not mix well with what we were drinking, but I was famished and attacked it with great gusto. And when the five-alarm fire went off in my mouth, I put it out with a healthy chug of the Jungle Juice.

A GI in a black leather trench coat walked past our table and tripped on a loose carpet edge, spilling his drink on Keith. Instead of stopping to excuse himself, the GI kept on walking.

"What the hell, man!" Keith said, shouting above the din and glaring at the GI. "Can't say excuse me? Didn't your mother teach you any manners?"

The GI stopped and looked at Keith with a dumbfounded expression but turned and walked toward the exit. Keith's outburst shocked me. It had been an accident, that's all. I could see how someone like Keith would end up on someone's shit list.

"Damn, I just had this jacket made last month." Keith grabbed some napkins and wiped up most of the alcohol. "Seems like every time I come here, something happens."

"Why is that?"

"These fucking GIs. They think they own the place. The locals put up with it because they have no choice, but it makes the rest of us look bad."

"I don't understand."

"Koreans got this love-hate relationship with us. There are a lot of older Koreans who love America thanks to us helping them out during the Korean War, but these days, a lot of younger Koreans resent America and see the US military as a necessary evil. Not everyone, though. Some women looking to have their meal ticket punched don't mind. Still, when a foreigner like you or me comes along, it doesn't make any difference if we're a GI or not. We're seen as one and the same."

"What's wrong with that?" I asked, frowning. "I was in the military."

"Sorry, man, I don't mean it like that. It's just that when a GI causes some shit, they lump us all together."

Truer words were never spoken. At the table next to ours, two GIs started arguing about some incident in their barracks and settled it with their fists. When they jumped up from the table, they knocked it over, sending bottles, glasses, and food into the air. A Korean woman sitting at the table came to the rescue of one of the GIs and got in a few punches before being pushed away.

"See, that's what I'm talking about," Keith said and then chugged the last of his Jungle Juice. "Let's get the hell out of here before the MPs and KNP get here."

"KNP?"

"Korean National Police."

I downed the rest of my drink and followed Keith toward the bar. We paid for our food and drinks, but as we walked to the exit, a large man stepped in front of Keith.

"Hey, asshole. Remember me?" The man said, jabbing a thick finger into Keith's chest.

"Sorry, I don't." Keith tried to walk around the man, but the man wouldn't let Keith pass.

"Isn't this the dude from the King Club?" The man asked his friend, who was standing behind him.

"Nah, he's not ugly enough," a man wearing a Pittsburgh Steelers stocking cap said.

Keith laughed nervously. "Lucky me, I guess. But I can see you've got the market cornered on it."

"Is that supposed to be funny?" The larger man said, furrowing his brow. He was built like a Mack truck.

"No, not all. But I take it you resemble that remark."

The man looked at Keith confusedly, unsure what Keith meant. Then he turned to me. "What are you looking at, asshole?"

"Nothing, man. I'm just leaving with my buddy."

"Come on, Moose. Fuck him," the man with the Steelers stocking cap said. "I think I see Carlos over there."

The man glared at Keith and then, probably thinking it wasn't worth it, pushed Keith out of the way.

"What was that all about?" I asked, following Keith down the stairs.

"I was at the King Club, this disco up the street from here, the other week. He got all medieval on me while I was dancing with this girl. Said he was going to rearrange my face. I guess it was his yobo or something."

"Yobo?"

"GI slang for a steady girlfriend."

"Ouch."

"I still got her phone number."

I smiled.

When we reached the first floor, which was crowded with GIs and Korean women waiting for the elevator, two MPs and two Korean police officers pushed through the crowd and proceeded up the stairs. Once outside, Keith and I headed up the street a few yards until we came to an intersection.

"Where to now?" I stuck a cigarette in my mouth.

"The Hill."

"The Hill?"

"Hooker Hill." Keith jerked his thumb to a narrow side street that climbed a small hill lined with small bars and clubs.

"Seriously?" I said, lighting my cigarette and gazing up the street aglow with pink and red neon signage.

"Yeah," Keith said, grinning.

"Lead on, Bro."

Named after cultural and geographical points of reference such as Rocky Top, Texas Club, and The Grand Ole Opry, these clubs seemed befitting for young red-white-and-blue-blooded male American GIs who streamed up and down the hill. AC/DC, Hank Williams, MC Hammer, and Bon Jovi boomed from inside these bars and clubs, while scantily clad women in tight-fitting hot pants or mini-skirts stood inside doorways shouting out to passersby inviting them to come into their establishments.

About a third way up the hill, Keith stopped in front of a club on the left named Cheers. "Where everybody knows your name."

Inside, several long-legged girls in hot pants sat with GIs in semi-private booths. The u-shaped bar was empty, aside from two girls sitting at the end looking bored. "Hotel California" played on the club's sound system—just in time for my favorite line from the song, "you can check out anytime you want, but you can never leave." Behind the bar, a chubby middle-aged woman with curly hair looked at Keith and glared.

"No trouble tonight," the woman said, setting a wooden bowl of what looked like puffed rice on the bar in front of us.

"No, no. I promise." Keith pulled up a stool and grabbed a handful of the puffed rice. He held up two fingers. "Two bottles of OB."

"OB?"

"Oriental Brewery. There are two kinds of beer in Korea. OB and Crown. OB goes down a little smoother than Crown. Not exactly your champagne of bottled beers, but it serves its purpose."

Still eyeing Keith with disdain for whatever he had done, the woman had walked to the end of the bar and grabbed two bottles of beer from a refrigerator.

"Damn, she looked pissed. What the hell happened?"

"I got into a squabble with a GI a couple of weeks ago. We broke a table. It was nothing, really. I paid for the table. That's the neat thing about being drunk in Korea. People are generally forgiving if you do something stupid, especially if you pay for it."

The woman returned with our beers and set them in front of us. I took a swig from the bottle and made a face. It wasn't Heineken, that was for sure. It went down smoothly, though the aftertaste in my mouth left something to be desired.

I glanced at the two women sitting at the other end of the bar. One of them looked in my direction and smiled. I smiled back. The next thing I knew, she had sidled up to the bar next to me.

"You Yongsan?" the woman asked, her voice monotone and dry as if she had asked this dozens of times. She wore a leopard-print blouse and a matching leather skirt. Smallish breasts with dark nipples peeked through the sheer fabric. She smelled of whiskey and cigarette smoke.

I turned to Keith. "Yongsan?"

"It's the Army base down the road. She must think you're in the military."

"No, I'm not in the military," I said, turning back to the woman. "I'm an English teacher."

The woman nodded politely, obviously not too amused with my answer, and snapped the gum she was chewing. "Buy me whiskey."

I knew the drill. I learned it on J Street in Panama City at the Ovalo Inn fourteen years earlier, my first night out on the town.

The night I had my cherry popped. Her name was Sarah. She was from Colombia, as were most of the hostesses. After she hit me up for several watered-down Cuba Libres, she came at me with the pitch. You and me, fuckee-fuckee, suckee-suckee? I didn't stand a chance. She took me back to her apartment and screwed my brains out.

Keith laughed. "She's not wasting any time, is she?"

What the hell. One drink wouldn't hurt. I reached inside my jacket and felt for the envelope of money Gilbert had given me last night. I took out a crisp ten thousand won bill and laid it on the bar. The woman behind the bar, who had been watching what was transacting between us, poured a drink and set it down in front of the woman. Ten thousand won.

"If I were you, I'd smell the drink first," Keith said, hoisting the beer bottle to his mouth.

"Why is that?"

"The hostesses will tell you they want a whiskey, but it turns out to be barley tea or some shit like that."

"No, kidding?" I picked up the drink and smelled the contents. It was definitely whiskey.

The woman's brow creased in a frown, and she stared at me, baffled. "You not trust me?"

"No, it's just —"

Keith laughed. "Looks like you've got everything under control."

While the woman I was sitting with, Mi-sook, tried her best to entertain me, Keith talked to a man and woman who had come into the club after we did. The man had his long hair tied back into a ponytail and wore a black leather jacket with the Harley Davidson logo patch sewn on the back. His female companion was tall and thin, wearing leather hot pants and a red jacket. The man whispered something into my roommate's ear and motioned to the door.

"Bro, are you good here?" Keith asked, getting up from the barstool.

"Yeah, what's up?"

"I need to step outside for a bit." He motioned to the man and woman standing by the door. "I've got to see this guy about something."

"Sure. No prob."

"And do you think you can spot me fifty thousand? I'm good for it. Payday is in a week."

"Yeah, sure. Whatever, man."

"There's this dude I owe money. He's been a real dick about it."

I pulled out five ten-thousand won notes from the envelope inside my jacket pocket and handed them to Keith.

"Thanks. You're a lifesaver." Keith shoved the bills into his pocket and leaned toward Mi-sook. "Hey, you take good care of my roomie. You got that?"

Mi-sook giggled.

"Be right back."

Keith fist-bumped me and joined his friends at the door. The woman said something to Keith, who arched his head back and laughed before the trio walked outside. After Keith and his friends left, I bought myself and Mi-sook another round, but seeing that I wasn't into anything more, she sulked back to the end of the bar where she had been sitting earlier. Sitting at the bar, my eyelids growing heavier by the minute, I bobbed my head up and down to the beat of AC/DC's "You Shook Me All Night Long."

When the song was over, I glanced at my watch. Almost midnight. The door opened, and a blast of cold air blew into the bar. I turned, expecting it to be Keith, but it was another customer. Between the Jungle Juice I had at the first place we stopped, the beers I had here, and the jet lag kicking my ass, I felt pretty messed up. All I wanted to do was get back to the apartment and crash.

"You might try Polly's," the woman behind the bar said.

"Excuse me?"

"Polly's Kettle House. It's at the top of the hill on the left."

I nodded, grabbed my smokes, and walked outside. The cold air sobered me a little, but I could hardly keep my eyes open. I fell in behind several soldiers staggering up the hill. A Korean woman standing outside the entrance to a motel, silhouetted in the reddish glow of the motel sign, shivered in a miniskirt and thin jacket, which barely restrained her ample bosom inside. She made eye contact with me as I passed.

"Hey, where you go? How about short time?"

I grinned and shook my head.

At the top of the hill, a large crowd had gathered outside several bars and clubs. It had this Bourbon Street vibe with all the noise and partying. Patrons streamed in and out of the largest one, Polly's Kettle House. I pushed my way through the revelers, looking for Keith. From inside the bar, I heard shouting and breaking glass above the din of the crowd and the Beastie Boys belting out their rock anthem, "You Gotta Fight for Your Right to Party." At the same time, I saw the man with the long ponytail Keith had been with earlier being helped out of the bar. Blood streamed down the side of his face. Someone came out of the bar holding a chair and smashed it over his head.

The crowd ebbed and flowed as people tried to get out of harm's way when a few GIs started exchanging punches. The next thing I knew, I was pushed and shoved along by the crowd away from the brawl. Then, I saw the two GIs that Keith and I had run into earlier at the Twilight Zone. One of them recognized me and said something to his buddy, who pointed in my direction. Somewhere down the hill, the shrill sound of a police officer's whistle pierced the cold air.

Behind me, I heard the familiar strains of Roxette's "Dangerous" coming from yet another club somewhere down a dark narrow street hemmed in by two-and three-story buildings. That's where I headed until the excitement died down. I walked a couple of yards when suddenly, a hand reached out from the darkness, and pulled me inside a tiny club bathed in pink and green light, called the Paradise Club.

FOUR

A TALL, FULL-FIGURED KOREAN WOMAN DRESSED IN A TIGHT red sequin dress hemmed a few inches above her knees had pulled me into the dimly lit club, no bigger than the one I had been in earlier.

"Welcome," she said. "Come, sit down."

On one side was a small, red and black vinyl padded bar with six stools in front of it. Behind it, a middle-aged woman with tightly permed hair sat hunched over on a stool with her head resting on the bar. The room reeked of kerosene from a heater that sputtered and crackled in the middle of the room. Strands of blinking colored Christmas tree lights hung from the ceiling, giving the place a cheery holiday vibe.

The woman hustled me to the back of the room to an unoccupied semi-private booth partitioned by pink and yellow plastic beads. She plopped me down on a stained red velvet couch inside the booth and sidled up to me.

"What's your name?"

"Robert."

"Joo-hee."

She was pretty. Black hair cascaded to her shoulders. Her

round face, whitened by powder, and complemented with violet eyeshadow, made her large, almond-shaped eyes alluring. She didn't look as worn out and disinterested as the woman in the last joint.

"Nice to meet you. Where you from?" Her voice was husky and inviting, like Kathleen Turner's. She shook a cigarette from a pack on the table and stuck it between her thin, painted lips.

"Chicago."

"Are you gangster?" She laughed.

"No." I smiled.

She lit the cigarette and took a short pull from it. "You GI?"

I shook my head.

"Businessman?"

"No."

She looked at me with a puzzled expression.

"I'm an English teacher."

She threw her head back and laughed aloud. She took another short drag from the cigarette, blowing the smoke out the corner of her mouth. The fruity smell of alcohol on her breath and the cloying sweet cloud of cigarette smoke in the air made me dizzy.

"You teach me English. I'm good student."

"Sure, why not?"

"And I teach you Korean, okay?"

"Sure."

She smiled. "Buy me one whiskey."

I could see where this was going. I should have stayed in that other club instead of wandering off to find my roommate. My head was spinning from all the alcohol I had, and the last thing I needed was more alcohol. I got up from the booth, but the woman grabbed my arm.

"Where you go?"

"Sorry, my mistake."

Her dark, thick brows furrowed together as she released her grip.

"I'm looking for my roommate. We came here together, but we got separated."

She pursed her lips in a little pout and made a crying gesture by wringing her hands in front of her eyes.

Oh, what the hell.

"Yeah, sure." One drink, and then I would go looking for Keith. I'm sure he wouldn't just leave me here. He was probably waiting for me back at the club we had been in earlier for all I knew, thinking I might have gone looking for him. On the other hand—

"You?"

"Beer."

"Fifteen thousand." Her voice was cold and mechanical.

I reached into my inside jacket pocket, took out two ten-thousand won notes from inside the envelope, and handed them to Joo-hee. I did the math in my head. I had already gone through a little over one hundred thousand today, including the fifty thousand I had loaned Keith. Another fifteen thousand wouldn't break the bank.

Sinead O' Connor's "Nothing Compares 2 U" softly filled the room. From where I was sitting, I could see Joo-hee leaning over the bar while the woman, who had woken up in the meantime, poured a glass of whiskey. Joo-hee's skirt crept up her thick thighs, exposing black lace panties underneath. I couldn't take my eyes away.

Just one drink, and then I'm out of here.

Joo-hee turned and walked toward the booth carrying our drinks. She had a signature walk, feline and graceful. Her stride measured, one stiletto placed delicately in front of the other, like a prowling tigress stalking prey. She was going to eat me alive.

She slid across the sofa and handed me my bottle of beer.

"Geonbae!" she said and clinked her glass with my beer bottle.

"Geon, what?"

"Geonbae!"

"What does that mean?"

"It's Korean for 'cheers.'"

"Geonbae!" I said.

"You speak Korean very well."

I smiled. "Thank you."

When Joo-hee took a drink, the sleeve from her dress slid up to her elbow, revealing an ugly red scar that ran the length of her arm. When she caught me looking at the scar, she pulled down her sleeve to cover it.

"You look like MacGyver."

How popular was this show in Korea for someone to think I resembled Richard Dean Anderson? I couldn't see the resemblance other than wearing my hair the same way as Anderson did in the show, only shorter.

"Thanks, I guess."

"How long you stay Korea?"

"I just got here yesterday."

She smiled, and her big brown eyes twinkled in the glow of the blinking Christmas tree lights on the wall.

"You married?"

"No."

"Girlfriend?"

"No."

"Can I be your girlfriend?"

I grinned.

"Robert?"

"Yes?"

She held up her empty glass. "Buy me one more whiskey."

"I really should be going. Like I said, I've got to find my roommate."

"Are you cheap, Charley?"

"Cheap… what? No, it's not that. I just got in yesterday," I said, pleading my case. "I'm pretty tired, too. You know, jet lag."

"Just one more." She put a hand on my knee.

What the hell. You'll only go through life once, as a beer commercial back in the 1960s proclaimed. Besides, I knew what she was up to. One more drink wouldn't hurt. I took out another ten-thousand won note.

She held up two fingers.

"Whatever." I handed her another bill.

Joo-hee plucked the bills from my hand along with the five-thousand won note on the table, change from the first drinks I bought. She sashayed to the bar, wiggling her backside with every step. She said something to the woman behind the bar and proceeded to a restroom down a darkened hallway.

I stuck another cigarette in my mouth, but I dropped my lighter when I tried to light it. Then, while leaning over and looking for the lighter on the floor, the door to the club flew open and frigid air invaded the space. When I found my lighter and sat up, I saw that a stocky man in a leather jacket had come in and sat at the bar. With his back toward me, I couldn't tell if he was Korean, but the bartender seemed to know him, pouring him a shot of some liquor without him having to ask.

Joo-hee also seemed to know him. When she walked out of the restroom and saw the guy, she walked around him as far away as possible, but he grabbed her arm and pulled her toward the bar. It was hard enough that it made her grimace.

She yelled something at him in Korean that didn't sound pleasant. He probably would have hit her had the bartender not motioned toward the back of the room where I was sitting. He didn't bother to turn around. He still held Joo-hee's arm with his other hand on her ass. She tried to get away, but his grip was too strong, his fingers digging into her arm.

I did not want to be in the middle of this. The sooner I got out of here, the better. Joo-hee yelled again at the man, and this time, he let go of her arm. Then she hauled off and slapped him on the side of the face. The woman behind the bar started screaming at Joo-hee. I thought for sure the man was going to retaliate, but he didn't budge. She grabbed the drink she ordered and returned to the booth.

"Are you okay?"

"I'm fine," she said, her voice throbbing with tension. She saw my cigarettes on the table and shook one from the pack. Her hand shook as she tried to light it with my lighter. I steadied her hand and looked into her eyes. She looked scared. Taking a quick puff from the cigarette, she blew the smoke out the side of her mouth. She picked up her drink and tossed it down.

"What was that all about?"

"He's a fucking prick." She took another puff from the cigarette and gazed toward the bar. "He do that to all girls. Fuck him."

She said it loud enough for the man to hear, but if he did, he wasn't going to do anything. Not here, at least.

"I'm sorry to hear that." I didn't know what she meant and didn't bother to ask.

The man at the bar finished his drink and collected his change. He slid off the barstool and glanced sideways toward the back of the room. Although he couldn't see me in the shadows, I could see him. He had a square jaw, offset by a broad forehead and a flat nose, the kind a boxer would have if someone had broken his nose several times. He looked like someone you would not want to tangle with on a dark street. But what was most striking about his appearance was the crescent-shaped scar on the right side of his face, which I could see in the glow of the lights above the bar.

Joo-hee, still seething from her earlier encounter with him, narrowed her eyes and took a quick drag off her cigarette. The man said something to the woman behind the bar before he left. A blast of cold air after the door had shut fluttered a calendar on the wall and swayed the strands of Christmas lights.

"Fucking bastard." Joo-hee squashed the cigarette in the ashtray. "Can you do me a favor?"

"What?"

"Come home with me."

"Oh, I don't know. I really should—"

"Please." She touched my thigh with her hand.

"Seriously. My roommate is probably worried that I won't be able to find my way back to our apartment." It was a lame thing to say, even in my drunken state. The truth was, I didn't want to get involved in whatever shit was going on between her and the man who had been sitting at the bar. Still, she was pretty hot.

"Don't worry. I'll help you get home." She squeezed my crotch. "Let's go."

Fuck it.

She grabbed a short white faux-fur coat from behind the bar. "Pay her fifty thousand won," she said, pointing to the woman behind the bar.

"Excuse me?"

"Fifty thousand won." She got close to my ear when she said this. Her breath was hot and moist.

I reached inside my jacket and took out the envelope. I counted out five bills, stopping twice when I had lost count. The woman behind the bar gave me the once over when I handed her the bills.

Joo-hee pushed me out the door. Outside, she wrapped her arm around mine as we walked down the road. From the time I had gone to the club until we left, the temperature plummeted. My leather jacket wasn't warm enough, but I had so much alcohol coursing through my veins that I didn't feel the cold. In the distance, a hubbub of laughter and shouting reverberated in the frosty night. The street we were on was dark, illuminated only by a lone street light; the further we walked toward her apartment, the quieter it got, except for the clicking of her high heels on the pavement and our breathing.

In my drunken state, there was no way I would find my way out of here without Joo-hee's help, but I wasn't going anywhere for a while. As if I didn't know what her designs were as soon as she pulled me into the club and sidled up to me in the booth. Worst-case scenario, I could always find my way back in the morning.

I thought I heard someone walking behind us and looked over my shoulder nervously, but no one was there. It was just the sound of my footsteps echoing off the buildings.

The road curved and dipped as we passed along buildings and homes behind stone and concrete walls with broken glass cemented on top of these walls. From behind one of these walled-in structures, a dog barked. We stopped at one of these buildings in front of a black metal gate—with a steel door—embedded in a six-foot-high concrete wall.

"We're here."

Joo-hee unlocked the gate that opened to a small courtyard and a downstairs apartment. On the right was an iron stairwell which we climbed to her apartment on the second floor. It was difficult climbing in my drunken state, and I slipped twice.

Once inside her tiny apartment, I sat on the edge of the bed and watched her put a cassette into a tape player on a dresser.

"Do you like Mariah Carey?"

I shook my head. "Never heard of her."

The song's opening guitar lick reminded me a little of the Eddie Van Halen guitar solo at the beginning of Michael Jackson's "Beat It," followed by Donna Summer-like "Love to Love You Baby" vocals.

"Seriously?"

I shrugged. It wasn't my kind of music, but I didn't mind. Definitely make-out music, though.

"Humph." She crinkled her nose and sang along to Mariah, all sexy-like with her throaty voice.

I saw several business cards on a nightstand cluttered with condom wrappers and a half-used tube of ointment. One of the business cards had an image of an eagle in the middle with "US Embassy" written underneath; another had a red four-leaf clover against a white background with "Eighth Army" written across it. At the bottom was the person's name, Major Paul Stephens.

"Soju?"

"I really shouldn't. I've had too much tonight."

"Come on. I won't bite. Yet." She had already opened a small green bottle of soju and poured two shot glasses. She handed me one and took hers. It had a sweet, sickening fragrance. We clinked our glasses.

"Dipshida!" Joo-hee said.

"Dip-shi what?"

"Dipshida."

"What does it mean?"

"One shot."

"One shot?"

"Drink it all."

"Dipshida!"

We clinked our glasses again. She tossed hers back in one swallow while I sipped mine. It went down a little rough at first, but the taste wasn't that bad. A fellow could get used to drinking this stuff. As Keith said, it was cheap and effective. Before I knew it, she had poured herself and me another one. She took a long drag from a cigarette before squashing it in a green ashtray.

When I turned around, she had removed her dress and pantyhose and slipped into a red negligee. When did that happen? Standing in the middle of the room, she danced to the music, swaying her large rounded hips from side to side in tune with the music. She hiked up her negligee just enough for me to see her thick triangle of black pubic hair before she finished her little dance. She laughed that throaty laugh of hers again. When she crossed the room to where I sat on the bed, her small breasts jiggled inside the negligee. As drunk and tired as I was, I felt myself getting hard.

Before sitting next to me, she pulled a nylon cord hanging from an overhead fluorescent fixture that turned off the light; she tugged the cord again, and a red light illuminated the room. The soju, the music, and the soft red glow of the light above made my head spin. She put her arm around me. We kissed. Her breath was hot and sweet. She told me to lie on the bed, and I felt her unzip my pants. She reached into my pants and grabbed my shaft. I felt the room spinning, followed by nausea rumbling through my body. I pushed her away, hurried into the bathroom, and puked my guts out.

I thought I heard her say something on the other side of the door. "Rob? Are you okay?"

"I'm okay. I'm okay."

But I wasn't okay.

When I woke up seven hours later, I was naked, she was dead, and I was fucked.

FIVE

After the blood-curdling scream ripped through the chilly air when she discovered the body, the woman I had passed walking up the stairwell ran outside the apartment and yelled to the old woman below. Whatever it was, it didn't sound good and, most certainly, did not bode well for me.

Out on the narrow street, I put my head down and walked away from the apartment as fast as possible. I had no idea where the hell I should go. All I knew was I needed to get away from here before the police arrived, but with all the screaming and shouting, it would not be long. Metal doors and gates opened and closed as residents walked onto the street to see what all the commotion was about. Several residents threw open windows from second and third-floor apartments and shouted down to the street.

The street curved, then dipped down a small hill. As much as I recalled walking to the woman's apartment last night, I was heading away from the bars and clubs, deeper and deeper into a residential area. My only hope now was to get back to the main road, wherever the hell that was, and catch a taxi back to my apartment. How hard could that be? Fuck, what was the name of the neighborhood where I lived? The teacher who showed me around told me yesterday. It was "cham" something. Why didn't I pay more attention? That's because, at the time, I didn't think I'd be running for my life twenty-four hours later. Cham…Cham… Chamsil! That's it! Hail a taxi and tell the driver Chamsil. I patted the inside pocket of my leather jacket, feeling for the yellow envelope.

It wasn't there. Shit.

Behind me, the heavy pounding of shoes on the street alerted me to another concern. All the yelling the two women had done earlier had gotten the attention of some good Samaritan who had given pursuit.

I looked over my shoulder and saw two men running down the street toward me. They were about fifty yards behind me and gaining fast. One of them carried an iron pipe.

At the bottom of the hill, I didn't see the police car coming down the street until it was too late. The officer behind the wheel slammed on the brakes and glared at me through the windshield. But when he and his partner saw my pursuers running down the street and yelling, they got out of the car and joined in the chase.

To my right, I saw a passageway between several buildings. With the two officers approaching and the two men behind me gaining ground, my only escape was down that passageway.

High cement and stone walls loomed on either side of the passageway. Behind these walls, pots clanged, and televisions blared. A brick-lined channel ran down the center of the passageway that emitted the strong nauseating odor of raw sewage and soap suds. The air was pungent from the strong odors of garlic, kimchi, and kerosene emanating from the residences. I hurried past dilapidated one-story wood and stone dwellings tucked inside these walls and followed the passageway for about fifty yards until it jogged to the right.

Several dogs behind these walled-in structures barked, alerting anyone in the area that someone was where they shouldn't have been. An elderly man in pajamas standing outside one of these apartments stared at me as I passed. I tried to look the other way, but our eyes had already met. He gave me a funny little smile and the "thumbs up" sign.

The passageway did not lead me to the street as I had hoped. Instead, it suddenly came to a fork, with one path leading to the left, another to the right, and one straight ahead. Somewhere behind me, I heard shouting and the squawk from a police radio. How the hell did the police catch up with me as fast as they did? I hadn't much luck finding a way out of here, so thinking fast, I took the one to the left. Hopefully, this one would lead to a street.

There was no wall here, and I could see into the tiny residences. As I passed several of them, faces looked out from dirty, cracked windows. It was like trying to swim in a fishbowl where everyone could see my every move. I feared at any minute that someone who lived in one of these residences was going to wonder why this foreigner was running around in their neighborhood and start yelling for the police. I saw people sitting on the floor around a small table eating; in another residence, a young girl studied in her room. She looked up from her book and waved. Then, from another one of these residences, a middle-aged woman walked out of one house carrying a red tub. She looked at me quizzically before she crouched over the tub filled with cabbages.

I forged on with wary agility, feeling like Alice descending deeper and deeper into the rabbit hole. A rat scurried across the path in front of me. It stopped and stood on its hind legs, with its nose twitching, and gazed in my direction before it ran off. An elderly man carrying a wooden frame on his back stacked with black cylindrical objects walked out of a ramshackle building and shuffled past me, but gave me no regard.

The passageway abruptly turned right, and I hurried down another narrow lane with crumbling residences behind walls with broken pieces of colored glass cemented on the top of the wall. I was so twisted around that I worried I would be heading back toward the woman's apartment. All I could hope for at this point was putting enough distance between the apartment, the police, and myself.

Then, I saw it.

Through a gap between two of the taller buildings that rose from these ramshackle stone and wooden dwellings, I saw Seoul Tower in the distance. Okay, now I had my bearings. All I needed was to find a way out of here now.

In some places, the ground, which was layered with rectangular stones, was uneven. I tripped over a loose stone and fell spread-eagle onto the cold ground. Grimacing from the pain, I quickly got to my feet and continued my flight along this narrow passageway. I limped for several yards and turned right. Then left. Laundry on a wire clothesline flapped in the wind. Then right. A house with a cracked window looked familiar. Had I already passed here? I continued down this passageway for another ten yards. Nothing looked familiar. Good.

Two other middle-aged women, dressed only in baggy pants and gray sweaters, their long hair lying wet and limp on their shoulders, came out of nowhere, stopping me in my tracks. Both women carried small plastic baskets which contained bottles of shampoo, conditioner, and bars of yellow soap. Surprised to have encountered a foreigner, one of them dropped her basket, scattering its contents on the ground.

Trying to put them at ease, I lifted my shoulders in a half-shrug as if to say, "sorry," and then hurried past them.

I came to another narrow passageway and continued until a sputtering motorbike with a man holding onto a metal box with one hand appeared out of nowhere. There was not enough room for both of us to pass. One of us would have to back up, and, by the look on the man's red, weathered face, it wasn't going to be him. He inched his motorcycle forward, forcing me to back into a recessed entrance to one residence, allowing him to pass.

Somewhere in this maddening labyrinth, I heard shouting. The guy on the motorbike must have ratted me out. All I knew was that the further I proceeded, the chances of finding a way out of it were diminished. One wrong turn and I might run right into the police pursuing me.

Maybe it would be better if I just stopped running and gave

myself up. Took my chances with the police. They would have to call someone from the embassy who could sort all of this out. Why hadn't I done that earlier? If only I had stayed in the apartment and had the woman I had seen coming up the stairs call the police. I'd be in a room somewhere explaining what happened instead of running around out here looking guilty as fuck the further I tried to get away.

I came to another dead end and about an eight-foot wall. I had no choice. I would have to take my chances as to what was on the other side. The trick was to get a good running start, leap at the right moment, grab the top, and pull myself over. Simple. I backed up several feet, eyed the top of the wall where I would grab, took a deep breath, and took off running for the wall. And I almost made it. I got enough speed and timed my leap just right, but not enough to escape whoever had come up behind me. I felt two thick arms grab me and pull me back. The last thing I remembered was something heavy cracking the back of my skull. It didn't hurt at the moment, but I knew it would hurt later. The world was spinning like it was last night. My knees buckled, and I saw the cold ground rising to meet my face. And then darkness.

SIX

Not far away, in Huam-dong, a neighborhood just north of a sprawling US Army base at the foot of Mt. Nam, in the center of the city, Chun Yong-chol stood in front of the cracked mirror in the bathroom of his apartment and removed the blood-soaked bandage from his right shoulder.

The wound wasn't too deep, definitely not serious enough to warrant a visit to a doctor. He got as close as he could to the mirror and turned sideways to examine the wound. It was about five centimeters long but not too deep. At least the bleeding had stopped. He would end up with another scar to add to the ones he already had on his stout body from a miscellany of fights over the years. He poured rubbing alcohol onto the wound and grimaced before applying a fresh bandage.

The cut underneath his jaw wasn't too noticeable. He'd be able to tell anyone who asked that he had cut himself shaving. Other reminders of last night's fracas were not too pleasant. His balls still throbbed with pain where the bitch had kicked him. He didn't expect her to come after him with any taekwondo moves, but she did, and he was paying for it this morning. One of them had swollen to the size of a tennis ball.

Before leaving the bathroom, he splashed some cold water on his dark, leathery face and gargled with mouthwash. The only problem was the woman who had stabbed him with a kitchen knife lay dead in her apartment.

———

LAST EVENING, Chun had only gone to the Paradise Club to confront the woman, Han Joo-hee, who had been running off at the mouth about him. Chun, who worked for an Itaewon crime boss and businessman, had heard through the grapevine that Han had been going around Itaewon telling anyone who wanted to listen that he was smuggling drugs. Although it was true about him trafficking and selling drugs, he had a hunch she was doing it to land himself in hot water with his boss.

He ordered a drink and sat at the bar, talking to the owner. Han was with a customer, and he didn't want to make a scene. But when she went to the bar to get another drink after she had gone to the restroom, he grabbed her arm hard enough to make her wince.

"I want to talk to you."

"I'm busy." She narrowed her eyes and tried to pull her arm free.

"Tell whoever it is to get lost."

"Go to hell."

The owner, who didn't want any trouble with Chun, shot Han a dirty look. "Han! Mal josimhae!" Watch your language.

Chun grinned and stared at Han. "That's okay. We can talk later."

He let go of her arm and watched her walk behind the bar to get herself another drink. When she walked past him on her way back to the booth where she had been sitting with the customer, she turned to him and whispered, "byeong-sin saek-ki." A deformed or diseased person.

Chun drew his lips back in a snarl. He raised his hand as if to hit her, but decided not. Instead, he lowered his hand and turned back to his drink. She was really pushing her luck tonight.

Without further incident, he finished his drink and left, but not before casting a veiled glance in Han's direction just to let her know he still owned her. He could barely distinguish the man's features through the beaded curtain and the dim light, but he was most likely a GI. No reason to get him involved.

He'd give her an hour, two at most, with her customer before he paid her a visit. No sense in passing up good money. Americans spend well, and knowing her, she could squeeze every dollar she could from whoever it was.

The cold air should have sobered him up, but there was no turning back once you started down a road paved with anger and revulsion.

He found a pojangmacha, an orange, rectangular-shaped tent bar on one of the side streets, and ducked inside. After all the bars and clubs had shuttered for the evening, the pojangmacha provided cheap eats and drinks for patrons who were not quite ready to go home. In the back, away from a couple having an animated and heated discussion about the current president, Roh Tae-woo, Chun sat at a table near a kerosene heater. He warmed his hands over the heater and ordered a bottle of soju. While an icy wind rattled the tent's walls and made a string of lights shake, it was nice and toasty inside. He listened to the couple still going at it about Roh. Apparently, the man approved of Roh's recent crackdown on student protestors, but the woman disagreed, referring to the president as a thug. Chun grunted his approval. The man and woman looked in his direction, but they knew better than to say anything when they saw his scarred face.

The middle-aged Korean woman, who owned the pojangmacha, asked him if he wanted anything to eat, but he refused. She cocked her head to one side, thinking that she knew him, but before she could talk to him again, a group of noisy, drunken businessmen stumbled inside and sat down at the far end of the counter. She sauntered down the counter to serve them, and Chun returned to his drink and the issue gnawing inside. He couldn't have someone like Han disrespecting him in front of people. The more he thought about her, the angrier he became.

Chun first met Han not long after she started working in Itaewon about five years ago. A friend of hers from her hometown had promised her a job with a department store in Myong-dong, an upscale shopping district in the heart of Seoul. However, when Han finally made it to Seoul, her friend, who had gotten married to an American GI, was long gone. Out of money and nowhere to go, she ended up in Itaewon and found work hustling drinks in one of Itaewon's hostess bars that catered to GIs and expatriates.

She spoke little English back then, but she was different. She was unique. Taller than most of the girls who worked the clubs, the way she moved and talked made her desirable. She was instantly a hit with wide-eyed soldiers who fell prey to her charms.

She also had a temper.

The night Chun met her, she had gotten into a fight with a GI at the Capitol Club, which resulted in the town patrol—two American MPs, an English-speaking Korean soldier, and a KNP officer—having to intervene. The GI, who took offense to the watered-down drinks he had been buying her at 10,000 won each, refused to pay the 100,000-won bar tab. Instead of paying it, he tried to run out of the club, but Han had thrown an empty beer bottle at him. Not only did she have a great body, but she also had a great arm. The bottle hit the GI dead square in the back of his head. Fortunately, Chun stepped in before things escalated further and smoothed things between the club owner and the GI.

The next time they met wasn't as amicable.

One night, after the clubs and bars on Hooker Hill had closed, he and Han, along with three other business girls from the Texas Club, played Go-Stop, a traditional Korean flower card game, and drank a bottle of black market Johnny Walker. He was drunk, but not as drunk as Han, and when he made a crack about her accent, she got angry and threw an empty soju bottle at him. He ducked in time, and the bottle crashed into a row of bottles behind the bar. She was feisty when she got angry, but she took that feistiness to a whole different level when she was drunk. She threatened him with a broken bottle and dared him to fight back.

"Waseo deombyeo ih gae-ja shik-ah!" Come on and fight, you bastard.

"You're not worth it," he said, turning away from her.

When she came at him with the broken bottle, he tried to wrestle the bottle free; however, in the struggle, he accidentally sliced her arm open from the wrist to the elbow. He rushed her to the emergency room, where it took thirty stitches to sew up her arm. He paid for everything and gave her 100,000 for the work she would miss. He even took her back to her apartment and stayed with her all night. He felt terrible for cutting open her arm the way he did. She might have made money for him, but he resented her talking back to him. Sometimes an example had to be made.

———

WHEN HE FIGURED Han and the American had finished fucking, he left the pojangmacha and walked up the dark, narrow street to her apartment. The winter solstice was approaching, and the sky was a clear dark color. At this hour of the night, most of the neighborhood had already gone to bed. Only a few lights shone from homes along the way. He could have just gone home and dealt with this another time, but Han had gotten under his skin. Aside from embarrassing him in front of the Paradise Club owner, he couldn't have her spreading rumors about him.

No, it had to be tonight.

He hoped the bottom gate leading to her apartment was not locked. It wasn't. Whoever had used the gate earlier had not latched it behind them. He slowly climbed the spiral staircase to the roof and stopped outside her apartment. He put his ear against the door and listened. He heard music softly playing inside, but no voices. He rapped on the door two times with the back of his hand.

Joo-hee opened the door a crack and looked outside. "You're not—"

"I want to talk to you."

"Ji-okk eh na-ga. Na-ba-ppa." Go to hell. I'm busy.

Chun had already stuck his foot between the door and the

doorframe to prevent Han from shutting the door. Then, pushing open the door and knocking Han off balance, he barreled his way into her apartment. He looked around the tiny apartment but couldn't see the American she had brought home.

Shutting the door behind him and locking it, he moved across the room to where Han was standing. "You've got a big mouth, Han."

"What are you talking about?"

"You know exactly what I am talking about. When will you learn your lesson?"

"Get out of here before I call the police."

"The police can't help you. You know better than that."

Joo-hee glanced toward the bathroom and backed up against a table. There was nowhere for her to run.

"You don't frighten me."

"If you're not careful, you might get hurt."

"Like the last time?"

Chun narrowed his gaze on her, his eyes thin slits in his flushed face.

"Maybe your boss would like to know what you're doing. I'm sure he would be happy to hear about your little drug operation."

"Are you threatening me?"

Joo-hee grinned. "What do you think?"

Chun grabbed Joo-hee around her chin, his fingers digging into her flesh. "You'd better watch yourself, Han. I'd hate to see this lovely neck of yours broken."

Joo-hee pushed Chun's hand away from her chin. "Na-ga dwi-jyeo!" Go fuck yourself.

Startled by her defiance, Chun did not see what was coming next. Using all her strength, Joo-hee brought her knee up and hit Chun in the crotch. He screamed in pain and backed away a few steps. However, before Joo-hee could escape, he lunged forward, grabbing the front of her negligee, ripping it, and exposing her breasts.

"It's time I taught you a lesson in respect."

He backhanded Joo-hee across the face and pinned her against the table. The sting of the slap stunned her for a moment. His breath, hot on her cheek and stinking of liquor, made her want to vomit. She groped for anything on a table behind her to use as a weapon. She felt for the chipped, glass green ashtray on the table and smashed it against the side of his head. Chun took a few steps back and winced from the blow, but did not release his grip around her throat. Seeing that the blow to the head had not stopped him, she frantically groped for another weapon. Something, anything, that could save her. Glasses, cups, and cutlery crashed to the floor until she found a knife.

"Come on, Han. Maybe this time, you'll get lucky, unlike last time."

She made a slashing motion in front of her body, daring him to stop her. When he moved to disarm her of the knife, she lunged forward and sliced him under his right jaw.

"Gae nyeon ah!" You bitch. He felt blood trickling down his neck.

Chun could see Han's dark eyes filled with rage in the yellow glow from a streetlight shining through the window. She came at him with the knife again. Unable to get out of the way in time, she stabbed him in the shoulder. Chun howled in pain. He grabbed her hand that held the knife with his left hand and backhanded her again across the face with his right. Spittle and blood flew from her mouth. Han dropped the knife and staggered back a few steps. She looked for something else to hit him, but it was too late.

He grabbed her by the throat, squeezed as hard as he could, and roared. "I should kill you!" Rage fueled him. He couldn't let go, even if he wanted.

Joo-hee's heart hammered in her throat. She clawed at his fat fingers and tried to pry them free, but his grip was like iron. She gasped, unable to catch a breath, but slowly she was losing consciousness. Seeing that she had enough and no more fight was left in her, he let go of her, leaving her to collapse on the floor. She curled into the fetal position and moaned softly.

"Get up, Han."

He pushed her body with his right foot.

"Il-eona, inyeon-ah!" Get up, bitch. When she didn't move, he grabbed her by the hair again. "I'm not through with you yet."

Han's legs and arms jerked and twitched.

"Shit."

Chun kneeled and slapped Han on the side of the face to revive her.

"Get up, Han."

When she didn't respond, he picked her up and dragged her across the room to her bed when the sound of high heels clicking on the iron steps outside froze him. Someone was coming. He lay her down, walked over to the door, and peered out through the peephole.

"Eoni?" Older sister. "Are you in?" a female voice said, banging on the metal door. "I forgot my key."

Through the peephole, he recognized the woman from the Paradise Club. One of Han's friends and, most likely, her roommate. She had a black leather miniskirt and a white sweater under a leather jacket that came down to her waist.

"Open up, Joo-hee. It's cold outside. I'm freezing my tits off."

The woman's voice was loud and gruff. Chun could tell she had been drinking. She was going to wake up the neighborhood. In the courtyard below, a dog barked.

"Are you in there fucking someone?" She banged on the door again. "I can hear music. I know you're in there."

"Ah shibal," Chun said. Fuck.

The woman teetered on her heels and almost lost her balance. "Okay, be that way. See if I care." She clutched her jacket and staggered back toward the stairwell.

Chun listened carefully and breathed a sigh of relief when he heard the metallic clicking of her heels on the iron stairwell as the woman left. But his relief was only momentary. Leaning over Han's body, he listened for a heartbeat and felt for a pulse, but there was none. He shook her, but she did not respond.

"Don't you go dying on me." In the red glow from the overhead light, her clouded, bloodshot eyes stared back at him. "Ah shibal."

He backed away from the bed. Before he left, he wiped down

everything he might have touched, cleaned his blood from the knife she had used to stab him, and locked the door behind him. However, in his haste to clean up everything, he hadn't noticed the narrow band of light under the bathroom door or heard the low growl of someone snoring.

After Chun finished dressing, he walked to a small Chinese restaurant near his apartment. Although he was the only customer, he sat at a table in the back near the kitchen. He ordered jjajangmyeon, noodles in black sauce, and a bottle of soju. The middle-aged Korean woman who waited on him smiled a wide, toothy grin when she brought him his food. He looked up at her and smiled back. He had been coming here for months, and this was the first time she had shown any interest in him.

The soju took the edge off last night and numbed the pain in his balls. He would go about his business today as if nothing had happened. He had a meeting with his boss later this morning, but before that, he had to square things away with the owner of the Paradise. It wouldn't be long before the police found out where Han worked and questioned the owner. They would most likely want to know who she was with last night and if there had been anyone else in the club. He and the owner had to get their stories straight. The last thing he needed was the police snooping around the club and asking questions. And as long as she stuck to her story, he would have nothing to worry about.

And just in case anyone asked about his whereabouts after he left the club last night, he would have the owner of the pojangmacha vouch for him. As for Han, he felt no remorse for what he had done. She had come at him with a knife. She got what she deserved. And if anyone else got in the way, they would get theirs, too.

Outside, a police siren wailed.

SEVEN

Park Chong-hun surveyed the crime scene in silence. He had worked several murder scenes in his ten-year career with the Korean National Police, but something about this crime scene seemed odd.

It was the way the victim, a young woman, lay in the bed, on top of a thick, hand-embroidered red silk comforter, with her red negligee smoothed down her body and her arms crossed over her chest as if the murderer wanted to make her look presentable. A person couldn't tell she had been murdered until they got up close and noticed the red marks around her neck.

What kind of person would brutally murder someone and then take the time to put them in bed?

Tall and thin with thick black glasses and wearing a gray down jacket over his blue suit, Park and his partner, Shin Song-su, had been the first to arrive on the scene. Together with two other officers and two technicians from the crime lab, they busied themselves processing the scene and collecting evidence, trying to determine how the victim had been killed.

"Looks like there was a struggle." Park pointed to an

overturned chair, various broken beer and soju bottles, and a cracked green glass ashtray on the floor.

Shin nodded. He had also noticed the ashtray and the broken bottles. Older than his partner by ten years, Shin had a square face with large jowls, a fringe of black hair around a balding pate, and a grim demeanor. He squatted and gingerly picked up the ashtray. He examined an edge where a piece had broken off, looking for blood or hair.

"What have you got there?" Park said.

"Can't tell. Looks like there's blood on it."

"Bag it and let the boys at the crime lab work their magic."

Shin nodded and placed the ashtray in an evidence bag. He looked at the kitchen counter and sink full of dishes, which looked as if they hadn't been cleaned in a week. Various empty bottles of beer and soju stood like silent sentries on the counter, along with an assortment of food-encrusted bowls and plates, most likely carry-outs from local Chinese restaurants. He opened the refrigerator and gagged when he got a whiff of food spoiling inside. An opened package of moldy hot dogs and a plastic tub filled with kimchi were on the top shelf. A few slices of processed cheese. Three bottles of beer.

Park turned his attention to a vanity table beside the bed cluttered with makeup, lipstick, several bottles of perfume, hair spray, and another ashtray filled with cigarette butts. Several packages of condoms. A faded photograph of a young Korean woman with short hair holding a girl was stuck between the mirror and the wood frame. He took down the photograph and examined it. He suspected the child was the victim and the older woman in the photo was her mother. He dreaded the phone call he would have to make to the victim's parents. They probably had no idea what line of work she was in. Or maybe they did.

Beneath the photo, a few name cards with embossed logos of foreign companies had also been stuck along the inside of the mirror frame. He recognized one of the logos on the name card and took it down. Eighth Army. He scoffed when he read the name. Captain Eric Brewster. Each one of these cards could lead them to a potential suspect. But something else got his attention—a yellow envelope underneath the bed.

He got down on his hands and knees and reached under the bed for the envelope. Inside, the envelope was stuffed with ten thousand won notes.

"What's that?"

"It's money." Park counted the bills. "A hundred and twenty thousand won."

"Guess it wasn't a robbery, then."

"Doesn't look that way," he said, placing the envelope in an evidence bag and handing it to one of the crime lab technicians.

Shin nodded and continued looking for clues. When he looked through a plastic trash bin next to the bed, he was repulsed by what he had discovered. "Oh, shit."

"What?"

"Used condoms. At least three that I can see. The one at the top looks like it was used recently."

Park grimaced. The last person she had sex with was most likely her murderer.

"What do you think happened?"

Park looked at the broken bottles, the cigarette butts on the floor, and the overturned chair. He tried to visualize the crime scene and the room as he pieced together a workable theory.

"It looks like it started here, in front of the table," Park said, pointing to the overturned chair. "Whoever the murderer was must have confronted the victim here. See the overturned bottles and the broken glass on the floor and the table? There was obviously some struggle here. First, I think the assailant must have pushed her against the table. That might have been when the murderer ripped her negligee. Then she must have grabbed a bottle or the ashtray to fight off her assailant. That was when things escalated. She might have tried to escape, but the assailant was too strong for her. Next, whoever it was grabbed her, which was probably when the chair was overturned. And then, that must have been when she was strangled."

"Whoever had done this had to have been consumed by rage."

"Exactly."

"Motive?"

Park shook his head. "Who knows? Money, perhaps, but then, that doesn't explain the money I found under the bed. Maybe she wouldn't do what he wanted. Maybe she made him feel like less of a man somehow. What puzzles me is that whoever did it took the time to pick her up and carry her over to the bed."

"Why would they do that?"

"Good question. Maybe the person knew her. Maybe they felt remorse."

"Or maybe they were trying to cover up the crime."

"Perhaps. Either that or someone startled them."

"Her roommate? Another customer?"

Park went through a pile of papers on the table. He found a document from a local health clinic stating that she did not have a venereal disease. He also found the victim's Korean National Identification card. "Han Joo-hee."

"What's that?"

"The victim. Her name is Han Joo-hee," Park said, looking at the identification card. "Twenty-eight. From Taegu."

Park shook his head and bagged the card and other evidence he had collected. He didn't want to jump to conclusions, but a business girl murdered in her apartment—he wouldn't be surprised if her murderer was a GI. That was their usual clientele. It had happened before. And it would probably happen again. Unfortunately, that was the price that came with the US military presence on the peninsula. A drunken GI out and about in Itaewon or another one of the camp towns where the US military bases were located lost their moral compass and thought they were above the law. Plus, they're trained to kill. The temptation and the risk must have been a powerful aphrodisiac for them.

Before becoming a homicide detective, he dealt with drunken and obnoxious GIs. Sometimes, a minor altercation between a shopkeeper or a taxi driver quickly spiraled out of control. Sadly, on one occasion, it escalated to assault with three GIs taking a taxi from Seoul to Uijongbu in the north. When they refused to pay the fare, they assaulted the taxi driver, stole his cab, and went joyriding around the city before the police finally stopped them. What were they thinking? Did they really think they could get away with it? With over 38,000 US service members stationed in and around growing metropolitan areas, the dark side of the US military presence on the peninsula was bound to raise its ugly head from time to time.

And sometimes, it ended tragically in rape or murder.

Last year, another business girl had been brutally murdered. She had been beaten to death by a heavy object. Then, to cover up the crime to throw off the police, the assailant had heinously desecrated the body by pouring laundry detergent over it and inserting a soju bottle into her anus. Desecrating a body in Korea was an unforgivable and unpardonable crime. A Korean would never do that; a foreigner, on the other hand, might. At first, a GI, the girl's ex-boyfriend, had been suspected of the murder. Brought in for questioning, he was later released when his alibi checked out, but not before student and pro-North Korea activists, who believed that the continued presence of US troops on the peninsula stood in the way of reunification, took to the streets clamoring for their withdrawal.

One year later, the murder remained unsolved. It still sickened Park, who was sure they had arrested the right man. It also intensified his disdain for anything remotely dealing with the United States Army or the United States military that started back when he was in the military. He had been a KATUSA, Korean Augmentee to the United States Army, because of his English skills. Stationed at the nearby Yongsan military garrison, he accompanied US Army MPs on town patrol in Itaewon. His job was to liaison with any Korean-speaking person involved in an altercation with a service member, which usually involved one of the hostesses or one of the club owners and the occasional Korean male civilian who had wandered into the area.

It was easy duty, even if it was sometimes awkward and embarrassing to patrol the "ville," US military slang for village. He still remembered two of the MPs he accompanied on town patrol,

Johnny Polk and Eddie Pilarski. They knew most of the girls who worked in the clubs that lined Hooker Hill and had picked up enough Korean for dealing with most of the incidents requiring their intervention. Only once did he have to act as a go-between. A drunken ajossi, a middle-aged Korean man, had wandered into the ville and started hassling a GI sitting outside a club with his Korean girlfriend. That also required assistance from a Korean National Police officer who accompanied the town patrol.

Although Johnny and Eddie taught him a lot of American slang and turned him onto American fast food on the military base where they were stationed, he didn't like how they sometimes embarrassed him when they were on patrol. He felt uncomfortable with how they joked with the bar girls and openly talked about sex with them, which usually involved whether they preferred being on the top or the bottom, or their preference for oral sex or anal sex. Nor did he like how Johnny and Eddie bragged about their sexual escapades with the Korean women they had slept with. Most of all, he despised how they looked down on the women who worked in the bars or the shopkeepers. Their arrogance and high-handedness represented everything he despised about the US military presence in Korea and, in turn, everything he despised about America. These camptowns, with the shops, restaurants, bars, and clubs, had all been built for American enjoyment, including the women who worked in them.

After he got out of the military and finished school, he joined the Korean National Police and climbed the ranks quickly. Thanks in no small part to his English-language skills, he was sent to America to study criminal psychology at the University of California, returning to South Korea just in time for the Seoul Olympics. Although he spent two years in America, that didn't change his attitude.

Park turned and gazed at Han's lifeless body on the bed. Who did this to you, Miss Han? Who would want to hurt you? Could this be the work of the same murderer? His gaze shifted to the scar on her arm.

"You see that scar on her arm?" Park pointed to the jagged

pink scar on Han's right arm that extended from the inside of her biceps down her forearm to the wrist.

Shin lifted Han's arm and examined the scar. "That's not a surgical scar. Someone must have used a knife or some other sharp object."

"Whoever it was must have been furious."

"But this time, it cost her life."

Park nodded solemnly and watched the technician from the crime lab dust for fingerprints but knew it was probably a waste of time. Given Han's line of work, there would be many matches. Maybe they would get lucky, though.

"We'll know more when we question the club owner," Park said, eyeing the name cards stuck inside the mirror again. "Find out who she was with last night."

Two men wearing blue jumpsuits entered the apartment carrying a canvass stretcher. After another officer had finished collecting evidence and photographing Han's body, the men in the jumpsuits wrapped her body in a sheet and carried her outside.

When Park and Shin finished their preliminary inspection of the scene, they walked outside, where an officer from the Itaewon police substation talked to Han's roommate and the landlady. Standing around them were several bystanders, mostly neighbors, who had heard all the commotion and rushed to the scene.

"Who do we have here?" Park asked the police officer standing with two women.

"This is Hong Hyon-ju. She is the one who discovered the body," the officer said, motioning to Hong, who stood shivering while she smoked a cigarette. "She was returning home when she saw a man running out of the apartment."

"Were you and Miss Han roommates?" Park said, gazing at Hong. She was a plain-looking woman with short black hair, a friendly round face, and small brown eyes. She did not have double-eyelid surgery, a type of eye surgery in which an upper eyelid crease was created, a rite of passage for many Korean youths.

Hong's right hand trembled as she took a drag off the cigarette, blowing a stream of smoke out the side of her mouth. "Yeah, that's right. We both worked at the Paradise Club."

"I'm sorry about your roommate," Park said.

Hong nodded.

"Did you get a good look at the man you saw running out of the apartment?" Park said.

Hong took another drag off her cigarette. "I'll never forget his face as long as I live. He had blue eyes and a hawk-like nose. Short brown hair. But what scared me the most was this wild look he had in his eyes."

"What was he wearing?"

"A leather jacket. Jeans and a sweater."

"Did he say anything?"

"No."

"Have you ever seen him before?"

"No."

"Anything else you remember about him?"

"I think he was a GI."

Park let out an exasperated sigh and looked at his partner. He hated it when he was right. "We'd better call the CID at Yongsan."

When he investigated the murder of the business girl last year, it also required working alongside the CID, the criminal investigative division of the US Army.

The landlady, patiently waiting to get a word in edge-wise, finally spoke. "I don't know why you're still here asking all these questions! The killer is going to get away!"

"And you are?" Park said, turning to the woman.

"Baek Kyong-ja. I'm the landlady."

"Is there anything else you care to add?"

"She was always bringing home men at all hours of the night. Sometimes there was screaming and shouting. Things breaking. Loud music."

Hong shot Baek a dirty look. "Maybe some people should mind their own business."

The landlady gasped.

"What about last night? Did you hear anything?" Park said.

"Of course I did. There was a lot of shouting. It sounded like a fight."

"Why didn't you investigate?"

"It's not my place."

"You might have saved her life."

The woman gasped again. "I didn't know."

"Never mind."

Another officer, who had been talking on the radio with headquarters, approached Park and Shin.

"Headquarters just radioed. A man matching the description of our suspect was just apprehended."

Park looked at Shin. "Lucky us. Let's go."

"Don't you want to hear more?" the landlady said.

"That's not necessary. Thank you for your time."

EIGHT

News of Joo-hee's death spread through Itaewon within a few hours, fueled by speculation and fear. Business girls, who would have typically slept in on a Sunday or gone to the local bathhouse, gathered in their respective clubs, talking about the murder.

"She was murdered in her bed," said one of the business girls, Kim Eun-ju, who worked in Rocky Top, a club halfway up Hooker Hill on the left. She was a tall woman with long, wet hair wrapped in a towel. She had been at a bathhouse when she heard about the murder from another business girl who worked at the Grand Ole Opry across the street and rushed to the club to be with her co-workers. "Her roommate discovered her body."

"Omo!" Oh My God. One of her co-workers, Chae Un-gyong, a short woman with permed hair and bulging eyes, said. "Keum jik hae." That's terrible.

"That's not all. The murderer ran right past her," Kim said. "He must have just killed her and was trying to get away when Han's roommate returned home."

"Omo!" Chae shuddered.

The third woman, Song Mi-yong, puffed nervously on a cigarette. "I would have been terrified if that had been me."

"How did she die?" Chae asked.

"I heard her throat had been slit." Song took a long drag from her cigarette before crushing it in an ashtray overflowing with cigarette butts on the bar. "There was blood everywhere."

Chae cringed and touched her throat.

"No, that's not what happened. He beat her to death with his hands." Kim poured herself and the other two women shots of soju. "Her face had been smashed in and her jaw broken."

"Oh, dear!" Chae's eyes widened at this revelation, and downed the soju in one gulp. "Who would do such a thing?"

Song shook her head. She had been walking back to her apartment after spending the night in a motel with a customer when an ajumoni who ran one of the brothels on Hooker Hill told her about the murder. "It's not safe anywhere these days. To think it could have happened to one of us."

All the business girls nodded and pondered their fates. They could handle the grab-assing or crude language their customers used most of the time, mostly eighteen-and nineteen-year-old GIs away from home for the first time. Still, sometimes things could get out of hand. Song was missing a tooth from a fight she had gotten into with a GI. Last month, Chae had bluish-purple bruises on her throat for a week from a GI who was into rough, kinky sex. And most of the business girls, once they picked up enough English and were jaded enough, had to be just as crude to defend themselves. Like Joo-hee, they had been forced into this lifestyle out of economic necessity and survival. Some had families to support; others hoped to save enough to have their own club one day or meet the right man who would take them away from all this. They accepted their fate, the same way a person who had been told they only had a few months to live, and prayed for a miracle.

"It's a terrible world we live in," Kim said softly. She poured herself and the other women more shots of soju.

Her co-workers nodded, their expressions solemn.

"Did the police catch him?" Chae asked.

Kim nodded. "Yes, he's in custody now. An American."

"Jin-jja?" Chae said. Is that so?

"Yes. A GI."

Lee Kyong-suk, the owner of the Paradise Club, had been a nervous wreck ever since Hyon-ju had woken her to tell her the news about Joo-hee's death.

Together, they sat at the bar, drinking from a bottle of Johnny Walker. The man Han had gone home with last night was pretty drunk, but he didn't seem like the one who might have killed her. Even if he was the dangerous type, Han was good at taking care of herself. Once, she gave a GI a black eye because he grabbed her ass while she was waiting to get a drink at the bar not long after she started working at the Paradise. She broke the nose of another GI who got rough with her. Han didn't take shit from anyone.

Until last night.

The brring-brring of a black phone on a counter behind the bar ringing unsteadily like a jumpy electrocardiograph startled both of them.

Lee walked around to the back of the bar and picked up the receiver. A chill coursed through her body as soon as she heard the voice on the other end. "We need to talk."

———

THIRTY MINUTES after Chun had called her, he came in through the rear entrance and joined Lee and Hyon-ju at the bar in the darkened club.

"What's she doing here?" Chun frowned when he recognized Hyon-ju as the woman who had been outside Han's apartment last night, sitting at the bar.

"We're just having a drink," Lee said. "In memory of Joo-hee."

"Beat it," Chun said to Hyon-ju. "I need to talk to Lee. Alone."

"It's okay," Lee said. "I'll be alright."

Hyon-ju glanced at her boss, a troubled look on her face as if to express her concern about Chun showing up suddenly. What was so important for him to come to the club? It was not like him to show up during the day, especially after last night. She doubted it had anything to do with paying his respects. And why did he want to talk to Lee in private? Like most girls who worked in the clubs, they steered clear of Chun if they could help it.

Instead of leaving through the back door, Hyon-ju slipped into a storage room at the back of the club. She opened the door a crack and listened.

"The police are likely to come here and ask a lot of questions about Han's death," Chun said. "Just make sure you tell them I was not here last night."

"I don't understand."

Chun noticed an empty glass on the bar. He picked it up, sniffed the inside to make sure it was clean and poured himself some Johnny Walker.

"If the police poke their noses where they shouldn't, there's no telling what they might discover."

Lee swallowed hard. "Why would the police want to question me?"

"You know goddamn why." Chun gave Lee a frosty look.

"I'm sorry, I don't."

Chun stared at Lee with hooded eyes. "Don't play dumb with me. You know exactly what I'm talking about."

Lee knitted her brow. "The police already have a suspect in custody."

Chun had expected a different reaction from Lee. He took a drink, but before he could swallow, he coughed upon hearing this revelation. "What's that?"

"The police arrested an American. He was in here last night, the same time you were. He went home with Han."

"Gu-rae?" Is that so? Chun lifted an eyebrow.

Lee nodded.

"Where did they arrest him?"

"Close to her apartment."

Chun put a finger to his chin and pondered this revelation about the American. How the hell did the police arrest an American for Han's murder? The only logical explanation was that this American had gone back to Han's apartment, and he got caught. If this American was a GI, and the police, with another murdered prostitute on their hands, it would have been easy for them to suspect him. But why would he have gone back?

"Hong saw him running from the apartment. That's when she discovered the body."

When he confronted Han last night, there was no sign of anyone else in the apartment. There had been no reason for him to check. The only explanation was that this American had been in the bathroom. But why wait in the apartment until the morning? But it occurred to him quickly. Did this American see or hear anything? And once the police questioned him, that would bring them right back here. This called for a preemptive strike. He needed to throw the police off his path, just in case.

"Now, here's what you're going to do. When the police question you—"

"Why would they want to question me? I told you they already have a suspect."

"No, they don't."

"Why?"

"I saw Han last night, and I don't want to be a suspect. You got that?" Chun's eyes burned into Lee.

"Omo!" Lee's eyes widened in horror.

In the storage room, Hyon-ju gasped at this revelation and had to put a hand over her mouth to keep from alerting Lee and Chun of her presence.

She knew all about the history between Joo-hee and Chun. Especially the night the two of them got into a fight at the Capitol Club when he cut her with the broken soju bottle. She hadn't been at the club that night, but she didn't believe it had been an accident when she heard about it. She knew what Chun was capable of doing if you crossed him.

Two days ago, when Joo-hee told her about stumbling upon Chun filling tinfoil packets with some white powder in the back room of the Paradise Club, Hyon-ju feared for her roommate's safety. She also knew about the rumors of someone trafficking drugs spreading around Itaewon. What Joo-hee told her confirmed her worst fears.

"I'm worried that he's going to think it's me going around telling people about it," Joo-hee said, confiding in her roommate.

"What are you going to do?" Hyon-ju said.

"I don't know."

"Maybe you should talk to Lee."

"She's probably in on it, too."

"Just watch yourself, okay? Maybe you should lie low for a while or go home. It'll be the holidays soon."

"That's a good idea."

As it turned out, that was the last time she and Joo-hee had talked.

Hyon-ju put her ear closer to the door and listened closely. She had to find out why Chun was interested in Joo-hee's death.

"What happens if I'm asked questions about the man they arrested? What do I say then?" Lee said, her voice edged with fear.

"Relax. They'll want to know how he was acting when he was here. So you tell the police that he was rude and obnoxious. That ought to do the trick." Throwing the police off his tail would buy him some time until he could figure out what to do.

"They'll know I'm lying. I can't do this."

"Sure you can. You have no choice. You don't want to lose this club of yours, do you?"

Lee was still into Chun for over twenty million won—money she had borrowed from him to open the Paradise Club. She had no choice but to allow him to use the club for whatever illegal purposes or operations he pursued. The back storeroom was filled with scotch and whiskey Chun had stolen from a US Army PX warehouse on a base in nearby Hannam-dong, and now he was using the club to peddle the drugs he had been trafficking. Although she didn't have to pay rent for the club, he still took his cut from the booze she sold or what the business girls made on top of her monthly payments to him.

"Yes, I understand."

"Good. Just do as you're told, and everything will be fine," Chun said. "Otherwise, you might end up like Han."

Hyon-ju gasped again. Next to where she was standing, there was a stack of boxes. On top were several empty whiskey bottles. When Hyon-ju heard Chun threaten Lee, she bumped the box, rattling the bottles. One toppled off the box, but she caught it before it crashed to the floor.

Outside, Chun turned and looked in the direction of the sound. "Did you hear that?"

"What?"

"Sounds like someone is in the back room."

Chun walked to the back of the club, where the sound had come. Hyon-ju silently shut the door and backed away. She slid behind a tower of stacked boxes and the wall and crouched down. The door flew open. In the dim light, she could see Chun standing in the doorway. Chun flipped on the light switch and walked inside the room. He got close enough that she could smell the whiskey on his breath. Chun moved a few boxes out of the way, but couldn't see her. Satisfied that no one was in the room, he turned off the light and shut the door behind him.

Hyon-ju breathed a sigh of relief, but not before fear gripped her again. If Chun had killed Joo-hee, she had to tell someone, but who?

NINE

When I came to, I found myself in an empty room, stripped down to my shorts, and handcuffed to a wooden chair. In front of me was a scarred, stained wooden table with a black gooseneck lamp on top. The bright light shone directly on my face. My vision was hazy, my head throbbing from where I had been hit from behind as I squinted into the harsh light.

Where am I?

I twisted my body to get a better look at where I had been brought. However, with my hands cuffed to the back of the chair, all I could move was my head, which took some effort, but at least it offered a reprieve from the light burning my eyeballs. In a few seconds, my eyesight adjusted, sharpening into focus.

What I could see was not promising.

Mildewed white wallpaper curled away from the mold-spotted walls. The orangish-brown vinyl sheet flooring, which looked like the same kind I had noticed in my bedroom, was marred with deep black scratches in several places, as if some heavy furniture had been moved out of the room. The one window in the room was covered with black tape. A dank, moldy smell, heavy and thick, suffused the air.

I couldn't tell if this was a police station or not. At this point, I was hoping it was because the alternative off the grid would be way worse.

A door opened and slammed shut behind me. As the sound of heavy footsteps echoing off the floor drew closer, my chest tightened, and my heart pounded. Two amorphous figures moved past me, but I could not make out who they were from the glare of the lightbulb, but I smelled coffee, cigarette smoke, and cheap aftershave lotion.

The taller of the two figures stomped around the desk and sat down behind the table, laying a large brown envelope in front of him. Although the light shining on my face made it difficult to see who this person was, I could make out a few details. A wrinkled navy blue suit hung limply on his frame. Thick, black-rimmed glasses clung to his head like moss to a cliffside. To his right, the other man leaned against the wall, his arms folded across his massive chest.

"I'm Captain Park Chong-hun," the older man said, his voice imbued with the bass of a dump truck rumbling down the highway. "And that is my partner, Sergeant Shin Song-su. Do you know why you are here?"

I squinted in the glare and nodded. Of course, I knew why I was here, but until now, no one had spoken to me, which meant that I hadn't been advised of my rights yet. I didn't even know if there was something like the Miranda Warning in South Korea. Judging from the room I was in and stripped down to my underwear, I didn't think I would be advised of whatever rights I still might have.

"Do you speak Korean?"

When I found out I was going to Korea, I went to Walden Books in the local mall back home and found some Korean language cassette tapes and a Berlitz Korean phrase book. I picked up enough Korean to say hello and goodbye and buy cigarettes.

I shook my head.

Park took a deep breath. "Alright then. Let's get started."

At least Park's English was good. That was one worry out of

the way. Maybe this wouldn't be as bad as I thought once I explained my side of the story. Still, I had run away from the police, but I was innocent. Once Park and his partner heard my side of the story, they would have no choice but to let me go. There was a logical explanation for the situation I now found myself in — I just had to find it.

He picked up the brown envelope and dumped the contents onto the table: my wallet, my Swatch wristwatch that my friend Gretchen gave to me as a going-away present, the Chicago Bulls keyring I had bought at a gift shop in O'Hare Airport, my lighter, cigarettes, and a pack of gum.

He picked up my wallet and started going through it. He took out my Illinois driver's license and read the information on the front. "Turner?"

"Y-Y-Yes, that's right. Robert Turner."

Park stared at my photo on the front of the license and then looked at me as if to make sure that we were the same person. The license was issued several years ago when I still wore my hair long. That's probably what threw him.

"LaSalle, Illinois." He pronounced "LaSalle" as "La-Sally." Illinois was a little more difficult, which he pronounced as "Ill-eh-noise."

"That's right."

"You're an American."

I nodded.

"GI?"

"No."

Park and Shin looked at each other with expressions of disbelief. I got the impression that they were hoping I was in the military.

"Only GI go to Hooker Hill."

"I wouldn't know anything about that."

Park frowned and looked at my driver's license again. "Thirty-two years old."

"Yes."

"I'm thirty-five." Park seemed pleased that he was older than me. That's nice, I thought. I wasn't sure what his age had to do with my age.

He slid the license back inside the license holder and flipped through the photograph holders. He stopped when he came to one photo.

"Who's she?" Park held up my wallet and pointed to the photograph.

I squinted again in the glare. It was a photograph of my friend, Mary Sue and I, taken at a party she had on the Fourth of July. "My friend."

"Girlfriend?"

"No, a very close friend."

Park looked at the photo again like someone would if they didn't believe you and flipped to the next one.

"Who's this?" He pointed to a yellowed, faded photograph of my mother taken back in the 1960s. She was sitting at the kitchen table with a Coke in one hand and a cigarette in the other. I don't even know who snapped the photo of her, but it was one of the few ones I had of her.

"My mother."

Park nodded approvingly. I figured he probably thought I must be a good son if I had a photo of my mother in my wallet. Maybe I had scored a few points with him. Seeing that there wasn't anything significant in the wallet, he shoved it and the rest of the items back into the envelope.

"Residence booklet?"

"My what?"

"Residence booklet. You know the law," Park said in an agitated tone. "All foreigners must carry their Alien Registration Booklet with them. Where is yours?"

I shook my head. "I don't have one."

"What do you mean, you don't have one?"

"I just arrived on Friday. I don't have what you're talking about."

Park arched an eyebrow and grunted his disapproval. He took

out a pen from a pocket inside his jacket and wrote something down in a notebook before looking at me again.

"Where do you live?"

"Chamsil."

He wrote the name in his notebook. "Where in Chamsil?"

"I don't know exactly. There's this big shopping center. Lotte, something."

"Lotte World."

"Yes, that's right."

Good. We were getting somewhere. Now all he or his partner had to do was contact my roommate, and this nightmare would be over.

"Danji?"

"Excuse me?"

"1 Danji, 2 Danji?"

"I don't know." Those big black numbers I had seen on my first night here didn't do me a damn bit of good now.

Park huffed out an aggravated breath. "Why did you come to Korea?"

"To teach English. I'm an English teacher."

"English teacher?" Park's eyes lit up.

I nodded. "I teach. I mean, I'll start teaching at the ELS school. I start on Monday. It's located—" I didn't know where it was located. I didn't even know the phone number. I hadn't even bothered to write down that information and stick it in my wallet. But then again, I didn't plan on getting arrested my first weekend in Korea. Perhaps Park had heard of it if it was as famous a language institute as I have been told. "I don't know where it is. Like I said, I just got here the other day."

"Yes, yes. You told me." Park said with the same agitated tone. "Is my English good?"

"Excuse me?"

"My English. Is it good?"

Why the hell was he asking me this? Was he just trying to be friendly or something? "Yeah, it's good. Great. You speak English well." What else was I supposed to say? His English was good enough for all this small talk. I hoped his English was just as good for the rest of the interrogation.

"My partner doesn't speak English. Good for you, I do," Park said and then grinned.

"Yes, I guess so."

"My English teacher was from Canada. Vancouver. Her name was Elizabeth."

"That's nice."

Park sat back and straightened his shoulders. He crossed his hands in front of his body on the table. "Now, let's talk about you and the murdered woman in the apartment. What happened?"

Smooth. He went from talking about his English teacher to the murder. "I don't know what happened. I woke up this morning, and…and…she was dead."

A frown creased Park's forehead. His eyes narrowed. "That's it?"

"Yes." I swallowed hard. "Someone was pounding on the door, and when I tried to wake her up, she didn't move."

"You found her that way."

"Yes." The image of the woman staring at me with her lifeless eyes was not one I would be able to get out of my mind anytime soon.

"You woke up in bed with a dead woman, and you don't know anything about it."

"Yes, that's what happened."

"Her negligee was ripped."

"I don't know about that."

"You didn't rip it."

"No."

"And the strangulation marks around her neck. I suppose you don't know anything about them either, do you?"

"I'm telling you, I woke up this morning, and she was dead! I don't know what else happened!"

"Take it easy, Mr. Turner. We just want to find out what happened, that's all." Park's voice was calming, but cold. "There's no need for you to get excited. All you have to do is tell us the truth. You can do that, can't you?"

Park's interrogation tactics unnerved me. While it might have seemed that he was trying to put me at ease, I got the feeling he was only setting me up to rip me a new one.

"Yes, of course." I took a deep breath.

"Better?"

I nodded.

"Good. I'm going to ask you again, what happened?"

"As I said, I woke up this morning, and I found her that way," I said, pleading my case. "I just arrived on Friday. I went out with my roommate last night. He wanted to show me around. We had dinner, then we went drinking, and he wandered off somewhere. I went looking for him, and that's when I met her."

"Stop!" The veins on his neck tightened as he pounded his fist on the table. "You will only answer the questions I ask you!"

Park's outburst scared me. What the hell? I was answering his question. My back, legs, and arms hurt from sitting on the wooden chair. My head still throbbed from the debilitating hangover, not to mention the back where I had been hit. It felt like my skull was going to burst through my head. My throat was parched and on fire.

"Could I have some water, please?"

"Answer the question first."

"Please."

Park motioned to Shin to get me some water. While his partner was out of the room, Park sat quietly and drummed his fingers on the table. He took a deep breath and exhaled slowly. When Shin finally returned, he approached me with a tin cup of water and held it to my mouth for me to drink. I took one sip and spat out what I had in my mouth. It wasn't water, but some kind of lukewarm brown tea. The second sip went down better, and I drank the contents of the cup. Shin set the cup on the table and stood beside the table next to Park.

"Let's try again. What happened?" Park changed his strategy and switched back to a more civil tone. "Start from the beginning."

"As I was saying, my roommate and I went out drinking —"

"What's your roommate's name?"

"Keith."

"Last name?" Park wrote Keith's name into his notebook.

"I don't know. I just met him."

Park snorted his disdain, his gaze a sneer that burned holes right through me. "He doesn't sound like much of a roommate to leave you alone."

"Yeah, I guess not. He borrowed some money, then wandered off with some guy that had a ponytail and a woman." I would be lying if I said I wasn't pissed off at Keith for leaving me like he did, but it was just as much my fault for looking for him. If I had stayed put, I wouldn't be in the predicament I was in now. "He'd said he would be right back, but I went looking for him when he didn't return. I was pretty drunk at the time. I know it was a stupid thing to do."

Park frowned. "Go on."

"When I went looking for him, there was this fight in front of this bar, and when I tried to get away, I ended up on this side street. That was when this woman pulled me into this small club."

"Miss Han."

I nodded. "Joo-hee. She said her name was Joo-hee. She was standing just inside the door."

"Then what happened?"

"Like I said, I was pretty drunk and tired, not to mention jet-lagged."

"But you stayed."

"Yes."

"Even though you had gone looking for your roommate."

"Yes, that's right."

"Doesn't seem like you were in too much of a hurry to find your roommate if you stayed."

I didn't like where Park's questions were leading. If I didn't know any better, he was trying to trip me up. "Yes, I guess not. Everything happened so fast. One minute I was outside this club, and the next thing I knew, I was sitting next to her."

A woman screaming from somewhere on the floor interrupted the interrogation.

"What was that?" I said.

"What was what?"

"Screaming."

"I didn't hear anything."

"Someone screamed. A woman."

"You worry about yourself. What happened next?"

I stared hard at Park. I was sure that was a woman's scream I heard. The next scream I heard might be my own if I didn't answer Park's questions. "We had a couple of drinks. Actually, she had a couple. I just had a beer."

Park screwed up his face. "Hmm… How long did you stay at the club?"

"I don't remember, but she told me she would help me get back to my apartment."

"In Chamsil."

"Yes, that's right."

Park made this disgusted breathing sound by sucking air through his teeth and exhaling the same way. He wrote a few more things down in his notebook. He was not buying anything I was telling him. Park, for whatever reason, was taking this interrogation personally. He had an ax to grind or something.

"What did you do when you got back to her apartment?"

"She put on some music, and we had a drink."

"Did you fuck her?"

The bluntness of Park's questioning unnerved me.

"I don't remember."

"You don't remember?"

"Yes."

"Yes, you had sex with her?"

"No. I said I don't remember if we had sex." Park had me so twisted around with his line of questioning that I could be confessing to her murder and not even know it.

"Then what?"

"She danced for me."

"Danced?"

I nodded.

"You liked that, huh?"

I would be lying to say that I didn't, the way she swayed and moved her large, rounded hips, but that was before everything went south.

"She danced for me. That's all."

"Then what?"

"We had something to drink. Soju."

"And?"

"We ended up on the bed together."

Park made another annoying, disgusting noise by sucking air through his teeth. He wanted this interrogation to proceed faster, but I wasn't giving him the chance.

"Go on."

"She touched me."

"Touched you?"

"She put an arm around me."

"And."

"We kissed and made out for a while. But, like I said, I was pretty drunk."

"What happened next?"

"She unzipped my pants and—"

"And you don't remember having sex with her?"

"No, I don't."

"We found several used condoms in the trash. One appeared to have been recently used."

"I wouldn't know anything about them."

"Hmm."

"I'm telling you the truth. We made out, but I don't remember having sex."

Park wrote more in his notebook and looked at me again. "Was it about money?"

"Excuse me?"

"Money. Maybe you didn't want to pay her."

"No, it wasn't about money."

"Or maybe you got a little rough with her." He glared at me from across the table. "Maybe you wanted to do something she didn't like."

"No, it was nothing like that."

"Did you two have a fight or something?"

"No, we didn't have a fight." I thought about the red marks around Joo-hee's neck and her ripped negligee.

"The woman who lives downstairs would disagree."

"What did she say?"

"She heard a lot of shouting and what sounded like someone fighting."

"There was no shouting. I told you what happened. We had something to drink and made out for a while. Then I got sick. I went to the bathroom and got sick. I must have passed out because the next thing, it's morning, and I'm in bed with her."

Park made an annoying clicking sound with his tongue.

"And when I woke up this morning—"

"How did you get that cut on your forehead?" Park pointed to the right side of my head.

"I don't know. I must have gotten it when I passed out. Maybe I hit it on the sink. Or when I was getting dressed. I fell and banged my head on a chair."

"Getting dressed?"

"Yes, when I woke up in bed with her, I was—"

"I was what?"

"Naked."

"So let me get this straight. You don't recall having sex with her, but you were naked when you woke up this morning."

"I don't know what any of this has to do with her death."

"I'm just trying to find out what happened. I'm just trying to figure out what is the truth and what is not."

"I'm telling you, I passed out. I don't remember. I must have gotten undressed before I got in bed with her."

"That's rather convenient, wouldn't you say?"

"I don't know what you mean."

"It's convenient how you have no recollection of what happened last night after you went to the bathroom."

"That's because I don't. We kissed and made out for a while. But that was as far as it went. I got sick and passed out in the bathroom. When I woke up in the morning, I was in bed. And she was dead. Why don't you believe me?"

Park translated what I said to this partner, who grunted his disdain for my explanation before turning back to me. "Do you really expect us to believe that's what happened?"

"Yes, that's exactly what happened."

Park heaved a heavy sigh. I could tell that he was losing his patience with me. "Then who killed her?"

Although it had been hours since I had thrown up my guts, thanks, in no small part to Park's interrogation, I felt my stomach doing somersaults. "I think I'm going to be sick."

"Just answer the question!"

"Please."

"Because if you didn't do it, someone else would have had to get inside her apartment and kill her."

"Yes."

"With you passed out in the bathroom."

I took a deep breath and willed myself not to throw up. "Yes."

"So, this mystery person came into her apartment, killed her, and then left without you hearing a thing."

"I guess so."

"Even though the woman downstairs heard a lot of noise from her apartment."

"I'm telling you, I didn't hear anything."

Park leaned back in his chair and steepled his fingers in front of his body. "That's right because you were passed out in the bathroom."

"I know it probably sounds far-fetched, but I've been telling you everything I know."

Park shook his head. "I don't believe you."

"But I'm innocent."

Park guffawed and shook his head. "You're not here to tell

stories, Mr. Turner. You're here to tell the truth, and if I were you, that's what I would start to do. For your own good."

"I did not kill her! I woke up this morning, and she was dead! Why is it so hard for you to believe me?"

My outburst startled Park, who motioned to Shin, who took out about a foot-long black baton from the inside of his jacket and walked up to me. He held the baton in front of me and pressed a button on its side. The baton buzzed to life. I spent some time on a farm back in Illinois when I was a kid. I know exactly what this baton was.

"Now, what's it going to be? The easy way or the hard way?"

I stared at Shin and the baton. "But I'm telling you the truth, I don't—"

Before finishing my sentence, Shin pressed the baton against my upper left thigh. A painful bolt of electricity shot through my body, sending me and the chair reeling to the floor. I lay there quivering in pain and felt a warm wetness spreading through my underwear. Shin placed the baton on the table and lifted me back upright in the chair. He grinned when he saw the pool of urine on the floor. My heart pounded in my chest, and my flesh tingled from the jolt of electricity that had shot through my body. I was breathing in short, little gasps, trying to catch my breath as if I had just run a race. But at least I didn't throw up.

"What the fuck, man? Why did you have to go and do that?"

"I warned you."

After a while, my breathing slowed and became more regular.

"Now, let's try it again. What happened when you got back to her apartment?"

I nodded and took a deep breath. I could see Shin tapping the baton on the side of his leg if I didn't tell them what they wanted to hear.

"She put on some music, and we had a drink. The next thing I knew, she had changed into this red negligee. We started kissing, and that's when I got sick. Not then, I mean, the room started spinning, and I went to the bathroom and threw up. And then I passed out. The next thing I know, it's morning and—"

"We have an eyewitness who saw you running out of the apartment."

The woman I passed on the stairwell.

"But I am innocent!"

Park sneered. "Then why did you run?"

"Because I was scared of what would happen if…."

"If what? If she or someone else found you in the apartment with a dead woman?"

"If you put it that way, yes. I know it was stupid for me to run. I panicked. What more do you want me to say? You have to believe me. I'm telling the truth."

"Truth? Do you want to know what the truth is, Mr. Turner?" Park leaned forward and pointed a finger at me. I could see my reflection in his glasses. "The truth is, we have a murdered woman in the morgue, and you are the primary suspect. Now I suggest you start telling us the truth, or this is not going to turn out well for you."

Park was good; I had to give him credit for that. He was going one on one with me with pretty decent English skills.

"I've told you everything that I know. Why do you have to be so stubborn and insist that I murdered the woman?"

"Because you're a liar!" Park jumped up from the chair and walked around the table to where I was sitting. Instead of Shin zapping me with the cattle prod again, Park slapped me hard, an open-handed blow to the side of the face that rocked my head back. "Why did you kill her?"

"I didn't kill her!"

"You can play dumb as long as you like, but we'll get to the truth eventually. And the sooner you cooperate with us, the better it will be for you. Do you know what we do to murderers in Korea? We hang them!"

I swallowed hard.

"That's right. Just like in your wild west movies." Park pointed his finger at me. "Confess now, and maybe the prosecutor will go easy on you. Maybe you'll only end up with life in prison."

I closed my eyes. I could not stand the glare any longer. My head pounded and my stomach twisted into knots as the horror of my situation gripped me.

This is not happening to me. This is not fucking happening to me. I'm going to wake up from this nightmare eventually. And when I do, I'm going to lay off the booze for a while.

"Open your eyes!"

I squinted in the harsh light. "I want to talk to someone from my embassy."

"Tell us what happened first."

I shook my head. "Embassy first. I have rights."

Park laughed. "Your embassy can't help you now."

This was absurd. It was something right out of a Kafka novel. No matter what I said in my defense, Park refused to believe me. It was almost as though they had already made up their minds that I was guilty before they brought me here. This was window dressing. It was them showing me they were in control.

"Again, what happened when you got back to her apartment?"

"As I've already told you, I have no idea what happened after I passed out." I wanted this to stop. I wanted to close my eyes and sleep. "I've told you everything I know. What the hell is wrong with you?"

"I'm losing my patience with you." Park motioned to Shin to use the cattle prod on me again.

"No, wait," I said, eyeing the cattle prod in Shin's hand. "Th-Th-There is something that I remember."

"What?"

"This guy came into the club when I was with Miss Han."

"Who was he? American? GI?"

"No. He was Korean."

Park furrowed his brow. "Korean men don't go into those clubs."

"He was Korean."

"Did you get a good look at him?"

"Not really. I only saw him from the side when he got up to leave."

"Was he tall or short? Big? Small?"

"Medium height, I guess. Kind of big. About the same build as your partner."

"That's not a lot to go on."

"It was dark. I was drunk and jet-lagged, as I said. I guess that's what he looked like."

Park shook his head in disbelief. "You'll have to do better than that."

"Wait. I do remember one thing about him."

"What's that?"

"He had a scar on his face."

"A scar?"

I nodded. "The kind you would get if someone cut you with a knife."

"What did he do?"

"When Miss Han went to the bar to get another drink, he said something she didn't like. She slapped him. He grabbed her arm and got rough with her."

"Got rough with her?"

"You know, talking bad. I don't know. It was in Korean. But when she came back to our table, she looked scared."

"Was he in there long?"

"No, he had a drink and left. Talk to the bartender. She saw everything."

"Okay, Turner. We'll question her. You'd better not be wasting our time."

"I'm not."

"For your sake, I hope she has something to say in your defense."

TEN

After leaving the Paradise Club, Chun drove to a nondescript three-story office building near the Han River in Bogwang-dong. The neighborhood was a mixture of residential and business, with the odd factory here and there. Chun got out of the car and pulled up the collar on his overcoat in deference to a raw, biting wind blowing in from the river. Overhead, fleecy grayish-white clouds dotted the turquoise sky that scuttled along the swift air currents.

Hopefully, this wouldn't take too long.

Chun climbed the stairs to a third-floor office. In the back of the room, cluttered with cases of Johnny Walker and Chivas Regal, cartons of American cigarettes, instant coffee, and other black market items pilfered from local US military bases, he found a seat and sat down. Sitting at a dark mahogany desk in the front of the room was Kwon Yong-ho, his boss. Kwon, who had silver-gray hair, wore a finely tailored wool suit from one of the oldest tailors in the city, whose clientele included Korean presidents, diplomats, and foreign dignitaries.

Kwon had built his business up from nothing following the

Korean War. While he made a fortune with his illicit activities—mostly prostitution and black marketing—he also had several legitimate enterprises, including exporting ginseng to Japan and China. Despite his underworld activities, he was a trusted and well-respected businessman. Twice he was Itaewon Business Man of the Year, was past president of the Itaewon Retail Association, and was a founding member of the ROK-US Friendship Association.

Kwon grew impatient with a middle-aged man standing in front of the desk. The man, Nam Yong-sik, had already taken up more of this time than he wanted.

"Business has been slow," Nam said in a low voice, fidgeting with a gray winter hat with earflaps.

Nam, who sold black and red lacquered mother-of-pearl inlay wardrobe cabinets and jewelry boxes in one of Kwon's shopping arcades, could not come up with this month's rent—the third time this year.

"It's two weeks before Christmas."

Nam lowered his head and said nothing.

"I understand you've been gambling again," Kwon said, looking past Nam to Chun. "Is that what you heard, Yong-chol?"

"That's right, boss." Chun shifted his large frame in the chair and stuck a cigarette in his mouth. "The only problem is, he always loses."

"Maybe that's why you can't make your payments again. Am I right?" Kwon said.

Nam nodded.

"Do you remember when you approached me a year ago and begged me to let you have a stall in the arcade? You knew the consequences if you couldn't pay your rent on time. What do you think would happen if word got out that I let people slide with their rent? I'm a fair man, but being fair can only go so far."

Chun grinned. He loved to watch Kwon make people squirm.

"I tell you what would happen. People would think that I was weak. And a guy in my position can't let that happen. Do you understand?"

"Please give me one more chance. I promise this won't happen again."

Kwon brushed away a piece of lint from his jacket sleeve and rubbed his chin while he thought about what to do with Nam. "Being it's the holiday season and all, I will do you a favor. Better yet, it's my Christmas present to you. Have the money here by the end of the week, plus ten percent interest, and we will be square."

Nam looked at Kwon with a dumbfounded expression while he quickly did the math in his head. "T-T-That's five hundred thousand won."

"Then I'd suggest you get back to your shop and start selling."

Nam bowed deeply in front of Kwon and waited to be excused.

"Remember, the rent plus ten percent by the end of the week, or my associate here will be paying you a visit."

Nam bowed two more times, then backed away with his head still lowered and shuffled out of Kwon's office.

"By the end of the week?" Chun stood and walked across the room to Kwon. "You've gone soft in your old age."

"It's the holidays. What can I say?"

"Do you think he'll make it?"

"Probably not. Just don't rough him up too much. After all, his wife is my cousin."

"Like I said, soft."

Kwon grunted and poured himself a shot of bourbon from a bottle on his desk. He gestured to Chun with the bottle if he wanted one, but Chun shook his head.

"What happened to you?" Kwon pointed to the cut on his chin.

"I cut myself shaving."

Kwon raised an eyebrow as if not to believe Chun. But, knowing Chun, he probably stuck his dick where he shouldn't. "You should be more careful."

Chun laughed. "I'll remember that next time. Anything else, boss?"

"Yeah, there is one more thing." Kwon picked up a pair of green metal Chinese Baoding balls embellished with a red dragon and rotated them in the palm of his hand. The metal composition of them alleviated the pain in his arthritic fingers. The hollow sphere contained a smaller ball that produced a pleasing metal chime when it struck the outer sphere. "What can you tell me about the business girl murdered last night?"

"Nothing that you probably already know. Her roommate discovered her body, and the police have a suspect in custody."

"Did you know her?"

Chun and his boss locked stares for a moment. "No, I didn't."

Chun set the Baoding balls back in their velvet-lined case. "A murdered business girl is bad for business."

———

CHUN, orphaned as a young boy, had run away to Seoul from an orphanage in Inchon not long after the Korean War. Destitute and hungry, he met some kids rooting in the rubble, not too far from Toksu Palace in downtown Seoul, looking for anything of value to sell. A young man had approached them and asked if they would like to make some money. He explained to Chun and three other kids that trucks brought in goods daily to the back of a department store used by the US military as a PX. Sometimes, the trucks sat at the loading dock for several hours before they were unloaded.

"I'll give you kids 15 hwan each to bring me as much as you can from the contents of those trucks."

Chun and the other kids nodded.

"Just watch out for the soldiers. They like to shoot thieves."

Chun couldn't be sure if the man was lying or not, but 15 hwan was more than he had ever seen before and had to be worth the risk. That night, Chun and the kids went to the department store across the street from the Myong-dong shopping district in central Seoul. When the coast was clear, Chun and the three other kids ran to one truck and looked inside the back. It was filled with boxes of cigarettes and whiskey. One of the older kids ripped open one box, grabbed as many cartons of cigarettes as he could, and passed them to Chun and the two other kids. Then they ran back to where the young man was waiting.

"See, that wasn't so hard," the man said, grinning. "Go ahead. Get some more."

The kids ran back to the truck, grabbed more cartons of cigarettes, and brought them back to the man. Chun loved the thrill and the money that awaited him. However, on the third trip, Chun was running back to the man when he tripped over a stone. One soldier guarding the trucks shone a flashlight in the direction of the sound. Chun lay as flat and silent as he could. The soldier got within a few feet of Chun, but turned around and returned to the dock. However, the other kids, seeing Chun on the ground and the soldier, dropped their cigarettes and ran in the opposite direction. The soldier shone his flashlight in the direction where the kids had run and took off after them.

Chun waited until the soldier was gone before he got up and limped to the man, remembering to retrieve the cigarette cartons he had dropped.

"You did good, kid," the man said, clapping Chun on the back. "What's your name?"

"Chun Yong-chol."

"Come on, let's get out of here."

"Pay me first," Chun said.

"What's the matter, kid? Don't you trust me?"

Chun shook his head.

"I like you, kid." The man took out two ten hwan notes from his billfold and gave them to Chun.

Chun's eyes widened when he saw he was getting paid five hwan more.

"How would you like to come and work for me?"

"Serious?"

"Yeah."

"Sure."

That man was Kwon.

Over time, Chun graduated from being a "slicky boy"—a slang term used by American service members stationed in South Korea to describe Koreans who made a living stealing items from GIs and selling the items on the black market—to a more esteemed position in Kwon's organization. Soon, Chun handled some of Kwon's more lucrative black market operations, including hijacking trucks from the Inchon Port Authority destined for US military bases. Cigarettes, booze, ox-tail soup, and toaster ovens soon found their way to one of Kwon's warehouses. He was also responsible for running one of Kwon's sweatshops that turned out hundreds of designer handbags for Japanese tourists. He even had his workers produce knock-off shopping bags that couldn't be detected even by the shrewdest customs agents who raided the Itaewon sweatshops from time to time.

Chun also built up a reputation as a person one didn't want to cross unless one wanted to end up dead. When one of Kwon's enemies tried to murder him in his office, Chun killed the assassin with a ceremonial Korean sword that Kwon had hanging on the wall in his office. Chun then hacked up the body in small pieces and buried them in hills south of the city.

Kwon made him his bodyguard and, later, his partner for his loyalty. There was no one more feared or respected in Itaewon than Chun.

Although he might have been Kwon's right-hand man, Chun wanted a bigger piece of the action. Kwon was too old-fashioned, preferring to make his money from prostitution, the black market, and the knock-off goods he sold and more legitimate enterprises, which included several shops in a shopping arcade on the main street through Itaewon. In a move against his boss, Chun had already been selling methamphetamine, or philopon, as it was called in Korea, to tourists and GIs in Itaewon and using the Paradise Club as one of his fronts for his operation. Business had been booming since the end of the Olympics. Itaewon was no longer a place for GIs and Japanese tourists. Instead, there was a new wave of tourism, especially backpackers and English teachers who loved to party.

Kwon didn't suspect a thing. The old man was too busy with strong-arming renters who couldn't pay their rent, running his sweatshops, or the mediocre black marketing that comprised most of his enterprise. And as long as Chun kept his little drug enterprise out of Kwon's sight, what the old man didn't know wouldn't hurt him.

Until Han caught him in the back room of the Paradise Club, filling tinfoil packets of methamphetamine.

ELEVEN

Later that day, after Lee had gone to a local Buddhist temple, where she lit incense and prayed to the Buddha—not only for Han but also for her tormented soul—Park and Shin were waiting for her outside the Paradise Club.

"My name is Captain Park Chong-hun, and this is my partner Shin Song-su," Park said, raising his hand in salute. "Are you Lee Kyong-suk?"

Lee nodded. "Yes."

"We have some questions we would like to ask you about the woman who was murdered last night, Han Joo-hee."

"Aigoo," Lee said, using an expression to express her shock—her voice trailing out the last vowel sound for several seconds, which intensified the depth of the emotion. Although she had mentally prepared herself for meeting the police, hearing Park refer to Han's death sent chills through her body again. "Please, come inside."

Lee unlocked the door and showed Park and Shin inside. She turned on several lights and the kerosene heater in the middle of the room. Park, no stranger to bars and clubs like this one when he was a member of the town patrol, looked upon the tacky red and black interior, the air heavy with the odors of cigarette smoke and kerosene with a strong sadness in his heart. He knew that most of the women who worked in these establishments had no other means of support. If they were lucky, they might find a way out by marrying a GI or a foreigner. Those who couldn't were doomed to a life of sexual servitude, abuse, and addiction.

From the corner of his right eye, Park saw several empty glasses and a beer bottle on a table in one booth. That was most likely where Han and Turner had sat last night.

"I can't believe someone would do something like this," Lee said, clearing away dirty glasses from the bar.

Park nodded, his expression solemn. "We have a suspect in custody. An American."

"You do?" Lee's eyes widened. "So soon?"

Park nodded again. "He was caught fleeing from her apartment."

"And you think he's the one who killed Han?"

"Yes, we do. The suspect said he had been here last night and gone home with Han. What can you tell us about him?"

"He came in late, right around closing time. Han was the only one working. The other girls had gone off with customers."

"I see. Was there anything out of the ordinary about him?"

"What do you mean?"

"How did he act?"

"He was drunk, if that's what you mean."

Park wrote that down in his little notebook. "Did he do or say anything that would have alarmed you?"

Lee shook a cigarette from a pack lying on the bar. Her hand trembled when she lit it with a disposable lighter. She took a quick puff from her cigarette and expelled it quickly, then drew another as if she couldn't get quite enough nicotine. She was putting on a good show for the officer—her life depended on it. Now it was time to lie, as Chun had instructed. "He was loud and obnoxious. He got a little rough with her."

"Rough?"

"He wasn't nice at all."

Park and Shin exchanged curious glances.

"He called her a bitch and told her to suck his dick," Lee said. "Right here in the club. I don't allow that sort of thing in my club. Some club owners do, but not me."

Park's face turned red as he wrote what Lee had said. "Anything else that he said or did?"

Lee thought for a few seconds and then nodded. "When he and Han left, he got angry when I told him he had to pay 50,000."

"What did he say?"

"He didn't say anything. He just threw the money at me."

"I see."

"Guys are like that sometimes."

"How so?"

"They think if a girl sits down with you and drinks with you, they like you. It doesn't work that way."

"Of course not."

Lee took a long draw from her cigarette. So far, so good. She had done everything Chun had ordered her to do. She knew how to deal with the police when it came to a curfew violation or fracas involving one of her girls and a GI, but lying to the police about Han was the hardest thing she ever had to do. She felt terrible about it, but she had no choice.

"There is one more thing. Was there anyone else in here last night at the same time as the American?"

Lee went quiet for a moment and then shook her head. "No, just this American. Why?"

"The suspect claims that there was another man in here at that time who he thinks might have something to do with Han's death."

"There was no one else in here. Like I said, it was just Han and this American."

"Well, that about does it. Thank you for your time. I know this hasn't been easy for you." Park closed his notebook and gave Lee a little salute.

"She was a good girl. I had no trouble with her."

"Excuse me?"

"Han, she was a good girl."

"Yes, I'm sure she was."

"She sent money home to her parents every month."

"She sounds like a very nice person."

"Sure, she had run-ins with unruly and obnoxious customers. Which girls wouldn't, right? It's the nature of our business."

"I understand."

"I don't understand why someone would want to hurt her?" Lee welled up with tears. "It just doesn't make sense. Everyone liked her. She bothered no one."

"Yes, of course."

"I wish I could have helped her more. Maybe if I had, she wouldn't be dead now."

Park raised an eyebrow, not quite sure what Lee was alluding to but thinking it had to do with her being overcome with grief, and nodded. "You can't blame yourself for what happened."

"I'm just happy they caught the guy who did this."

"Yes, I know how you feel, and I'm sorry for your loss."

"One more thing."

"What's that?"

"I hope the person who did this rots in hell."

"Yes, I'm sure he will."

TWELVE

My mother hadn't been thrilled when I told her I had quit my job and found another one teaching overseas and that I wouldn't be home for Christmas. Outraged would have been more like it.

"Two weeks before Christmas?" She might have been eight hundred miles away in Dallas, but she could have just as well been in the next room when her voice screeched through the receiver.

"Why did you quit your job?"

"I wasn't happy."

"Couldn't you find something closer to home?"

"This is what I do. I teach English."

Actually, that wasn't true in the strictest semantic sense of the word. Until my buddy Ray told me about his experience in Korea, teaching English overseas hadn't even been a blip on my radar screen. Although I had taught two ESL classes in graduate school, it was only to make some extra cash. However, the chance to teach for a year or two overseas and see some of the world was enticing, to say the least. Who knows? Maybe I would like it so much that I would make it my career. I explained the benefits I would get, but my mother wasn't buying anything I said in my defense.

"Do they even celebrate Christmas over there?"

"Of course they do."

"Is it even safe to live there?"

"Of course, it's safe. If it wasn't safe, would these schools hire teachers from overseas?" I lied. I had to confess that I knew little about South Korea. My general knowledge about the country had been limited to the 1988 Olympics and the TV show M*A*S*H. I had an uncle who fought in the Korean War, but he never talked about it.

Had I known the current tense standoff between the two Koreas, I might not have been so quick to accept the job offer. Prior to the Olympics, North Korean spies had blown up a South Korean airliner, killing everyone on board in an attempt to scare countries from participating in the games. And then, earlier this year, another infiltration tunnel dug by the North Koreans had been discovered under the DMZ. And if you had asked me who Kim Il-sung was, I wouldn't have been able to answer. Well, you know what they say, ignorance is bliss.

"You weren't worried when I was in the military."

"That's different."

"No, it's not."

"I heard they eat dogs in Korea."

"I don't know, Mom. Maybe they do." I don't know how my mother knew all this about South Korea. Her way of staying up-to-date with what was happening around the world was what she could glean from the National Enquirer she picked up at her local grocery store or morning talk show radio hosts. "What difference does it make it? If they do, there's probably got to be a pretty good reason."

The literature Gilbert had sent me about living and working in Seoul had mentioned nothing about eating dogs. However, it was suggested that teachers bring underarm deodorant or sanitary napkins because both were hard to find in South Korea.

"Don't get snippy with me."

"I wasn't snippy."

It didn't make any difference what I said in my defense. I didn't feel like going around and around with her over this because it wouldn't have done either of us any good. We'd end up right back where we started. However, my mother wasn't about to walk away from this without getting in a few more words edge-wise.

"It's always got to be about you, doesn't it?"

"It's a job. Why can't you be happy for me?" I was losing my patience trying to justify my career decision. "Maybe it would have been better if I hadn't told you, seeing how it has ruined your day."

Silence. I could just imagine her chain-smoking whatever brand of cigarettes she was smoking these days and tossing back a tumbler of vodka or gin. I should have kept my mouth shut, as I had intended, but the damage was already done.

"Why can't you be more like your brother?"

There it was. My mother never disappointed, especially when it came to throwing up my brother, Randall, to me.

Randall was my younger brother, who, in recent years, had become a saint in my mother's eyes. He had moved to Texas in the early eighties at the height of the oil boom and did quite well for himself. He got a job installing drywall and, in a few years, worked his way up to the top with a contracting company out of Houston. In the meantime, my mother had also moved to Texas. At the time, I was still going to college after dropping out several times before settling on a major I liked. In all the years my mother and brother lived in Texas, we only got together once. That was three Christmases ago when I was in graduate school. When my mother's boss found out that we hadn't spent Christmas together in over eight years, he paid for my airfare. But on the drive down to Houston from Dallas, it was Randall does this and Randall does that. Randall was promoted to foreman. Randall bought a new boat. Randall's wife, Debbie, was crowned Miss Spring Creek in 1986. Randall's wife is a paralegal. Randall and his wife bought a new house. Randall. Randall. Randall. The worst Christmas ever.

"I'll be down for Thanksgiving."

"Thanksgiving?"

"Yeah. I'll spend a couple of days."

As it turned out, it was one of the most civil holidays we had

had in years. She laid off the sauce for most of the week and did a complete 360 when talking about Korea. She introduced me to this middle-aged Korean woman who lived in the same apartment complex. The woman, originally from Seoul, had been living in the States for several years. I practiced some of the Korean I had been studying, and she gave me the phone number and address of a relative who lived in Seoul.

The night before I left, I called my mother and told her I would call her as soon as I settled in. If and when I could get word to her about what had happened, I could just imagine how heartbroken she would be; either that or I would get one of her trademark "I told you so" lectures.

———

I HEARD a door open behind me and footsteps coming toward me. It was another round with Park and Shin. Park, who looked like he had slept in his clothes, sat down again. He placed a manila folder on the table and folded his hands. I couldn't see his partner, but I knew he was there because of the cheap aftershave lotion he wore, which reminded me of those pine tree air fresheners people hung from their rearview mirrors.

"You talked to the bartender, right? She told you all about the man, didn't she?" I said, staring at the folder on the table.

"Yes, we talked to her," Park said, pushing his glasses back up on his nose. "Turns out she is the owner. She was very helpful."

"See, I told you." I sighed and felt vindicated. The club owner would corroborate my story. The police would have to release me, no worse for the wear, as my grandmother used to say. "It was the man in the bar, wasn't it? She told you that Miss Han slapped him, right? And that he had gotten rough with her. He must have followed us to her apartment. He must have been—"

"In fact, her version of what happened last night differs greatly from your account."

"What do you mean?"

"The owner said that only you and Han were in the bar."

"What? She's lying."

"What would she have to gain by lying?"

"Maybe she's trying to protect the man. I don't know."

"Her account of what happened last night is very interesting. She said you were loud and obnoxious and feared that you might harm Han."

"That's a lie."

"She also said you got angry when it came time to pay the bar tab. She thought you were going to hit her because you were so angry."

"That's not true. Joo-hee told me I had to pay the woman fifty thousand won, that's all. So I paid her, and we left. I didn't say anything to the owner."

"Not according to her."

"You still don't believe me, do you?"

"There's your account of what happened last night and the owner's account. Two different stories. One murder."

"I tell you, she's lying!" I would have jumped up off the chair if I hadn't been cuffed to it.

"You've wasted enough of our time, Turner."

Park looked up at his partner and gave a slight little nod. I felt Shin's huge hands on my head to keep me from moving and keep my head still. Park got up from the table and walked around to where I was sitting. In his hand were several photographs. He held one of them just inches from my face.

"Look at her, Turner! Look what you did to her!"

Although the photograph was black and white, I could see the extent of her fatal injuries I had not seen when I first discovered her body. A bruise stretched across her forehead and extended down her nose and left eye. Dark-colored strangulation marks stretched around her neck.

I shuddered and felt sick again. I clenched my eyes shut and tried to look away.

"Open your eyes, Turner!"

"No, please. Take the photos away. I'm going to be sick."

I felt Shin remove his hands from the side of my face. The next thing I felt was my ear ringing and my face stinging from the big-gest slap I'd ever felt. My eyes bulged open. The force of the slap almost knocked me and the chair over. I grimaced from the pain.

"Look at her, Turner. Look what you did! And then you were sick enough to pose the body for us when we found it! Why did you do it?"

"Please! Why don't you believe me? I had nothing to do with her death. The last time I saw her, she was sitting on the bed next to me. The next thing I know, it's morning, and she's dead. Please, you have to believe me!"

"Look at her!" Park threw the photographs at me. "And to think, you almost got away with it."

"I swear I didn't do it."

"Come on, Turner. You can do better than this. You're tired. We're tired. Why don't you do yourself a favor and spare yourself any more of this treatment?"

"Embassy." I could barely get the word out. "I want to talk to someone from my embassy."

"There is nothing your embassy can do to help you. Only you can help yourself now," Park said, his voice fraught with anger. "Think about it, Turner. We have all the time in the world. It's all up to you."

THIRTEEN

How long had I been here? Twelve hours? Twenty-four hours? By now, my roommate must have contacted someone at school who, in turn, would have contacted the police. And once my school got involved, it was only a matter of time before someone contacted the US Embassy. But where the hell were they? Why hadn't anyone come to help?

Then, I had a terrible thought. Maybe my roommate hadn't told anyone. Perhaps he didn't even bother to see if I had come back. After all, I had told him I had been in the military. Maybe he thought I had gone off with the woman I had been with at the first bar. Considering how fucked up this was, that was a possibility.

My head drooped, and my eyelids got heavy, but dozing off was impossible even for a few minutes—not with the bright light still shining on my face. Even when I closed my eyes, I could feel that searing light burning into the back of my brain.

At any moment, I expected Park and his partner to return for another round of interrogation and torture. Around and around we had gone. And the more he grilled me, the angrier he got when I didn't come out and admit to killing the woman. Someone had gotten into that apartment and killed that woman, but try explaining that to Park. He was convinced I had done it, but all he wanted or needed me to say was that I did it.

And Shin, that son-of-a-bitch. He had already used his cattle prod on me twice to move things along. And each time he zapped me, he had this smug expression on his face. If only my hands weren't cuffed to the chair, I would love to have the chance to wipe that expression from his face. It would be worth getting zapped again. Or better yet, take that cattle prod of his and shove it up his ass.

Park was a real piece of work. If I didn't know any better, he had some personal issues with Americans. His favorite expression was, "you foreigners think you can get away with anything you like. But not anymore." Yeah, he was a real piece of work. A real prick. The more he questioned me, the more I despised him. Why wouldn't they let me talk to someone from my embassy? There had to be some international law about that, like the Geneva Convention. Name, rank, and serial number. All they had on me was fleeing from the apartment and the statement from Joo-hee's roommate and the club owner.

But then there was the eight-hour gap in my story from when I went to the bathroom and passed out until I woke up in the morning. As Park put it, blacking out and not remembering anything was a convenient alibi that any prosecutor worth his salt would be able to tear apart.

I thought I heard screaming and shouting several times from the floor above me. I pitied the poor son-of-a-bitch, who was most likely enduring the same interrogation methods. Reminded me of the expression, "misery loves company." I wondered what they did to be on the receiving end of an interrogation.

But the bigger question was, what did Park and Shin have in store for me next?

———

"ALRIGHT THEN, TURNER, FROM THE BEGINNING." Park's voice was raw and raspy. His eyes were red and puffy. He looked just as bad as I felt, but he wasn't the one cuffed to the back of a chair wearing nothing but soiled underwear. "What happened when you went back to her apartment?"

Here we go again.

Although Park's tone seemed less threatening when he and Shin returned, a lot had to do with him being tired than being civil.

"As I've told you before, we had a drink, and then we made out on the bed before I got sick. I went to the bathroom and threw up. The next thing I know, it's morning, and she's dead. You can ask me a hundred times. No, make that a thousand times, and I'll still tell you the same thing."

"Yes, of course. You're going to stick to your story. And it's a good one. I would probably feel the same way if I were sitting where you are. But I have a better story for you. Would you like to hear it?"

"Do I have a choice?"

Park shot me a dirty look. "These two boarders were living in a boarding house in Seoul back in the early 70s. They had come to the city looking for work, as many people did, hoping for a better life, but it didn't always work out that way. One night, while they were drinking in one of their rooms, they had an argument about something. In a fit of rage, one boarder killed the other. The boarder who committed the murder panicked. He didn't know what to do with the body, so he chopped it up into pieces to dispose of them around the city. Working throughout the night, he chopped off the hands, and the feet, and then the legs and the arms, and finally the torso. It took him several trips to dispose of these body parts. Each time he left the boarder's room with another body part, he was afraid that at any moment, someone would catch him with the grisly evidence, but no one did. Finally, by morning he was finished, all except the head. Unable to dispose of the head during the daytime for fear of being seen and having to go to work, he wrapped the head in a towel and put it in the closet. He would take care of it that night.

"That evening, just as he was coming home from work, the boarding house owner met him outside of his room with two police officers. Apparently, several boarders had complained about the noise the previous night. Upon investigation, blood was discovered in the victim's room. Worried that he might be suspected, this boarder concocts this elaborate story about how he and the victim had been drinking in the victim's room the previous evening, and yes, they had argued. However, when he went to bed early, the victim was still in his room and very much alive. And after a while, he begins to believe that was exactly what happened. He had convinced himself that was what happened and thinks he had gotten away with it. But the problem was, the police didn't believe him. While questioning him, his story changed each time he was asked about what had happened that night. Not a lot. Just a little here and there. Maybe in one version, it was 8:00, but several hours later, it was 8:30. You know, little things like that. And all the while, the victim's head is still in the closet. Finally, when the police searched the boarder's room, he broke down and—"

"I know the story."

Park furrowed his brow.

"I know the story. I studied it in American literature. But it was the heart, not the head."

"Excuse me."

"Your story. It's like Edgar Allan Poe's 'The Tell-Tale Heart.'"

"I don't know what you're talking about. This really happened. I must have been ten or eleven at the time. It was in all the newspapers. They talked about how the head of the victim still had its eyes open. Really gruesome."

"You were right. It was a good story, but it's not going to work."

"What's not going to work?"

"I might be tired, but I know what you're trying to do, and it's not going to work."

"Doing what?"

"Whatever it is you're doing to make me confess."

"I'm not making you do anything. I'm just trying to figure this all out." Park narrowed his eyes.

I sensed that he still had something left up his sleeve. The story was just a diversion. He had been saving his best for last.

"The one thing that bothers me the most is why would anyone in your shoes brutally kill this poor woman? Here you are, you just arrived in Korea. You've got a job and a nice place to live in Chamsil. You go out and have a few drinks. I suspect you're having a good time. Your roommate disappears, as you said, and you go looking for him. When you can't find him, you end up in the Paradise Club with Han. Maybe what the owner said is true, that you were rough with her. Maybe not. We'll just leave that as it is, but when you go back to her apartment, something happened."

Park stood and walked around the table to where I was sitting. "What could she have done that would make someone angry enough to kill her?"

I swallowed hard. If this was another one of Park's interrogation tactics, I did not like where it was going.

"Then it dawned on me. You didn't have any money."

Where was he going with this?

"When I went through your wallet, I noticed you didn't have any money in it. I thought that was rather strange. You had just arrived here and had been out drinking with your roommate. You couldn't have spent all your money. After all, you had just paid the owner of the Paradise fifty thousand won. And then I thought, what would have happened if you caught Han going through your wallet?"

As he explained his theory, Park circled the chair like a hawk waiting to swoop down on its prey. I was right. I didn't like where he was going with this.

"So, here's what I think happened. After you vomited and came out of the bathroom, you caught her going through your wallet. She figured you were so drunk you were an easy target. It's been known to happen before with business girls and drunken customers. Usually, the men don't realize they have been robbed until the next morning when they've sobered up. Of course, by then, it's too late. But in your case, you caught her red-handed, as you say in English."

I followed Park with my eyes as he circled around me.

"That's when you got angry. You demand your money. She tells you she has no idea what you're talking about. That's where the shouting comes in—what the woman downstairs hears. You call her a liar. She calls you a liar. But it escalates, doesn't it? You can still leave at this point, and other than an empty wallet and a lesson learned, the only thing you're going to wake up with the next morning is a hangover and a bruised ego. But that's not what happens. Maybe you slap her. Not too hard, but she doesn't back down. Maybe you even push her around a bit. Instead, she comes after you."

Park stopped behind me and put a hand on my shoulder. He squeezed it hard enough that it made me wince.

"That's when you lose it. You're not going to let this woman push you around. After all, she just stole from you. You choke her, but she is stronger than you thought. She grabs an ashtray that we found on the floor and hits you on the head. That would explain the cut on your forehead. We found blood on the ashtray, which I'm certain will match yours."

"No, that's—"

Park released his grip and walked around to the front of the chair.

"You could have gotten out of there when you had the chance, but now you are consumed by rage. That's when things get out of hand. You strangle her again. But she can't fight you off this time, and you kill her. Now you've got a bigger problem. You got a dead woman on your hands, and you don't know what to do. The owner knows you went home with Han. She can identify you. You panic. You could have run then, but you didn't. I think that's when you put her in bed and made it look like nothing was out of the ordinary. But before you could leave, her roommate came home. That must have been rough sitting in her apartment with Han's dead body and her roommate outside. I'm surprised you didn't shit your pants."

"Stop it! Please stop it. That's not what happened! You've got it all wrong!"

Startled by another one of my outbursts, Park stopped and stared at me. "Excuse me?"

"You've got it all wrong. I had money. Not in my wallet, but in my jacket."

"What are you talking about?"

"My school gave me three hundred thousand won the night arrived, but I lost it."

"Lost it?"

"It was in an envelope. It was in my jacket. I must have lost it in her apartment."

Park turned to his partner and nodded. I sensed they had found the money during their investigation.

"You found my money, didn't you?"

"Found what?"

"The money in the envelope. I had around one hundred thousand left. My roommate borrowed some, and I spent the rest on drinks and Joo-hee. You see, there's no way I could have killed her over the money."

"Or maybe you caught her going through the pockets on your jacket looking for it."

"But I didn't."

"She knew it was there. She probably saw you take out money from the envelope when you paid for her drinks."

"But that's not what happened."

Was this guy for real? There was no winning with Park. Every time I said something in my defense, he came back at me immediately with one of his barbed accusations. I could not keep up with him. Everything I said, Park twisted it around. How much more of this interrogation would I have to endure? I'd say anything to make them stop.

"We've been over this a hundred times. I passed out, and when

I woke up, she was dead. What the fuck is wrong with you? Why can't you get that through that thick skull of yours?"

Oh, shit.

I didn't see Park's hand until it was too late. It wasn't a hard slap, not as hard as Shin's earlier, but hard enough to sting and probably leave what I'm sure was a red mark the size of his palm on the side of my face. I recoiled in pain and glared at Park.

You bastard. You fucking bastard. If I ever get out of here, I'm going to make you pay for this.

"And that's another thing." Park took off his jacket and laid it across the table in front of me. "You keep on saying that you passed out. Why didn't she check on you?"

"I don't know."

"She just sat there on the bed, and when you didn't come out, she went to sleep? I would think that she would be concerned about you, am I right?"

"I guess so."

"So, why didn't she check on you?"

"I don't know."

"You know what I think? I don't think you passed out at all."

"But I did!"

"I think you've been making this all up."

"Someone else must have come into her apartment and killed her."

"Who?"

"The man at the club."

"Oh yes, the man at the club. The one, according to the owner, who wasn't there."

"The owner is lying to protect him."

"Do you really expect us to believe that?" Park rolled up one of his sleeves.

"But that's what happened."

"If what you say is true, that someone had entered the apartment while you were passed out, how did that person get inside? We checked the front gate. The person would have needed a key to get inside. The landlady who lives downstairs she's a light sleeper. She didn't hear anyone else come in after you and Han did."

"I don't know how the person got inside. Maybe they climbed over the wall."

"And that's another thing. You claimed the man you saw at the club, the one who got rough with Han, might have been the one who killed her. If that were true, he would have known that she was with a customer, you. So why risk catching you and her together by going to her apartment? Do you see where I am going with this? You're good, Turner. But not good enough."

"But that's what must have happened."

"Or, as I said, maybe you're just making this all up."

"But I'm not making it up!" I watched Park roll up the other sleeve. What did he have in mind for me next?

"And this landlady, she heard a lot of shouting. I'd think that you would have heard it, too."

"But I passed out!"

Park huffed. "Again, how convenient? I'm sorry, I don't remember anything because I passed out," Park said, imitating me in a condescending, sing-song voice. "Come on, Turner. Tell us the truth!"

"But I have been telling you the truth!"

"Why did you do it?"

"Please, I'm tired."

"Maybe you're one of those psychos who gets off on killing a woman with their hands."

"Stop it!"

"Did it excite you? Having all that power."

"No!"

"Tell us now, and all this will be over."

"I just want to sleep." I closed my eyes and lowered my head.

Park grabbed a handful of my hair and yanked my head up. "No! You will not sleep until you tell us what happened!"

"I didn't do it. Please, no more."

Park kicked the chair over, sending me sprawling onto the floor.

"Confess, Turner!" He kicked me in the side of the ribs. "Confess, you miserable piece of shit."

"No more. No more."

He kicked me several more times. I thought I was going to pass out.

"Confess!"

The baton in Shin's hand buzzed to life again.

FOURTEEN

I READ SOMEWHERE, I THINK IT MUST HAVE BEEN FOR THIS psych class I took back in college, about the effectiveness of sleep deprivation as a means of torture during an interrogation. After a while, when a person is kept awake for long periods, their reasoning is clouded and undermines their will to stay alive. Given a choice between sleep, food, and water, most people would rather forego food and water than sleep.

There was no doubt in my mind that keeping me awake for almost two days affected the way I remembered events from the time I left the club with Joo-hee until I woke up in bed next to her dead body in the morning. No matter how many times Park asked me what happened that night, I stuck to my story: After we got back to her apartment, I went into the bathroom, puked my guts out, and then passed out, and then at some point, I came to and staggered out of the bathroom and got into bed. Eight hours later, I woke up, thanks in no small part to Joo-hee's roommate showing up and banging on the door.

And then, my world turned upside down.

It was, as Park made it clear to me several times, a very convenient explanation. But that's all I had for my defense.

Could I, as Park suggested, have been capable of reacting violently if I had caught her looking for my money? That was as good a motive as any. But could it have escalated to murder? Ah, there it was. That was the rub. That was what Park wanted to believe; that was what he wanted me to believe.

There was more. If I thought someone had entered her apartment while I was passed out in the bathroom, why didn't that person check to see if anyone was inside? Surely they would have noticed my jacket or shoes.

The thing was, after two days of going around and around with Park, it started to make sense. Not all of it, but some of it. Enough that I believed Park more than myself. Indeed, his theory might not have been convincing, but it could be enough for a prosecutor and a judge to consider. I was pretty loaded that night. More than I had been in a long time. And then, on top of all the booze I had, I was jetlagged. Anything was possible.

After all, I have blacked out before from drinking too much and then later, not remembering anything I had done.

There was that time when I was stationed at George Air Force Base when I blacked out after getting drunk at the NCO club celebrating my promotion to sergeant. I was living off-base at the time. How I drove the ten miles to my apartment without crashing my car in the desert, I'll never know? When I got home, I popped several TV dinners into the oven, turned on the TV, and plopped down on the sofa. I woke up naked ten hours later in the upstairs bedroom, not remembering having gone to bed. When I walked downstairs, it felt like I had entered a blast furnace. The oven was still on, and those TV dinners were still cooking inside, having been reduced to a pile of charcoal.

Could the same thing have happened? Could I have been so inebriated that I killed Joo-hee and not remember? I thought about the photos that Park had shown me. There were bruises around her neck where someone had choked her. Could I have done that?

Don't even go there, man. That's what Park wants you to do. Park wants you to believe that you were capable of doing this.

They have nothing. All they have is you running out of her apartment. But if I didn't kill her, who did? Could that man from the club have gone to her apartment and killed her? Could he have killed her when I was passed out in the bathroom? But then I would have heard something. Remember what Park said? The woman downstairs said there was a lot of shouting. Park said there was a used condom in the trash. I woke up naked. Remember, when you first realized she was dead—you thought that you might have been responsible. Why would you even think that? Unless—

Stop it, Turner! You're going to make yourself a nervous wreck!

One thing was for sure, after a while, Park had me so turned around with his questions I was starting to believe him. He was pretty convincing, that was for sure. I had to give him credit for that. He knew I was tired and reeling from the effects of jet lag. He kept on pushing and pushing. He was relentless in his pursuit of the truth and a confession. He was obsessed with breaking me. After nearly two days of being interrogated, I would have admitted to anything just so Park would stop. I wanted to sleep. I wanted to crawl into my bed and sleep for a week.

According to what I read, some psychologists believe a person will confess to a crime they didn't commit to get out of the interrogation room. The hope was, when more facts came to light, they would be cleared. Studies have been done to prove this. At some point, a person just breaks down and will say anything for the interrogation to stop.

Had I reached that point?

———

MY EYELIDS GREW HEAVY, and my chin slumped to my chest. I thought I could hear my mother's voice calling my name, telling me to wake up. I was back home, sleeping in my bed. I scrunched up the blanket around my face and breathed in the sweet smell of the Downey fabric softener she used. Just a few more minutes, Mom.

Park let me sleep just enough before he slapped me on the back of the head.

"Open your eyes, Turner. Don't you go sleeping on us. Tell us what happened!" Park grabbed a handful of hair again and jerked my head up.

I winced from the pain, but I was too tired to tell him to stop.

"We know you killed Han. You know you killed her. Just confess, and this will all be over. Confess now, and I promise you will be sleeping in a warm bed soon."

"Sleep. Yes, I want to sleep."

"Good, Turner."

"But I didn't kill her."

"Goddamnit! I'm losing my patience with you! Confess now!"

Park slapped me on the side of the head. He slapped me so hard my ears rang, and my head felt like it would explode. I tasted blood in my mouth. He would have slapped me again, but his partner restrained him.

"What's it going to be, Turner? What's it going to be?"

I opened my mouth to say something, but the words did not come out. I was too exhausted. That was when I broke. I could not take any more of this.

Park held a sheet of paper in front of me. There was something written in Korean on the front. No doubt my confession. "Sign this. And this will be all over."

I nodded. I would have signed anything for the interrogation to stop.

Shin helped me up from the chair. Park handed me a pen, and I scribbled my name at the bottom of the paper. When I looked up at Park, he had this smug look of satisfaction. He had won. He had broken me.

After that, everything happened so fast. I was dragged out of the room and dressed in an orange jumpsuit. My arms were tied with ropes. Pushed down a dark hallway past several rooms by two officers, I couldn't see Park or his partner. Where the hell was I being taken?

The two officers led me down two flights of stairs through a dark lobby and out a pair of glass doors covered with black tape. Once outside, I squinted in the bright sunlight and gulped in huge mouthfuls of the fresh, cold air. After two days cooped up inside, I could not believe how pure the air tasted. My body ached in a hundred places, and I had trouble walking as two police officers helped me inside the van. My ankles were shackled to the bottom of the bench seat just in case I tried to make a run for it—as if I would get very far with my arms tied to my sides and two armed officers sitting in the front.

As it turned out, I hadn't even been at a police station. The four-story building, covered with grimy yellow rectangular tiles, had no visible signage showing what kind of building, other than the faded outline of what looked like a rock with wavy lines above it. All the windows were covered with tinted glass. It was set back from an alley near a railway freight yard. Park and Shin climbed into the van and sat behind me. Park said something to the driver, and we pulled out of the parking lot.

A few minutes later, we were headed down a busy boulevard. For two days, it had been the Park and Shin show, and I enjoyed this brief respite of freedom, even if my arms were bound and my ankles shackled. Traffic grew thicker, and the van slowed past two- and three-story buildings covered with the same grimy tiles I had seen earlier and big box stores. Some signs were in English, and not very good English at that. One sign simply said, "Cock and Rest," which I took as a weird abbreviation for "cocktail and restaurant," or so it seemed. In my frazzled state, anything was possible, but I found it amusing just the same. I had better luck with Korean. I picked out a few of the Hangul characters from my study of the language courtesy of the Berlitz phrase book. Tambae. Cigarette. Keopi. Coffee. My body craved both.

Thirty minutes later, we pulled into the parking lot of a gray, official-looking building. I was taken to an office on the sixth floor where a thin, dour-looking middle-aged man in a dark blue suit sat behind an oversized dark brown desk. The man motioned for the two officers escorting me to remove the ropes around my arms.

"I'm Kang Jae-min, the Chief Public Prosecutor," Kang said.

Although his English was just as good as Park's, his voice was cold and mechanical. "I'll be the one prosecuting you in your murder trial. But, before discussing the charges against you, I thought we would have something to eat first. Are you hungry?"

I nodded.

"Good," Kang said something in Korean to one of the officers, who immediately left the room.

Apparently, Kang or someone had already ordered food because the officer who had left the room returned a few minutes later with a delivery man who carried two large metal boxes. The delivery man set the boxes down on the floor, removed four plastic bowls from compartments inside, and set them on a coffee table between four large, dark brown upholstered chairs. The man also removed several smaller bowls and plastic containers containing kimchi, chopped onions, yellow disc-shaped vegetables, and wooden chopsticks. After finishing, the delivery man bowed to Kang and left the office.

"Let's eat," Kang said.

Kang motioned to one officer to bring me to a chair where I was told to sit. Park and Shin sat on one side of the table while Kang sat beside me. The two officers picked up one of the covered bowls and chopsticks and sat on a sofa behind me.

I watched Kang, Park, and Shin remove the plastic wrap covering the bowls, revealing black sauce and thick noodles. The men grabbed a pair of chopsticks, split them apart, and rubbed them together before mixing the black sauce and noodles.

"Can you use chopsticks?" Kang asked.

I nodded.

"Please, eat." Kang motioned to the bowl of noodles.

I was famished. While being interrogated, the only thing I had been given to eat was some hardtack crackers and water. Park and Shin, with their heads down over the bowls, attacked the noodles with great gusto, making loud slurping sounds. Park and Shin were almost finished by the time I had removed the plastic wrap and attempted several times to swirl the noodles around my pair of chopsticks. Even though I was hungry and did my best to eat as much as possible, I was too nervous about what lay ahead. After a few mouthfuls, I gave up.

Once the bowls had been collected and set outside the office and the table cleaned, an officer led me to a chair in front of Kang's desk.

"Okay then," Kang said, working a piece of meat free from one of his teeth with his tongue. "Do you understand the charges which have been brought against you?"

"Yes, but—"

"But what?"

"But I'm innocent. I didn't kill the—"

Kang glared at me and held up a finger on his right hand to stop me from speaking more. "Please let me finish. You have been charged with the murder of Han Joo-hee based upon evidence collected at the scene, the testimony of several eyewitnesses, and in the statement you gave to detectives Park and Shin."

What evidence at the scene? The used condom? My brand of cigarettes in the ashtray?

"But I didn't kill Miss Han. I signed whatever it was they gave me so they would stop interrogating me."

Kang cast Park a sideways glance before he turned back to me.

"Come now, Mr. Turner. You're not making matters any better for you. If you cooperate with us now, it will be better for you in the long term."

"There's no way that I murdered that woman! Park and Shin coerced that statement out of me. They kept me awake for two days. They beat me. And Shin used a cattle prod on me! You wait until I tell my embassy how you have treated me."

I still had some fight left in me, but not much.

Kang looked over at Park and Shin to see their reactions to what I had just said. Both men stared straight ahead with blank expressions on their faces. Then, Kang turned back to me. "Please don't interrupt me. As I was saying, all the evidence points right back at you. So unless you are ready to face the death penalty or spend a very long time behind bars, I suggest you cooperate with us. Do you understand?"

Again, what evidence? And then there was that word cooperating again. I signed the confession. What else was I supposed to do to cooperate? I felt helpless sitting here in front of the prosecutor, who had my life in the palm of his hands. The death penalty. Park had said the same thing.

"What do you mean by cooperating?"

"By showing remorse."

"Is that what this is all about?"

Kang nodded. "Showing remorse now will go over well with the judges."

"How am I supposed to show remorse for a crime I didn't commit? You've got the wrong man."

"Did you not confess to the killing of Miss Han?"

"I was tired. I wanted Park and Shin to stop."

"I'll ask you again, did you not confess to the murder of Han Joo-hee?"

"I just wanted them to stop."

"Let me explain how this works. I am going to present this case before several judges. Now, the manner in which I present this case could determine your sentencing, which means you need to cooperate with us. So what's it going to be, Mr. Turner? Did you confess to the murder?"

"Yes."

"See, that wasn't so hard, was it?"

"But you don't understand."

"Understand what?"

"There's no way I could have killed Miss Han. I tried explaining this to Detective Park and his partner several times. I passed out in the bathroom. When I woke up the next morning, she was already dead. Someone else entered the apartment when I passed out and killed her."

"And still you persist."

"Tell him, Park." I glanced at Park, who avoided eye contact with me. "Tell him about the man I saw at the Paradise."

"Tell me what?" Kang asked.

"There was another man in the club while I was there. He got rough with the woman. He was a big guy. Had a scar on his face. Tell him, goddamnit!"

"That's enough, Turner! I've read Park's report. There was no man in the club."

"What do I have to do to get you to believe me? The real murderer is going to get away. What's wrong with you people?"

Oh, shit. I fucked up again. I knew it as soon as I said it.

Kang glared at me. "'What's wrong with you people?' What is it with you foreigners who come to Korea and think they can come here and get away with anything they want? Ever since we held the Olympics, more and more foreigners have come here. Many are like yourself, coming here to teach English. But once they get here, they think they are above the law. For example, just last month, I prosecuted an American for mailing himself some marijuana cigarettes from the Philippines. And then, after he was arrested picking up the package at the post office, he dared to tell me it was someone else who mailed them. Can you believe that?

"But you know what? We're not some poor, backward country anymore. We're not, as some people have liked to describe our country, a shrimp caught between two whales. We have over 5,000 years of history. So, in response to your little outburst, I would think someone in your position would be wise to choose their expressions carefully to ensure there is no misunderstanding that could further complicate these proceedings. Do you understand?"

"Yes."

"Is there anything else you want to say on your behalf?"

"I want to talk to my embassy now."

"Yes, we'll notify them."

FIFTEEN

Before I was transported to a detention center, Kang quickly arranged a press conference. How nice of him. The murder of Han and the arrest of an American responsible for her death were big news. With the large media turnout, I got the impression that this was being touted as the crime of the century.

Park and Shin led me to the front of the room, where a podium was located. Cameras flashed around me, and there was nothing I could do to avoid their glare. My hands had been tied with rope, so there was no way that I could raise my hands to hide my face. That's all I needed was some international news service like the Associated Press to wire my photo back to the States. Dateline, Seoul, South Korea. An American English teacher was charged with the brutal murder of a Korean woman. Although the accused murderer, Robert Turner of LaSalle, Illinois, has no recollection of the murder, police authorities are confident he is their man. All I could do was put my head down as far as I could, like a turtle withdrawing into its shell, to hide my face.

Kang approached the podium and stood behind it.

"We are happy to report that the murderer of Han Joo-hee has been apprehended and charged thanks to the efforts of Captains

Park Chong-hun and Shin Song-su," Kang said, reading from a prepared statement. "They are a credit to the Seoul Metropolitan police force."

He spoke for a few more minutes, outlining how Park and Shin apprehended me and got my confession. I'm sure he left out the part about how Park and Shin, who stood on either side of me, nearly electrocuted me with a cattle prod and kicked me senseless to coerce the confession from me. I kept my head down and imagined them smiling and gleaming for the cameras.

A few members of the press asked questions that Park and Shin took turns answering. I'm sure they responded I was a cold-hearted killer and probably would have killed again if I hadn't been apprehended. Or maybe they described their interrogation methods and how they kept searching for the truth. No one was there to translate for me, so they could have been making everything up for all I knew.

And then, a voice like an angel asked a question directed at me.

"Are you sorry for what you did?"

The question caught me off guard. Not because it was in English, but because the woman who asked me it had already assumed I was guilty. She was standing near the front, dressed in a gray pantsuit with short hair and glasses. I could feel everyone in the room looking at me while cameras clicked and speed lights flashed. My fate might have already been sealed, but I was not going to let an opportunity pass me by.

"I did not do it. I'm an innocent bystander in all of this. They arrested the wrong man! Someone, please notify the US embassy!"

It was worth a shot.

This was followed by more clicks and flashes. The noise of the crowd reached a crescendo. However, this so-called press conference was not over yet. Another reporter, who knew a little English, yelled out a question. "What do you mean?"

Before I could answer, Park and Shin whisked me to a back room and closed the door.

Park shot me a dirty look. "That was a foolish thing to say back there."

"The reporter asked a question, and I answered it."

Park snorted his disdain and pushed me down onto a wooden chair. Police officers walked in and out of the room, staring and sneering at me while Park gathered some documents. Now that I had been formally charged, the only thing left was for me to be taken to some jail or detention center. My body shook with fear. I wish I could go back in time to the interrogation room, where I still had some control over my fate. Could I have held out for another day? Could my intransigence have broken Park and his partner? Would they have gotten tired and given up? I would never know now.

When Park was finished, he walked over to where I was sitting and helped me to my feet. Then, he and Shin escorted me to a van waiting outside. Once inside and handcuffed to my seat, I looked out through a dirty window at Park and Shin standing in the parking lot. Park had this smug expression on his face that filled me with anger. I had a strange feeling that this was not going to be the last time I saw him.

From the Seoul Prosecutor's Office, I was transported to a detention center on the outskirts of the city. It was an uneventful ride, sitting between two officers who appeared to take no joy in escorting me. My first real glimpse of the Korean countryside, and I was on my way to jail.

Urban sprawl gave way to rolling hills covered with pine trees and barren rice paddies lying fallow for the winter. Long, narrow, cylindrical structures covered with white plastic—greenhouses, I guessed—dotted the landscape. We passed through quaint, idyllic villages, no more than a cluster of rectangular-shaped concrete and wooden structures topped with orange and brown tile roofs and wisps of smoke rising from brick chimneys. Round, brown pots of various sizes were stacked outside many of these buildings. Dark orange fruit, which I took for persimmons, hung on brown string from the wooden eaves, drying in the sun.

I remembered something my roommate Keith had said about some teachers coming to Korea expecting the country to conjure up images of a Pearl Buck novel. I wondered if my journey through the Korean countryside would qualify, though I don't think Buck wrote about anyone carted off to prison.

Once at the detention center, the two officers released me into the custody of two guards. One mean-looking guard with a pock-marked square face and shaved head sneered at me with contempt. He pushed me along a corridor until we came to a waiting room where other prisoners sat. I felt both terrified and shocked at what awaited me inside. While I had denied my guilt up to this point—even though I had signed a confession—I hadn't even fathomed what would happen if this went to trial. It was right there that it finally hit me that I could go to prison for a long time.

I gazed at the other prisoners sitting on the wooden bench and thought about that proverb, misery loves company. I was the only American. No one said anything. They just sat there staring straight ahead or at the floor in front of them. The man beside me had bruises and lacerations up and down his thick arms. I wondered what he did or didn't do to be on the receiving end of those injuries.

Exhausted, fatigued, frazzled—there were barely any words to describe my mental and physical condition. After two days of torment and no sleep, I wanted this nightmare to end, but it was just beginning. The uncertainty of my future loomed heavily in the darkness of the night.

My mouth felt parched, like old dried-out leather, and I wished I had drunk more water and eaten more when I had the chance back in Kang's office. There was no telling when I would eat again.

Why hadn't someone from the US embassy called? Surely by now, they had been contacted by the police or someone at my school. Unless the embassy got around to helping me, there was no way that I was going to get out of this situation.

One by one, myself and the other prisoners were called into an adjoining room. Inside, a guard motioned for me to strip naked. I stood there freezing and humiliated as the guard, who had a small flashlight in his mouth, had me bend over to check for any contraband in my anus. My knees trembled while he poked and prodded until he was satisfied I was not sneaking anything inside.

All the while, I kept on thinking, this can't be happening to me.

After being issued my dark blue prison garb and a pair of slippers, I was finally brought to my cell on a lower level of the detention center. The air reeking of piss, shit, and body odor gagged me. Curious prisoners looked out from their cells at the latest additions to the detention center population as the other prisoners and I were marched to their cells. I shuffled along, my eyes lowered as I passed each cell, but I could sense all the pairs of eyes peering out from these cells, burning a hole into my tortured soul.

One prisoner spoke a little English and called out to ask what country I was from, but I pretended not to hear. And then he followed with, "I was only trying to be friendly."

When I reached my cell, which was in a different section of the cellblock, segregated from the Korean prisoners, I stood shaking in front of the entrance. My stomach twisted into knots. I tensed at the grating sound of metal against metal as the guard turned the key inside the lock. The heavy door slid open with an equally metallic grinding sound, and I was pushed inside my cell. The door slid shut with a bang.

A metal cot with a thin mattress on top was in the corner of my tiny cell. I sat down on the edge of the cot and put my head in my hands. A myriad of troubling thoughts bounced around my head, not the least of which was how I had ended up in this predicament. When I replayed the events that had occurred that night inside my head, it was all too surreal to comprehend. From the time I wandered into the Paradise Club until I woke up in bed with the murdered woman in the morning, it was like one of those movies where everyone knows what will happen next except the protagonist. If only I hadn't wandered off looking for my roommate. It was funny how a person's life could change in an instance: wait for Keith to come back, and I'm back in my room to sleep off my drunk; go looking for him, and the next thing you know, I'm being charged with murder and spending my first night in prison.

Somewhere down the cell block from my cell, I heard someone whimpering. Another person farted.

I lay down on the smelly, ratty mattress and covered myself with an equally smelling and tattered blanket. Curling up in the fetal position, I cried myself to sleep.

SIXTEEN

Three thousand university students took to the streets around the US embassy in Kwanghwamun, a district in downtown Seoul. They protested against the US military in Korea and the murder of the Itaewon business girl. An American flag and an effigy of George Herbert Walker Bush were burned. Fifteen thousand riot police were deployed around the downtown area, including the embassy.

Han Joo-hee had quickly become a martyr for a militant student organization that used her death to vent their anger at the US military presence on the peninsula, which they believed prevented North and South Korea from reunifying.

Students pumped their fists into the air in synchronized, robotic motions and shouted anti-American chants. USA out of Korea. Justice for Han Joo-hee. Yankee Go Home. There was no mention the American who was arrested was not a GI. It was assumed that it had to be a GI because the murder took place in Itaewon.

"Ii nara-neun uri-nara-ya! Hanguk e-seo na-ga!" The student organization leader pumped his fist and shouted through a bullhorn. This country is ours! US out of South Korea!

"Miguk beom jwe meom cheo-ra!" Stop US crimes!

"Han Joo Hee reul gi eok he-ra!" Remember Han Joo-hee!

Several students carried enormous posters of Han through the crowd of demonstrators. Unfortunately, a recent photograph of her could not be found, so they were forced to use one from high school. Blown up to cover the poster, the grainy black-and-white photograph of Han staring straight ahead expressionless, in her high school uniform with a short, pageboy-style haircut, cast an eerie, surreal pall over the demonstration. To an untrained observer, it would have appeared that one of South Korea's young, angelic teenagers had her life shortened by a brutish, cruel, long-nosed American.

The US military command, completely caught off guard by accusations that a US service member had murdered the Korean woman, had issued no statement, further fueling anger and the possibility of a cover-up. Several hundred more students protested outside the main gate of the Yongsan Garrison, the large US Army base in central Seoul, demanding justice for Han.

Students who usually would have gone back to their hometowns after taking their final examinations stayed in the city to participate in the protests and clashed with riot police late into the night. In choreographed moves, protestors wearing handkerchiefs and bandanas over their mouths and noses to protect themselves from tear gas first pelted the riot police with stones and chunks of concrete. The riot police, who wore padded gray uniforms with ominous Darth Vader-like black helmets and wire mesh screens over their faces, deflected the stones and other projectiles with their long gray shields. Then, another group of students charged the line of police tossing Molotov cocktails, which exploded with a hollow sucking whoosh sound into dozens of fireballs on the street. Some landed on their intended targets, splattering officers with the burning liquid, which was quickly extinguished with small fire extinguishers the police carried on their belts.

Finally, students wielding iron pipes assaulted the line of the police, who held their ground. "Skull Busters," a special unit of riot police, who got their name for cracking the heads and bones of protestors with their wooden batons, rushed out from the ranks, headlong into the fray. Wearing blue and white motorcycle-like helmets, padded denim jackets, and elbow and knee pads, they chased down individual protestors and smacked them several times before dragging them behind the lines.

When the protestors failed to disperse, the pop-pop-pop of tear gas launchers mounted on top of several black vans fired salvos of tear gas canisters into the crowd echoing off the buildings lining Sejong-ro, the main thoroughfare through the heart of the city. In the heat of the battle between the protestors and police, a riot police bus was overturned and set on fire. Students tossed Molotov cocktails into the US Embassy compound. One brave soul tried to climb over the wall and was promptly pulled down by three riot police officers who beat him with iron pipes.

A Christmas concert at the Sejong Cultural Center across the street from the embassy was disrupted when protestors ran into the building to escape riot police. Hundreds of concert-goers fled from the building, with hands and handkerchiefs covering their mouths and noses to avoid the thick tear gas in the air outside.

Fifty protestors were sent to local hospitals with a miscellany of injuries. Ten riot police were injured. Thirty protestors were arrested.

SEVENTEEN

THE FOLLOWING DAY, THE US EMBASSY SENT ONE OF ITS consular officials to meet with me. When I was brought into a windowless room, sitting at the table was a tall, neatly dressed man with short black hair. He looked ten years younger than me, probably fresh out of college. In front of him was a manila folder. He looked at his watch and sighed. Not a good sign when the person you hoped could get you out of this jam was on a tight schedule.

"Mr. Turner." The man stood and held out his hand. "I'm Lawrence Baxter from the US Embassy."

"Thank God," I said, gripping his hand and shaking it. I wanted to say about fucking time, but I remained calm. "You have no idea how happy I am to see you."

Baxter nodded and motioned me to take a seat.

"I just found out about your case this morning. Actually, your school contacted us, and then we read about it in the paper. It's terrible, Robert. Or do you prefer being called Bob?"

"Bob is fine."

"As I was saying, Bob, this is all very terrible. Of course, it's also a real tragedy, but how the Korean press has covered it has been most unsettling."

"What are they saying?"

"They're calling you the Itaewon Murderer. It's not even original. Maybe they think it'll sell more newspapers. I wouldn't let it bother you, though. The Korean press likes to blow everything out of proportion. Do you know what I mean? The proverbial molehill into a mountain. I have to admit that they have pulled out all the stops with this one. They've already got you tried and convicted in the minds of their readers. But you probably already know that, right? How long have you been here?"

"What? In jail?"

I suddenly got the strange feeling that he had drawn the short straw at the embassy. He had no idea who I was other than what he had read in the paper. If this was the best my embassy could do, I was screwed.

"No, not in jail. I'm talking about how long have you been in Korea?"

"I arrived on Friday."

"Last Friday?"

"Yeah."

"Oh man, that's too bad."

"No shit."

"I thought you'd been here for a while."

Enough of this small talk. "Can you get me out of here?"

"I'm afraid that's not how it works."

"What do you mean, that's now how it works? I've been wrongly accused of murder. You've got to do something!"

"We have no jurisdiction over cases involving a US citizen suspected of committing a crime like you did. However, we can provide you with a list of Korean attorneys, help you contact family members, and get any medication you need. You're not sick, are you?"

"You mean other than the beating and electrocution by the cops for two days? No, I'm not sick."

Baxter pretended not to hear that. "At my last post in Thailand, we had an American locked up for running over a Thai national with his motorcycle on the island of Koh Samui. Have you ever been there?"

I shook my head.

"Too bad. Lovely place. Anyway, this guy ate a bunch of those magic mushrooms, which are really popular on the island, stole a motorcycle, and went joyriding around the island until he ran over this elderly guy walking along the highway. The old guy lived but ended up spending six months in the hospital. Well, this American turned out to be diabetic, and it was hard as hell to get him his insulin."

"Are you even listening to me?"

"Calm down. I know this is not easy to take. You see, if we get involved, the South Koreans might think we're trying to meddle in their affairs. Whether you're guilty or innocent is not the issue here. This has to play out according to Korean law, and therefore, we cannot get involved."

I didn't know what Baxter's angle was. Aside from his feeble attempt at being witty, he came across as a by-the-book bureaucrat who didn't want to step on any toes. He made it seem that it was all my fault without hearing my side of the story.

"But I'm innocent! I didn't kill anyone. You've got to believe me. The only thing I'm guilty of is being in the wrong place at the wrong time."

"But you signed a confession."

"I only signed it so the police would stop interrogating me."

"Stop right there."

"What?"

Baxter leaned forward and lowered his voice. "You can't talk about the case with me."

"I'm just telling you why I signed the confession. Why are you even here, then?"

Baxter held up his right hand to shush me. "I understand, but you have to realize our hands are tied in this. We can't even advise you what you should or shouldn't do. It's a real Catch-22."

I couldn't believe what I was hearing. My own country was going to hang me out to dry.

"But the prosecutor is going to ask for the death penalty!"

"Please, calm down, Bob. You're not making matters any better by getting all worked up."

"That's easy for you to say."

"You know what I mean."

I took a deep breath and sighed. Baxter was right. I might not be able to talk to him about my case, but I could feed him some information.

"There was this guy in the club where I had been. I think he might have killed the woman."

Baxter sat up. "What?"

"There was this guy. He was in the club at the same time that I was. He got rough with the woman. I told the police about him, but they —"

"Hold it right there, Turner. I told you I can't discuss the case with you."

"I know. We're just talking here. Just talking about sitting in a bar, and then this guy comes in and —"

"Well, don't." Baxter sighed and then looked around nervously. "People could be listening."

"What?"

"People could be listening," Baxter said, lowering his voice and gesturing with his head to a vent in the corner of the room.

I glanced in the direction where Baxter had indicated, but I couldn't see anything.

"I don't know if I should tell you this—you're probably going to find out about it eventually—but last night, university students took to the streets protesting against the US military in South Korea."

"What's that got to do with me?"

"Plenty."

"What do you mean?"

"Somehow, they think you're a soldier. There aren't too many foreigners in Korea other than the US military. When the police paraded you in front of the media yesterday, these students assumed you were a soldier."

"With hair like this?" I pointed to my head.

"Yeah, I can see that."

"I still don't understand how this deals with me."

"About a year ago, there was a similar case involving a GI and the murder of a business girl in Itaewon. Really brutal and gruesome. The body was desecrated, and her room was set on fire to cover up any evidence. Makes your murder pale in comparison, if that's any consolation."

I shot Baxter a dirty look.

"Sorry. I don't mean to make light of your situation."

"What happened?"

"A GI was eventually arrested, but the police botched the investigation and had to release him. Although the police were convinced he was the one, he had an alibi. But the public didn't see it that way. They thought because he was an American GI, he got preferential treatment. And now, with the death of another business girl, the public will demand that justice be served this time."

"Oh my God."

"Like it or not, you're the man of the hour, Bob. The police and the Prosecutor's Office will not make the same mistake twice."

"But I'm not a GI."

"That doesn't make any difference. We believe the Prosecutor's Office might use you as an example. The bottom line is that this will not go away quietly. To begin with, women are not treated too well in Korea. When a foreigner does anything to one of them, all hell breaks loose. Between you and me, most Koreans couldn't care less about some murdered prostitute, but have a foreigner charged with it, the press is going to make her out to be a saint. The police, the prosecutor's office, and the press will milk this for everything it's worth."

Great. Just fucking great. I was going to be used as an example for a crime I didn't commit. And worse, my own country couldn't lift a finger to help.

"These anti-American activists are going to make you a poster boy for everything they hate about America. The current president is pro-US, but his part in clamping down on a democratic uprising ten years ago has come back to haunt him. It's a real shit sandwich if you can excuse the reference."

I recalled my roommate telling me the same thing about anti-American sentiment the night we had gone to Itaewon.

"Between the press and the Prosecutor's Office, this is quickly turning into a diplomatic cluster fuck. Frankly, it's a real burr up the Ambassador's ass, but you didn't hear that from me. Maybe they'd be happy if we all went home. Just think how fast ole Kim Il-sung would be down here if that happened with the whole North Korean army behind him."

For a guy who wasn't supposed to talk about my case, he sure had a lot to say and not what I needed to hear. Too much information overload from the guy who should have been helping me assuage my anxieties, not compound them. "What about me?"

"What?"

"Me. What about me? What do you think is going to happen next?"

"Your case will go to trial. It probably won't last long given all the press it has gotten, not to mention your confession."

"But there is a chance it won't go to trial, right?"

"What?"

"I mean this guy I saw. If someone —"

"Stop it." Baxter looked over his shoulder at the guard standing outside the room. "I told you about that."

"We're just talking here."

Baxter opened his mouth, then, as if changing his mind about what he wanted to say, cleared his throat. "Who would you like for us to contact?"

Any other time, I would have said my mother, but there was not much she could do. It would have to be my brother, even though we had not spoken to each other in two years. That's when I said a few things that I probably shouldn't have, like how he had our mother wrapped around his little finger. Our mother might have put him on a pedestal for being the perfect son, but that was far from the truth. When he first went to Texas, he promised to take care of our mother if she joined him. Then, after she sold most of her belongings, packed up the rest in a U-Haul trailer, and went to Dallas, where my brother was living, he took off for Houston, leaving her high and dry in Dallas. At least when I screwed up, I did it to myself and didn't hurt anyone.

I imagined the phone call I would have with my brother. "You've gone and done it now, haven't you?" he would say. "Mom was right about you all along. You think only about yourself. I always figured you'd go and do something stupid like this one day. And you didn't disappoint me. Murder, huh? If it were up to me, I would let you rot in prison over there. But I have to think about Mom and what this will do to her. She's not getting any younger, you know. She's going to be a nervous wreck when she hears about this. I suppose you're going to need money, too."

And then I would say something like we're family, and we have to look out for each other, which probably wouldn't go over well with my brother, who would be the one who would have to come up with the money.

"I'm only doing this because of Mom. I'm not doing it for it you. But if I do this, you and I are done. Don't ever bother calling again."

"Bob?"

I snapped out of my thoughts and stared across the table at Baxter. "I'm sorry. What was the question?"

"Who do you want us to contact?"

"My brother, Randall. I don't know his phone number, but he lives outside of Houston in some town called Spring Creek."

"I think we can handle that." Baxter opened the manila folder, took a sheet of paper, and slid it across the table toward me. "This is a list of attorneys who might be able to defend you."

"Do you think they can help me?"

"I don't know."

"Who do you recommend?"

"You know I can't answer that question."

"Do you know if anyone has contacted any of these attorneys before?"

Baxter sighed. "You know I can't answer that, too."

"Yeah, you wouldn't want to do anything that would jeopardize US and Korean relations, now would we?"

"It's the way it is, Bob."

I looked at the list of names. Three attorneys named Park. Two named Kim. One Lee. One Choi. One of Kim's first name was Daniel. An English name meant he probably spoke English. Maybe he even studied or practiced in the US. I sighed. Hiring an attorney meant money—money that I did not have. Money that my mother or brother did not have. I slid the list back to Baxter.

"And what happens if I can't afford one of these attorneys?"

"The court will appoint a public defender."

"Then I guess that's how it's going to be."

Baxter nodded. "We'll offer you moral support every step of the way."

"Right, as long as I don't tell you I'm innocent."

Baxter pretended not to hear that, too. "And if there's anything you need, like writing paper and pencils, we'll make sure you get it."

"But you can't get involved."

Baxter pursed his lips. "I'm glad you understand."

Understand what? That my own country couldn't lift a finger to save one of its own.

"In the meantime, we'll contact your brother and be in contact with you again shortly," Baxter said, picking up the sheet of paper and putting it back inside his briefcase. "I know things might look pretty bleak now, but every dark cloud has its silver lining. I know how you feel. Here you are, halfway around the world with everything collapsing around you, and no one can help you. Hopefully, the public defender will be able to help you. If you're lucky, you'll get off with a reduced sentence, which is better than the alternative."

"Lucky? Do you call getting off with a reduced sentence for a murder I didn't commit, lucky?"

Baxter stood and walked toward the door. "Chin up, Turner. You're an American. Show a little grit. There are worse things that could happen to you."

EIGHTEEN

Sitting in the front seat of his black Hyundai Grandeur in a parking lot near the Wonhyo Bridge in central Seoul, Chun Yong-chol's mind was uneasy and perplexed beyond expression. What he still couldn't wrap his mind around was this American, who had been caught fleeing from Han's apartment, had confessed to her murder. Now why the fuck would he go and do that?

All things considered, it was a stroke of good luck for him and bad luck for the American. Although he had coached Lee on what to say when questioned by the police, what remained troubling for Chun was whether this American could identify him from the Paradise Club. That's what he needed to find out, and if need be, to make this problem go away. Fast.

From where he sat, he could see the Yongsan district of the city spread out before him, like an urban amoeba glowing and twinkling in the misty night. Headlights streaked by noiselessly on Kangbyeonbuk-ro, the expressway that meandered along the northern side of the Han River as workers returned home to their boring, unassuming cramped lives, unaware of the true mechanisms that ran the city. Something that a man in Chun's position never had to worry about.

In the bluish glow from the dashboard lights, he glanced at his watch and then looked in the reflection of the rearview mirror. Nine o'clock. The appointed meeting time. From his vantage point, he could see the road that led to the parking lot and anyone approaching. A few seconds later, he saw a car's headlights turning down the road toward the parking lot. He got out of the car and walked to a walkway along the river.

The car pulled up alongside his car. The driver got out and approached Chun.

"This better be good, Yong-chol," Kang Jae-min said, shoving his hands into the pockets of his dark blue down jacket when he reached Chun. He looked around nervously for any other vehicles in the parking lot. "You know what will happen if people see you and me talking together."

"What's the matter, Kang? You seem a bit on edge." Chun cared little for Kang's attitude. And he certainly cared little for his manner of speaking. "Is that any way for two old friends to talk?"

"Okay, I'm here. What was so damn important that you couldn't tell me on the phone?" Chun had said nothing when he called earlier and told Kang to meet him that evening, but knowing Chun, who only called when he needed a favor, probably wasn't good. "It's my daughter's tenth birthday."

"Sibal, dak-chyeo!" Shut the fuck up and listen. Chun stared at Kang with hooded eyes. "What can you tell me about this American charged with the murder of that business girl?"

"Is that why you had me come down here tonight to talk about that? Couldn't you have read about it in the paper?"

"Don't get smart with me, Kang. Just answer the question."

"He's guilty, if that's what you want to know. I'll ask for the maximum, but if he shows remorse, the judges will probably give him life imprisonment."

"And he said he did it?"

"He claimed there was someone else in the bar that night who might have done it, but there wasn't."

"Hmm…."

"So, what's your interest in the case? Was she one of your

—" Kang's eyes widened with horror. In the light which fell from a lamppost, he stared at the scar on the side of Chun's face. "Oh, dear God. You were the one in the club that night."

"That's right."

Kang shook his head, unable to make sense of the revelation that Chun had been the one who killed Han. "No, no. This is not happening."

"Jin-jeong hae, sibal." Calm the fuck down.

"How can I calm down? Turner has been right all along. He claimed that a man came into the club and got rough with Han. He insisted that this man was the one who killed her, but when the police questioned the owner of the Paradise, she denied everything."

Chun grinned.

"You got to her, didn't you? You told her to lie for you."

"It helps to have friends in the right places."

Kang frowned. "You bastard. How can you be so smug and calm about all of this? You murdered the woman."

"I had no choice."

"No choice?"

"Let's just say she poked her nose where she shouldn't have, which would not have turned out well for you and me. She knew about the drugs I had been smuggling. Started going around, running off her mouth about them. She threatened to go to Kwon and tell him everything."

Kang shuddered and felt sick. He leaned over the railing and vomited the samgyeopsal, the grilled pork he had eaten with his wife and daughter earlier in the evening. When he finished, he used his handkerchief to wipe his mouth. He took a deep breath, but didn't feel any better. Murder had never figured into any of the illegal activities he had done for Chun, but now he was complicit in one murder and perhaps one more. He felt sick again, and dry heaved.

"You okay?"

"No, I'm not fine." Kang closed his eyes and took a few more deep breaths until the nausea passed. "What the hell were you thinking?"

"She knew all about our little operation. And you know what would have happened if Kwon found out about us. The police would find us at the bottom of the Han River. So it wouldn't hurt to show a little gratitude."

Kang stared at the dark waters below. Several weeks ago, Chun approached him with an offer he could not refuse. He couldn't, even if he wanted. Chun had arranged to have several packages sent from Japan to a shop he used as a front for some of his illegal activities in Itaewon that, under no circumstances, could be delayed by local customs authorities. "All you have to do is make sure they reach their destination," he had told Kang, who in turn called in a few favors to ensure the packages arrived without any problems. Later, he was furious when he discovered the packages contained philopon. The penalty for trafficking drugs in South Korea was death. Although he was paid handsomely for his efforts, Chun's hooks were into him deeper.

Kang didn't like where this was going. "Go on."

"I went to the club to confront her, but she was with a customer."

"The American?"

"That's right. So I left and returned to her apartment later that night."

"What happened?"

"I had to do what I had to do. I only wanted to scare her. But things got out of hand. The next thing I know, she's coming at me with a knife. What a crazy bitch. She stabbed me in the shoulder. You know what happened next."

"Oh, dear God."

"Don't give me any more of that 'oh, dear God' crap. I told you I had no choice. But if it makes you feel any better, it was an accident. I acted in self-defense."

"Acted in self-defense? Are you kidding me?" Kang said, his voice fraught with anxiety. "Do you have any idea what you've done?"

"Shut up. And this American. He has no idea what happened?"

"Although he signed a confession, he insists he did not murder the woman. He said he blacked out in the bathroom and didn't hear anything. The police didn't believe him, and eventually, they got him to sign the confession."

"Hmm…interesting."

"Interesting? How can you be so smug about this?"

"Shut up." Chun rubbed his chin and pondered the situation at hand. He didn't mind someone taking the fall for him. Still, the fact that this American could possibly identify him made him feel a little uneasy. That was a liability he could definitely live without. "What would it take for this to go away?"

"Whoa, hold on, Chun. I don't appreciate you dragging me into another one of your messes. You don't make something like this go away. As I've already said, I was going to ask for the maximum. Maybe you haven't heard. The public is up in arms about the murder of Han. They've been clamoring for the death penalty."

"Yeah, there's that, isn't there?"

"You don't understand the gravity of the situation. I'm going to help put away an innocent man to cover for you."

"That's your problem, not mine."

Kang shot Chun a dirty look.

"This American, what is he, military?"

"No, he's an English teacher. He teaches at a language school in Kangnam. At least he was supposed to teach at the school. He just arrived the other day."

"Talk about your bad luck."

"No more, Chun. No more. I told you before that I'm done helping you."

"Are you threatening me?"

Kang opened his mouth as if to say something, but didn't. He knew he had stepped over the line with his friend.

"You're done when I say you're done."

Chun and Kang knew each other from the Star of the Sea Orphanage, located in Inchon, where they lived for several years following the Korean War. Whereas Chun had left the orphanage and fallen in with the wrong crowd with Kwon, Kang studied hard and eventually went to Yonsei University, one of the top universities in the country. Although they lost touch after Chun left the orphanage, their lives became intertwined again in the 1970s.

Chun had taken advantage of their special friendship and background and made it a point to keep the middle-aged prosecutor on a short leash, just in case he needed a special favor. Kang could not escape his past when it came to helping his friend. In the beginning, it was for something minor. Chun had been arrested for assaulting one of Kwon's rivals. There was no question Chun was guilty. He had been caught with a bloodied hammer he had used to smash the fingers of the rival.

It wasn't one of Kang's proudest moments, but he got the case thrown out because he argued Chun had acted in self-defense. Later, when he became a public prosecutor, Kang helped Chun several times by alerting Chun when law enforcement authorities cracked down on illegal activities in Itaewon.

Once Chun's hooks were into Kang, there was no turning back.

And just to be sure that Kang never refused one of his requests, he had enough dirt on Kang to bury him. Kang often frequented a high-end room salon, a drinking establishment that also provided sexual services for its clientele in Chongno in downtown Seoul, and had a thing for one of the hostesses, Sun-hee. It didn't take much persuasion from Chun to make sure Sun-hee did more than peel fruit and pour his drinks—and plenty of them—while one of the staff waited behind a two-way mirror with a camera, instructed to take photos of Kang and the woman. After some high-end whiskey, he was like putty in her hands. All she had to do was make sure that the staff member behind the two-way mirror got both her and Kang's good side while engaged in various lewd sexual acts.

A car drove down the road and slowed when it passed where Chun and Kang were standing. They both turned around to avoid their faces being seen. They waited until the car had driven down the road before speaking again.

"Does this American have an attorney?"

Kang shook his head. "He couldn't afford one. He's been appointed a public defender."

"See, nothing to worry about. You just do what you have to do and make sure that this doesn't become a problem. You got that?"

"I can't do this anymore. I want out."

Chun laughed. "Perhaps I wasn't clear enough. Maybe Mrs. Kang would be interested in these photos I have of you."

"You wouldn't." Chun had threatened him before with the compromising photographs, which would surely derail his career and marriage.

"Just remember who you work for."

Kang said nothing. Instead, he turned and walked back to his car. Before he got in, he turned and looked back at Chun, who gave a little wave.

"I'll be in touch, Mr. Prosecutor."

Chun watched Kang pull out of the parking lot and head down the road that led to the freeway. Whether Kang honored his part of the bargain wasn't that important. He enjoyed making the prosecutor squirm just to let him know who was in control. As much as he depended on Kang to help him in situations like the one he was in now, he had become too much of a pain in the ass, not to mention a liability. They might have known each other since they were kids, but the fact was that Kang was no longer of much use to him. It was time to send him on his way. And in due time, that was what he would do.

NINETEEN

My second night in the detention center was worse than the first, now knowing that my embassy wouldn't be able to get me out of here. I barely slept at all, if you would even call it that. Three cells down from where I was, a prisoner talked in his sleep, crying out about something in a language that sounded Filipino. Several prisoners, yelling in other languages, tried to get him to stop.

Maybe I would be the next one, screaming in my sleep.

I replayed the night I had gone home with Joo-hee over and over in my mind. If only I had stayed in that bar and waited for my roommate. Why the hell did I have to go looking for him? What was I thinking? Now, there was no way I was going to get out of here unless the court-appointed attorney could prove my innocence.

The closest I had come to being in a similar predicament, if you would call it as such, happened when I was stationed in Panama. My buddy, John Hill, and I went joyriding in his dune buggy in a restricted area and got stopped by the military police. I thought for sure we were in some deep shit, looking at the very least, an Article 15, which meant losing a stripe and a reduction in pay. John, who was a smooth, fast talker, explained how he had taken the wrong road to avoid the rising tide, which was why we ended up in the restricted area. The police bought it and sent us away with a stern warning to go joyriding somewhere else.

My stomach rumbled and churned. I could barely stomach the food which was brought to my cell. The rice was cold, and some kind of soup, if that was what it was supposed to be, smelled like dirty socks. A piece of greasy fish and sour kimchi rounded off my meal.

Other than the person who tried talking to me my first night, the other prisoners on my cellblock left me alone. The guards who brought my meals and let me outside for an hour only grunted.

Lying there on my cot, I stared at the dark ceiling. The prisoner who had been talking in his sleep finally quieted down.

I thought of the night before I left when I called my former college roommate, Luke, who was now in graduate school in Kansas.

"Don't go doing anything stupid over there," Luke said.

In college, Luke had hung a bedsheet out of our third-floor window with "US Out of Nicaragua" scrawled in black marker. The guy had balls, given that our college, Eureka College, was then-US President Ronald Reagan's alma mater.

"Yeah, right, man," I said.

"Seriously, Turner. Don't fuck up."

———

IN THE MORNING, after another meal I could barely stomach, I was told I had a visitor. Maybe things had changed overnight, and the embassy had worked out a deal. Instead, when I was brought back to the same room I had been in yesterday, a middle-aged man with pockmarked skin and a receding hairline was sitting at the table in a disheveled charcoal suit, as if he had slept in it. He also had a terrible cold and kept clearing his nose and throat with an annoying phlegm-filled sound.

If his morning had started out bad, judging from the serious, almost deathly expression on his face, my day was about to get much worse.

"Mr. Robert?"

"It's Turner. Robert Turner."

"Yes. Mr. Turner, I see," the man said apologetically. "My name is Moon Jung-ho. I'm your court-appointed public defender."

That was fast. I smiled and nodded. My fate hung in the balance with this guy, and he didn't even know my name. Lucky for me, his English was good. I hoped he was just as good as an attorney.

"I just found out about your case last night. I wish I had better news for you."

"What do you mean?"

Moon looked down at his hands in front of him for a few seconds and then looked at me with dull brown eyes. "I'm really sorry to have to tell you this, but I have some bad news for you. Kang, the Chief Prosecutor called me this morning. He explained that given the heinous nature of your crime and your refusal to show remorse, he's going to ask for the maximum penalty for the crime."

I swallowed hard, and a chill coursed through my body. Even though Kang had threatened me with this possibility two days ago, it felt like a knife had been plunged into my heart.

"Isn't there anything you can do?"

Moon looked at me with a helpless expression. "With the evidence they have and the statements from the club owner and the victim's roommate, there's not much I can do. I can only beg for leniency."

"Beg for leniency? That's your strategy?"

"It all depends on the judges. Sometimes they can be quite fair. Though in your case, it's hard to say, given the heinous nature of the murder."

"Yes, you've made that clear already. Nothing like throwing me under the bus."

Moon lifted an eyebrow. "Excuse me?"

"It's just an expression."

Moon cleared his throat. "Okay then, let's get started. I would like to go over a few things with you. Is there anything you would like me to say in your defense?"

"How about I didn't kill the woman?"

"Please, Mr. Turner," Moon said, furrowing his brow. "Part of begging for leniency means showing remorse. Judges have been known to reduce a sentence if you show remorse."

"How can I show remorse for something I didn't do?"

"I'm sorry. I know how you feel."

"No, you don't know how I feel! I'm innocent! It's what I've been trying to tell everyone since I was arrested. I passed out, and when I woke up in the morning, the woman was dead." It was the Park and Shin show all over again. "I didn't do any of that. Why doesn't anyone want to believe me? There's no way that I could have killed that woman."

"If you are innocent, as you claim, why did you run away from the crime scene?"

"Of course, I ran. I was scared. I panicked. I knew it was wrong," I said, trying to make sense of my actions. "I thought if I could call my roommate, he would know what to do."

"Why didn't you call the police?"

"I didn't know how to call the police. Besides, they would have detained me, and I probably would have ended up in the same predicament I am in now."

"Good point."

"I know it was wrong, but I didn't know what else to do."

"And what about the confession you signed?"

"The police made me sign it!"

"Made you sign it? Oh, no. That's not what the Chief Prosecutor said."

"Whose side are you on?"

Moon's brow dipped into a frown. He opened his mouth to say something, but I interrupted him.

"You've got to help me. I did not kill that woman."

"I wish I could do more for you, but as I've said, the case

against you is strong. If you just show remorse, the judges might reduce your sentence to life imprisonment."

"Life imprisonment for a crime I didn't commit?"

"I'm terribly sorry, Robert."

"Have you ever defended someone accused of murder before?"

"No, I haven't."

That's not what I wanted to hear.

"Great. Just fucking great. The police don't believe me, and my embassy can't help me for fear of starting some international incident. And now you tell me you've never defended someone charged with a felony."

"Robert, please."

"What's the point in having an attorney assigned to me if you can't do a fucking thing for me? Well, fuck you, too."

I didn't mean to snap at Moon. It wasn't his fault. He could only do what he could. I just needed someone to listen to my side of the story. Park and Kang wouldn't. Baxter couldn't. My only hope was Moon, who probably couldn't do anything, but he could listen to me at the very least.

"I'm sorry about that. It's just I don't know why no one wants to believe me."

Moon looked at me from across the table with this sad, troubled look. He cleared his throat and shuffled the documents he had removed from a folder. What I said must have struck a chord with him.

"Let's start from the beginning. Tell me everything that you told the police."

Good, now we were getting somewhere. I told Moon how my roommate had taken me to Itaewon to show me around, how we had gotten separated, and how I ended up in the Paradise Club and, later, Joo-hee's apartment.

Moon scribbled a few notes in his notebook. "What happened when you arrived at her apartment?"

"We had a couple of drinks, and then I got sick and passed out in the bathroom. When I woke up, I was in bed with her."

"And you don't remember getting into bed with her?"

I nodded. "That's right."

"And then what happened?"

"I woke up several hours later when I heard someone banging on the door. That's when I realized she was—" For the past three days, I had been trying to prove my innocence, but the one constant in all of this was that a woman had died, and I hadn't been able to stop it. "Oh, dear God. It was awful. Seeing her on the bed like that. Her lifeless eyes staring at me."

Moon looked at what he had written and then looked up from the paper at me. "That's okay, I understand."

"I just can't get her face out of my mind. The police and the prosecutor say I did it, but I could never hurt anyone. It was just so awful. So horribly awful."

Moon stared at me silently for a few seconds before he spoke again. "I can only imagine how awful it must have been for you. And you're sure this is all you remember?"

"Yes, but you should be investigating the guy I saw at the club."

"What guy?"

"When I was in the club, this Korean man came in. When Miss Han went to get us another drink, he got rough with her."

"What do you mean, rough?"

"She grabbed her arm like this." I reached across the table and grabbed Moon's arm the same way that the man at the club had grabbed Joo-hee's arm. Moon tried to pull his arm away. "Sorry, I didn't mean to scare you."

"That hard?"

"Hard enough that I could tell she was in pain."

"Then what?"

"She slapped him. I thought for sure he was going to hit her."

Moon's eyes widened. "Did you tell Park or Kang about this man?"

"Of course, I told them, but they didn't believe me. And then, when they talked to the club owner, she said there hadn't been anyone in the club when I was there."

I could see by Moon's expression that he was trying to

process what I had just explained. There could be no other logical explanation. I certainly didn't kill her, and from what I had been able to piece together from that night, the man who had been at the club had most likely been the one who killed Han.

"I see. And you think the owner is lying?"

"Of course she's lying. She was right there at the bar. She saw and heard everything."

"This man, did he see you?"

"I don't think so. I was in a booth with Miss Han. There were these hanging plastic beads that partitioned the booth. I don't know how clearly he could see me."

"But you could see him."

I nodded.

"What did he look like?"

"He was of medium height. Husky."

"Husky?"

"Heavy set, but not fat."

"Anything else?"

"Yeah, he had a crescent-shaped scar on his right cheek."

"Do you know what Han and this man fought about?"

"Not really. When she returned to the table where we were sitting, she was pretty worked up about it, but I don't know what they were fighting about."

Although I told Moon everything I had pieced together since that night, I sensed that he still wasn't convinced. But, at the very least, he was listening to me with some compassion—more than I could say about Park and Kang.

"And you think this man had something to do with Miss Han's death?"

"Don't you see? He got rough with her, and after we left, he followed us to her apartment, and then, I don't know, he waited outside, and then he came into the apartment and killed her. That has to be what happened. You've got to find out who this man is."

Moon knitted his brow. "How did he get into her apartment and kill her? Where were you at the time?"

"I told you I was sick. I went to the bathroom to throw up and passed out."

"Then you don't know for sure if this man followed you to her apartment and if he was the one who killed her."

"No, I don't. All I remember was the woman, Joo-hee, was really scared when this man came into the club."

"Why was she scared?"

"I don't know. That's what you've got to find out."

"And you heard nothing when you were in the bathroom?"

"No, I didn't."

Moon sighed heavily. "I really would like to help you, but a man you think might have followed you and this woman to her apartment and then broke in and killed her while you were passed out in the bathroom, but spared your life makes little sense."

"What do you mean, it makes little sense? The man I saw in the club had to have been the one who killed Miss Han! Maybe he didn't know I was still in the apartment. Maybe he thought I had already left. Haven't you been listening to a word I've been saying?"

"Yes, I see, but—"

"But what? What's there not to understand?"

I jumped up from my chair, knocking it over. The noise summoned one of the guards who had been standing outside. He rushed into the room, ready to wrestle me to the floor, but Moon waved him off. Seeing that there was no immediate danger to Moon, the guard picked up the chair and gave me a dirty look before he pushed me down onto it.

"Please, settle down, Robert."

"You're not the one being charged with murder!" I rested my head in my hands and closed my eyes. When was this nightmare going to end? I opened my eyes and looked across the table at Moon. "Listen, you've got to tell Kang. He seems more understanding and level-headed than Park. You've got to tell him that the real murderer is still out there."

Moon sighed. "I'll do what I can. If what you say is true—"

"Of course it's true! Why doesn't anyone want to believe me?

All I did was go home with this woman, and I found her dead in the morning. The next thing I knew, I'm charged with murder. You've got to help me, dammit! You've got to help me!"

"I'll see what I can do." Moon gathered his belongings and walked over to the door. He turned as if he wanted to say something else, but then motioned to the guard to let him out.

TWENTY

The following day, Moon followed up on the claim Turner had made that the man he had seen at the Paradise Club might have been the one who murdered the woman. He knew it was a long shot, the police having already questioned the owner, but maybe there was something the police missed.

At the same time, he couldn't understand why the club owner would lie to the police about the man Turner had seen in the club. Could the owner have been scared about something, which was why she lied? And if so, why would the owner want to protect this mystery man? Could she also have been complicit in the murder?

His meeting with Turner had shaken him up. Usually, he wouldn't be sticking his neck out for a client by doing a little police work, but something didn't add up in this case. An English teacher, not even in the country for forty-eight hours, goes to a part of town frequented mainly by soldiers and murders a prostitute? He barely knew where he was. Now he was looking at the very least life imprisonment for murder. Yet, as he tried to explain to Turner yesterday, signing that confession sealed his fate. But if he was coerced into signing the confession, that changed everything. Or so he hoped.

As for this man Turner claimed was in the club at the same time he was, even if he could prove that there had been another man in the club, that didn't mean this man had killed Han. But if he could prove that this mystery man was connected to Han's murder, the Chief Prosecutor might re-open the case. That was the most he could hope for, all things considered.

As far as he knew, most bars and clubs in Itaewon were off-limits to Korean males. It was strictly a GI or foreigner enclave. A Korean male would not usually go into a bar or club alone and fraternize with the business girls unless he had business there. The question was, what kind of business would he have in the club? And why would he get rough with Han the way that Turner described?

There was only one way to find out. He had a friend, Hwang Young-su, who had been a police officer assigned to the Itaewon substation until he suffered a debilitating leg injury in a traffic accident. Now he owned a small antique shop on the western side of Itaewon that catered to American GIs and tourists.

"Moon Jung-ho, long time no see," a short, portly middle-aged man with thinning black hair styled in a bad comb-over said. He slowly walked towards Moon when he recognized his friend in his shop. "To what do I owe to the pleasure of your visit?"

"It's good to see you too, my friend," Moon said, looking around to make sure no one was in the shop. "Is there somewhere we can talk?"

"I see. You're here on business."

"Something like that." Moon smiled and held out his hand.

"Yoo-ri, could you watch the store, please?" Hwang said to a tall woman with black hair, which came down to her waist, dusting antiques on a shelf.

"Yes, father."

Hwang pointed to a room partitioned by a curtain at the back of the shop. "It's private back there."

Moon nodded and walked to the back of the shop with his friend.

"She's grown a lot," Moon said, looking back at Hwang's daughter. "Last time I saw her, she was still in middle school."

"She starts Ewha next year."

Moon smiled. Ewha Woman's University was one of the top private universities in Seoul. "You must be proud."

"Yes, I am. Would you like some tea?" Hwang said.

"No, thank you."

"What can I do for you?" Hwang motioned to a chair for Moon to sit down.

"Information."

"What kind of information?" Hwang sat on a padded chair and rested his bum leg on a box.

"What do you know about the girl who was murdered here the other night?"

"Nothing out of the ordinary."

"What does that mean?"

"You know, the usual. These poor girls who end up working in these bars and clubs have no idea what they're in for when they come to the city. They come here hoping for a better life, and it doesn't always end up that way for them. If it's not the thugs who own half of the district, it's the clientele that takes advantage of them. An American GI out on the town. Has too much to drink. Thinks he is above the law. Sadly, I've seen this too many times when I was the Itaewon Police Station captain."

"The man charged is not a GI."

Hwang furrowed his brow. "Not a GI? But I read in the newspaper that he was."

Moon shook his head. "He's an American English teacher. He just arrived. Went out with his roommate, and the next thing he knows, he wakes up in bed with a dead woman."

"That's awful." Hwang looked at Moon with a puzzled expression on his face. "What's your interest in this American?"

"I'm his public defender."

"Good luck with that."

"Thanks, but there's just one thing —"

"Let me guess, the American says he is innocent."

Moon grinned. "You're right. The thing is, he doesn't remember what happened. Only that when he went to the woman's apartment, he passed out, and when he woke up in the morning, she was dead."

"But the newspaper said the police caught him fleeing from the scene. Seems like they caught their man."

"That's just it. It's not a strong case. The police have statements from two witnesses, one that places him at the scene running out of the apartment and the other claiming that he was rough and obnoxious to the woman earlier in the evening."

"Any other evidence?"

"The police found a used condom in a trash can. They also found blood on an ashtray that the woman might have used to hit the American to defend herself. Still waiting to see if it's a match to him."

"Hmm." Hwang rubbed his chin. "That's not a lot to go on."

"He also confessed."

"Why would he confess?"

Moon gave a half-shrug. His dark eyes had a troubled, hooded look.

"Oh, I get it." Hwang massaged his leg. "Old habits die hard, I guess."

Moon nodded.

"Back in the day, I knew a few officers who were cruel, sick bastards. They beat suspects with wooden batons, electrocuted them, and even used water torture to get a confession. Different times, different methods. Sometimes they got what they wanted. Sometimes they didn't. The suspects died."

"That's terrible."

"And the thing is, they got away with it." A sad look crossed Hwang's seamed face. He was silent for a few seconds before he spoke again. "By the way, how did the woman die?"

"Strangulation."

"And he doesn't remember a thing."

Moon nodded.

"There's something more, isn't there? Otherwise, you wouldn't be sticking your neck out for him."

"The American claims there was this other man in the club at the same time he was with the girl. This guy got a little rough with the woman."

"Rough?"

"Grabbed her, slapped her around."

"And the American thinks this might be the murderer."

"Uh-huh."

"If this man murdered the woman, how did he get inside the apartment if the American was inside?"

"That's what I'm trying to find out."

"Didn't the police investigate?"

"They did, but the bar owner claimed that there was no other customer at the time."

"Despite that, you think your client is innocent?"

"What he says makes sense, but—"

"You want to be sure."

"Yes."

"Who was in charge of the investigation?"

"Park Chong-hun."

Hwang rubbed his chin, trying to remember if he knew this man. Then his eyes widened when he remembered. "I know him. He's a good cop, but he's more concerned about making grade than anything else. He's not the type to stake his reputation on any half-cocked theories. He's completely by the book."

"My client would beg to differ."

Hwang grinned. "He probably wants to redeem himself."

"Redeem himself? Why?"

"There was another murder here about a year ago. A business girl was brutally murdered. Park was in charge of that investigation."

"What happened?"

"The suspect, a GI, had an alibi, a flimsy one, but an alibi. The police had to let him go. Park took a lot of heat for that one. Never found the killer."

"I see."

"Which brings us back to this man the American claimed he had seen at the bar. Did your client get a good look at him?"

"Not really, but he said that man had a scar on the side of his face. It was crescent-shaped."

Hwang's eyes widened. "A scar. A crescent-shaped scar?"

"Yes, that's right."

Hwang leaned back in the chair. His expression turned sullen. "There's this one fellow. He's a bodyguard for a local businessman. A real piece of work. He'd sooner kill you than tell you the time of the day. I had a run-in with him once when I was on the force. Some shopkeeper who was late with his rent was found half-dead. I figured him for the assault, but the shopkeeper wouldn't press charges."

The shop door opened, and a tiny bell above the door jingled, startling the two men. Then they heard Yoo-ri talking in Korean to a man. Hwang put a finger to his lips to shush his friend. He got up, walked to the curtain hanging over a doorway, and pushed it open several inches to see who had come into the shop. The bell jingled again, and the door closed.

"Who was it?"

"Don't know. Never saw him before." Hwang closed the curtain and returned to the chair he had been sitting in. "Now you got me feeling all paranoid."

"Sorry. What about this bodyguard?"

Hwang sat back in the chair. "His name is Chun Yong-chŏl. He got started early when he was a kid stealing from the US military right after the war. He used to be a 'slicky boy.'"

"Slicky boy?"

"Back during the Korean War, these kids were good at stealing from the US military. They were clever, sneaking in and out of places without being detected. You know, who's going to bother their heads with a young kid? But these kids were stealing the US military blind. Later, Kwon Yong-ho, a local businessman with ties to organized crime, offered him a job. After that, Chun graduated to black marketing and counterfeiting. He also became Kwon's muscle. Rumors have it he's killed several men, hacked up their bodies, and scattered the parts around the country, but we could never prove anything. Now, as I understand, he's moved up in the organization. He's Kwon's number-two man. We tried several times to bring Chun in on various charges, but he always squirmed his way out of them. Once a slicky boy; always a slicky boy."

"What about the man he works for? Why couldn't you bring him in for questioning?"

"He's untouchable. As long as his not-so-legitimate enterprises don't cause too much of a stir, no one bothers him. You can't just waltz into Kwon's office and start questioning him about one of his employees. He's a respected businessman. He has a lot of friends in high places, if you know what I mean."

"What would you do if you were me?"

"If this American is sure that the man he saw was Chun, you've got to convince the club owner to change her story and go on the record. But my guess is the owner either works for Chun or is afraid to talk. Beyond that, I don't know what to tell you."

Moon was silent for several seconds, pondering what his friend had told him.

"Just one thing."

"What's that?"

"If Chun is responsible for the murder of the business girl, you want to be very careful who you talk to and who you trust."

Moon walked out in the cold afternoon air and shoved his hands into his jacket pockets. As he walked up the main street that ran through the heart of Itaewon, he passed a black Hyundai sedan parked outside Hwang's shop with the motor running. He got about twenty yards up the street when the car pulled away from the curb and slowly followed him.

TWENTY-ONE

A LIGHT SNOW FELL AS MOON CLIMBED HOOKER HILL TOWARD the Paradise Club. Although Chun might have been the one who murdered Miss Han, the only way he could be sure was by pressuring the club's owner, as his friend had suggested.

Be very careful who you talk to and who you trust.

Since talking to Turner yesterday, he had made a few inquiries about Han. He learned she was from Taegu and had come to Seoul several years ago, enticed and allured by life in the big city and the promise of a better life. She had worked in several clubs before she ended up working in the Paradise Club. He understood that many girls who worked in the clubs economically depended on the GIs who frequented them. They were tough in how they talked and moved, hardened and calloused by the fate that befell them.

He was haunted by the photograph he had got from the police. It was your standard black and white, "don't smile and look serious" identification photographs, but it was how she stared at the camera with her wide, dark eyes that haunted him. It was as though she had seen her own death.

Although it was in the middle of the afternoon on a weekday, several clubs had their lights on, open for business. Two young men, wearing satin jackets with tigers embroidered on the back, strolled up the hill, pushing and jostling each other. Standing in the doorway of the Capitol Club, a middle-aged woman in a tight-fitting leopard pattern mini-skirt and permed hair yelled out to the men.

"Hey, where you go? Come in and have a drink."

"I don't know, mama-san," one of the men said. "You're old enough to be my mother."

"Fuck you!" The woman said, giving him the finger.

The two men continued up the hill, laughing.

When Moon passed the woman, he looked at her with an apologetic expression.

At the top of the hill, Moon turned right and walked about twenty-five meters. Like the other clubs he had passed on his way up the hill, the Paradise Club had its lights on. He was surprised that the club was open, considering it had only been a few days since the murder.

He walked out of the cold, biting weather and into the warmth of the club, heated by a kerosene heater in the middle of the room. It took a while for his eyes to adjust to the dim light inside. Behind the bar, a woman was stocking a cooler with bottles of OB and Budweiser.

"We're not open yet," Lee said, not bothering to turn around. Her tone was curt and rough.

"That's okay. I just want to ask you a few questions."

Startled by Moon's voice, Lee stopped what she was doing and turned around. She had on a white sweater and a black leather mini-skirt. On her chubby legs were fishnet stockings. She wore thick makeup that barely covered the wrinkles and blemishes on her face, giving her a ghostly appearance. Moon placed her somewhere in her early fifties, and that was being generous.

"I'd like to talk to you about Han Joo-hee," Moon said, warming his hands over a brass kettle that sat on top of the heater.

"Are you the police?"

"No, I'm a lawyer representing the man accused of killing her."

Lee glared at Moon. "Accused? He killed her, that's for sure. What else is there to talk about?"

"You don't seem to be shaken up about it."

"What do you mean?"

"You're still open for business."

"Business is business."

Moon thought about saying something about how cold and callous her response had been, but decided not. "I just want to ask you a few questions about that night."

In the back of the room, Han's roommate, Hyon-ju, had been sleeping in one of the booths when Moon's voice woke her. She lifted her head to see who it was.

"What's there to ask? He went back to her apartment and murdered her. I've already told everything that I know to the police."

"Yes, I am aware of that. But was there anyone else in the club around the time the suspect was with Han?"

Lee gazed at Moon with a blank expression. "It was late. We were closing."

"Do you remember a middle-aged Korean man who might have been in here around the same time?"

The color drained from Lee's face. She tapped out a cigarette from a pack lying on the bar and stuck it in her mouth. She lit the cigarette with a pink disposable lighter and blew out a mouthful of smoke.

"What good will it do? Han is dead. I don't know why you're trying to save him. I hope the American gets everything he's got coming to him."

Moon, who did not smoke, waved the smoke away with his hand. "You didn't understand my question."

"I heard you. Nothing I say is going to bring her back."

"I understand how you feel. It's just my client claims there was another patron here that night and that this patron and Han had some kind of argument."

"He's lying."

"He said that she slapped this man and that you intervened."

Lee took a short draw on the cigarette and blew the smoke out from the corner of her mouth. "I'm sorry. I have no idea what you are talking about. There was no other man in here that night. Only that American. I've already told this to the police."

"Are you sure? He came in right around closing."

"Mr. —"

"Moon."

"Mr. Moon, I don't know what else to tell you. It was just Han and this American. He was not nice to her. He wanted her to do unspeakable things. Right here in the club."

"She slapped this man."

"Please, I've told the police everything I know, and I don't appreciate you coming in here and accusing me of lying."

"I'm not accusing you of anything. I'm just trying to find out the truth." Moon sensed he had unnerved the owner with his questions. She was hiding something. And she was afraid.

"And I'm telling you, there was no one else in the club."

"You told her to stop. You must remember that."

"Listen, I don't want any trouble, okay?"

"He was a heavy-set man. He had a scar on the side of his face. Does that help?"

"I told you there was no one else in here."

"Who are you trying to protect?"

"I'm not protecting anyone. I've told you everything that I know. Now, if you don't mind, I would like for you to leave before —"

"Before what? Before you call the police? I'm sure they would be very interested in hearing how you lied."

Lee's lips quivered as Moon watched her take several quick puffs at her cigarette.

Hyon-ju sat up when she heard what Moon had said. She wrapped an overcoat she had been using as a blanket around her shoulders and reached for a pack of cigarettes on a nearby table.

Outside, a car door slammed, startling both Moon and Lee.

"Are you scared? Is that why you don't want to talk to me?"

"Please leave." Lee looked toward the door with a nervous expression on her face.

"If you're scared, I can protect you."

"Just like Han?" She squashed the cigarette in an ashtray.

Lee lifted her eyes with a helpless expression across her face. Moon opened his mouth to say something else to make the woman feel better, but decided not. Moon sensed she knew more about what happened to Han that night than she was letting on. He also had a hunch that someone had gotten to her and told her not to talk.

He took out a name card from the inside pocket of his coat and handed it to the woman. "Just in case."

The woman looked at it before she tucked it inside her bra.

"I'm sorry about Han's death."

Moon stared at the woman for a few seconds, thinking she would say something, but she didn't. He turned and walked outside.

Hyon-ju waited until Moon was gone before she threw on her coat and ran outside. Moon was halfway down the block when he heard someone walking behind him.

"She's lying," Hyon-ju said.

Moon stopped when he heard the voice. He pivoted around and faced Hyon-ju. "Excuse me, what did you say?"

"Lee, the woman from the club. She's lying." Hyon-ju looked around nervously in case anyone had seen her talking to Moon.

"And how do you know this?"

"I heard her talking to him."

Moon's eyes widened. He had a hunch that Lee was hiding something. "Talking to who?"

"Chun Yong-chol. The man who was in the club the night Joo-hee was murdered."

"You know him?"

"Unfortunately."

"When?"

"Not here."

"What?"

"I don't want to talk here."

"Where?"

"I'm hungry. I know a place close to here."

As they walked toward the main street, which ran through Itaewon, Moon thought he saw the same black Hyundai he had seen outside his friend's shop, with its motor running at the end of the block. But when he looked again, the car was gone.

———

FIFTEEN MINUTES LATER, they were in a cramped, drafty shiktang, a Korean restaurant, at the end of Bowang-ro, the major thoroughfare leading south out of Itaewon, near the Han River. They found a table in the back, away from the handful of customers. The girl, who introduced herself as Hong Hyon-ju, ordered a large bowl of ramen. When the ajumoni brought the steaming bowl of ramen to the table, Hong put her head down and slurped the noodles without looking until she finished. Then she tipped the bowl over her mouth and drank the broth at the bottom. She smacked her lips and dabbed them with a thin sheet of tissue paper.

"Feel better?"

Hyon-ju nodded and poured herself a cup of boricha—barley tea—from a brass kettle on top of a kerosene heater.

"What do you know about the man who was in the club the night Miss Han was murdered?" Moon said, keeping his voice low.

Hyon-ju cupped her hands around the white plastic cup of boricha and held it in front of her face. She breathed in the warm vapors before taking a drink. "After the police questioned me, I went to the Paradise Club to tell Lee that Joo-hee had been murdered."

"Why did the police question you?"

"I was her roommate. I was the one who discovered her body."

"Oh, I didn't know that. I'm sorry."

Tears welled in Hyon-ju's eyes. "I can't believe anyone would do that to her. She wasn't like the other bar girls. She knew how to make men feel good about themselves. She didn't deserve this."

"What happened after you went to the club?"

"As I was saying, I told Lee that Joo-hee had been murdered. We had a couple of drinks to remember her and drown our sorrows."

"I understand."

"We had gone through about half a bottle of Johnny Walker when Chun called. I didn't know it was Chun. But Lee looked scared when she answered the phone and found out who it was. He showed up about thirty minutes later."

"How well do you know him?

"I've seen him before, if that's what you mean. He's been in the club several times. He and Joo-hee had a history."

"What do you mean?"

"A couple of months ago, they got into a fight. Chun cut her with a broken soju bottle."

"A fight?" Moon couldn't believe what he was hearing.

Hyon-ju drank more of the boricha and nodded. "And then she found out that he was dealing drugs. She didn't say anything about it, but then someone was going around Itaewon spreading rumors about it, and she was worried that Chun would think it was her."

"Drugs?"

Hyon-ju nodded.

"What kind of rumors?"

"Rumors about a big shipment of drugs from Pusan or Japan."

Moon pondered what Hyon-ju had said. "What kind of drugs?"

"Philopon."

In recent months, there had been several articles in the newspapers about an increase in drug use in South Korea, specifically philopon. Although he didn't have all the details yet, based on what his friend had told him, it might be possible, if Turner was telling the truth, that he got himself caught up in the middle of something.

"I don't think Chun's boss knew about it, and that's why Joo-hee was scared."

Moon thought about what his friend had told him about Chun's boss. If Chun was going behind his boss's back selling drugs without his knowledge, Moon could see why Chun would resort to anything to ensure his boss didn't find out about it.

"What happened after Chun arrived at the club?"

"Chun asked Lee what I was doing there, and she told him, just having a drink. He didn't seem too happy that I was there and told me to beat it. Said he had to talk to Lee about something. Alone."

"What did you do?"

"I wanted to know what he wanted to talk to Lee about, so instead of leaving, I slipped into a storage room in the back of the club and cracked the door open."

"What did you hear?"

"Plenty. Chun talked about the American who the police had arrested."

"What did he say about him?"

"He told Lee that if the police asked her about the American, she should make something up. You know, to throw the police off his path. Something like that."

"Are you sure that's what he said?"

Hyon-ju nodded. "He also told her she'd better keep her mouth shut if she knew what was good for her and something about the police poking their noses where they shouldn't."

"Do you remember anything else?"

Hyon-ju looked around to make sure no one was listening to their conversation and leaned across the table. "He said he had gone to her apartment that night."

Moon couldn't believe what he was hearing. But there it was, right in front of him. This revelation that Chun had gone to Han's apartment the same night Turner had gone home with her also placed him at the crime scene. However, it only proved that Turner had been telling the truth about the man he had seen at the club. The police and the Seoul Prosecutor's Office would have no choice but to reopen the case and investigate Chun. This revelation that

Chun was trafficking drugs was undoubtedly the motive for killing Han if that, in fact, was what happened. And when Chun found out Turner had been with Han, he was going to let the American take the fall for the murder. That was why he told the owner to cover for him—to lie about him being in the club and about Turner being rough with Han.

It was all making sense now. While Turner was passed out in the bathroom, somehow, Chun had gotten into the apartment, murdered Han, and then left. Turner, in the meantime, had woken up and gotten into bed with Han, not knowing what happened until he woke up several hours later. Once the police arrived on the scene, Turner didn't stand a chance.

"Why didn't you go to the police?"

"I was scared."

"The police have charged an innocent man. The prosecutor is going to ask for the death penalty. You have to go to the police."

Hyon-ju shook her head. "I can't. You don't know Chun and what he's capable of—" She stopped mid-sentence. A look of horror washed across her face. "Oh my God!" She put her hands to her face and started sobbing. "I could have stopped it."

A few patrons stopped and turned to see why she was crying.

"What are you talking about?"

"The night she was murdered, I had left early with a customer. We went to the King Club and then we had something to eat. I got back to our apartment late. I was drunk. I didn't have my key with me. I banged on the door and yelled for her, but no one came out. I figured she was in there with a customer, so I returned to the club and slept there until I figured Joo-hee was done."

"Did you hear anything?"

"I just heard music." Hyon-ju grabbed a handful of tissue from a plastic container on the table and dried her eyes. "Maybe Chun was in the apartment at the time. If I'd only gone home earlier—"

Tears ran down Hyon-ju's cheeks as she sobbed uncontrollably.

Moon reached across the table and gently held her hands. "You can't blame yourself for what happened. And even if you thought she was in danger and tried to stop whoever it was, you could have been murdered, too."

Hyon-ju grabbed more tissue and dried her eyes.

"Would you be willing to go to the Seoul Prosecutor's Office and tell them everything you just told me?"

"I can't."

"I understand your concerns. I would feel the same way if I were in your position, but right now, an innocent person is charged with her murder while the real murderer is still out there. Do this for Joo-hee."

"You know what will happen if I talk to the police."

"The Prosecutor's Office will protect you."

"I don't think so. Chun knows people."

"Who? His boss?"

"No, not his boss. Other people."

"What other people?"

Hyon-ju looked around the restaurant again to ensure no one was eavesdropping on her and Moon's conversation.

"People in high places."

Hwang had told him the same thing. "The police?"

Hyon-ju shook her head. "That's all I'm going to say. I've said too much already." She shook a cigarette from a pack on the table and stuck it in her mouth. She tried to light it, but her hand trembled too much.

Moon reached across the table, took the lighter out of Hyon-ju's hands, and lit her cigarette. His solemn gaze roved over her frightened face. There was no need to press her any further. She had told him more than enough. Hopefully, it would be enough for Kang to reopen the case and release Turner from custody.

Hyon-ju bit down on her bottom lip. "I'm sorry."

Moon took out his name card and gave it to her.

"If you change your mind, please call me."

She looked at Moon's name on the card and shoved the card into a pocket on her overcoat.

When they were getting ready to leave, Moon took out his wallet and handed her several ten thousand one notes.

"What's this for?"

"Get out of town for a day or two."

"Why?"

"For your own safety."

Hyon-ju stuffed the bills inside the pocket of her jacket. "Thanks."

"Be careful."

TWENTY-TWO

Snow swirled around the taxi Moon had taken as it passed Seoul Station and headed downtown. It slid around a corner and almost hit a pedestrian running across the busy, snowy street. The taxi driver honked the horn and yelled a few expletives. The near-miss jolted Moon, who had been contemplating the case and the information he had learned.

Thanks to what he learned from Hong, Turner might be an innocent bystander in all of this. He had been telling the truth all along about someone else being in the apartment and killing Han. Turner had just been in the wrong place at the wrong time. Turner was lucky he had passed out in the bathroom. If Chun knew Turner was in the apartment, Turner would also be dead.

And if his friend and Hong were right about Chun, not only was Turner's life in danger, but also the owner of the Paradise Club and Hong. The sooner he got to his office and shared this information with Park and Kang, the better he would feel. The problem was he needed Hong to tell them what she had told him. Maybe there was a way they could bring her in and protect her like they did in the American movies he watched.

Ten minutes later, the taxi turned down a side street in the

Chongno area and pulled up in front of a five-story nondescript building with a grimy, yellow-tiled façade. Moon paid the driver and hurried inside the building.

Down the street, the black sedan that had followed Moon from Itaewon pulled off the street and stopped in front of a Chinese restaurant down the block. The driver switched off the lights but kept the motor running. He leaned forward and looked out the windshield at the building Moon had entered. His gaze ran up the front of the office building and was greeted by fifteen office windows. Several lights were on in offices on the second and third floors. He waited in the likelihood the lights were turned on in one of the darkened offices.

Moon dashed up the narrow stairwell to his tiny, third-floor office. He didn't even bother to take off his coat. He looked for Park's phone number, which he had written on a pad of paper, and picked up a black phone on his desk. Glancing at a clock on the wall, which read 5:30, he hoped Park had not gone home for the day.

Outside, somewhere down the hallway, he heard a door open and someone walking down the hall. His office was on the same floor as two other offices, Joy Travel Service and Paik Consulting. He listened carefully and heard high heels clicking on the tile floor. That would have been Helen Kim, the owner of the travel agency. She was probably on her way home.

Park picked up on the seventh ring.

"Detective Park, this is Moon Jung-ho. I'm Robert Turner's attorney."

"Yes, Mr. Moon. What can I do for you?"

"I need to talk to you about Turner?"

"Turner? What about him?"

"Is there a place where we could meet?"

Park was silent for a few seconds. "I was just on my way out. Can't this wait until morning?"

"No, it can't wait until the morning. There's something you should know about the murder. Turner's life might be in danger."

"Danger? What the hell are you talking about?"

"I was in Itaewon today. I stopped in at the club where the murdered woman had worked. When I asked the owner if she remembered a middle-aged man being in the club around the same time as Turner, she got scared. And then I talked to this business girl. She was Miss Han's roommate. She told me—"

"What the devil were you doing in Itaewon?"

"My job."

"This is a closed case, Moon. If you have any questions or concerns, I suggest bringing them up with Prosecutor Kang."

"I understand, but—"

"I'm sorry. Maybe you didn't hear me. This is a closed case."

"Turner was right."

"Right about what?"

"The man at the bar."

"What about the man at the bar?"

"I know who he is." Then, outside, he heard the elevator stop on his floor. "Wait a minute."

Moon set the phone down, but Park kept on talking. "Listen, Moon. I'm a busy man. If you have new information, call Kang. Moon? What do you mean, you know who it was? Moon? Are you there?"

Moon walked over to the door to his office and cracked it open. He looked up and down the hallway, but whoever it was had already left.

"Who's there?"

The only sound was a hissing sound from a radiator in the hallway. The lights were off in Kim Consulting, as well as Joy Travel. It was too late for anyone to visit Joy Travel. Besides, he was confident that Helen Kim had already left for the evening.

Footsteps echoing on the stairs sent a chill through his body. He shut the door, slowly locking it so as not to make a sound, and switched off the lights. Then he walked back to his desk and picked up the phone.

"Moon, I don't have time for this—"

"I think someone's outside my office," Moon said, cupping his hand around the receiver.

"What?"

"When I went to Itaewon to make some inquiries, I saw this black car down the street with the engine running. And after I talked to the owner of the Paradise, I saw the same car parked down the street. I think whoever it was followed me here."

"Can you leave?"

"No, I can't."

"Where's your office located?"

"It's in the Kolon Building, across from Pagoda Park. Third floor."

"Lock the door. I'll have a unit dispatched to your office. I'll be there —"

The doorknob on his office door jiggled, and Moon's heart hammered against his ribs.

"Someone's outside —"

The door flew open, and in the silhouette from a light in the hallway, Moon saw a large figure rush into his office like a gust of wind. Before he could react, Chun grabbed Moon from behind and ripped the telephone receiver from his hand.

"Moon? Are you there? What's happening?"

Moon could hear Park as Chun got behind him and wrapped the telephone cord around his neck. He tried to put up a fight, but was no match for Chun's strength. Chun wrapped the cord tighter and tighter around Moon's neck. It dug into his neck, squeezing his larynx and windpipe. Moon's eyes bulged out, and he fought to breathe. While he struggled and gasped for air, he tried to get his fingers between the cord and his neck to set himself free, but Chun was too strong. When that didn't work, Moon, in a panic, realizing he was about to die, clawed at Chun's face and gouged him in the right eye. Chun howled in pain and loosened his grip around Moon's neck, but not enough for Moon to get free and escape. Disregarding the pain in his eye, Chun tightened his grip around Moon's neck and planted his knee in Moon's back to make the cord even tighter around his neck. Whatever fight Moon still had in him was not enough to save his life. The last thing Moon saw was his reflection in the window, his arms flailing above his head in one last feeble attempt to stop his attacker.

Releasing his grip on the telephone cord, Chun grabbed the side of Moon's head and twisted as hard as he could. Then, a grisly snap signaled the end of Moon's life. He had more fight in him than Chun expected as he let Moon's body drop to the floor. Turning his attention to the telephone, Chun unwound the cord from around Moon's neck and put the receiver to his ear. Park was still on the other end, screaming for Moon to answer.

"Moon? Are you still there? What the hell is going on?"

Chun grinned and hung up the phone. There was no time to waste. He had to dispose of the body before the person he had overheard Moon talking to on the phone came to the office. However, as he dragged Moon's body out of the office, he heard the elevator approaching the floor. Thinking fast, he saw the bathroom at the end of the hallway. He dragged Moon's body into the restroom and put it into one of the stalls. When he was finished, he hurried down the stairs.

———

TEN MINUTES LATER, two KNP officers, who had been dispatched to Moon's office, got off the elevator and walked down the hallway to Moon's office. One of them knocked three times on the door. When Moon didn't answer, the officer opened the door and stuck his head inside.

"Hello? Is anybody here?" The officer looked around the room. He closed the door and turned to his partner. "He's not here."

The two officers exchanged confused glances. They had been instructed to check on Moon but couldn't understand why he had left his office. The first officer unclipped his radio from his belt and radioed headquarters.

"Dispatch, this is Kim Hae-chul," the officer said, speaking into the radio. "My partner and I are at the address you gave us, but the person you wanted us to check up on is not here."

"Copy that. There's a detective on the way. Please stay on the scene."

"Roger."

Five minutes later, Park got off the elevator and approached the two officers.

"What's going on?"

"The guy is not here," Kim said.

"Did you check the floor?"

The two officers shook their heads.

Park looked down the hallway and saw that the light was on in the bathroom.

"Did you check in there?"

"No," Kim said.

Park walked to the end of the hallway and stood in front of the restroom door. "Moon? Are you in there?"

He opened the door a few inches.

"Moon? Didn't you hear me yelling for you?"

Park opened the door the rest of the way and walked into the restroom. Water dripped from a leaky faucet. A light bulb flickered above the sink. He looked underneath the first stall door but couldn't see anyone. Then he looked underneath the second stall door and saw a pair of black shoes pointing outward at a funny angle.

"Moon?"

Park pushed the door open and found Moon slumped over on the toilet. Moon's eyes bulged like two golf balls, and his tongue lolled out of his mouth like a dead fish.

"Oh, shit."

TWENTY-THREE

ON THE OTHER SIDE OF THE CITY, IN THE UPSCALE neighborhood of Apkujong, Kang Jae-min and his family were in the living room of their twelfth-floor apartment, watching television when the intercom buzzed.

"I wonder who that could be at this hour of the night?" Kang's wife, In-sook, said.

Kang got up from the sofa and walked to the intercom on the other side of the room. "Ne?" Yes.

"It's me, Park. I need to talk to you."

"Park?"

"Can I come up?"

"Yes, sure." Kang pressed a button that unlocked the main door to the apartment building below.

"Who was that?" In-sook asked.

"Someone from work."

"Couldn't it wait until the morning?"

"I guess not."

Kang walked to the foyer in front of the door to their apartment. It was unusual for a detective to come to his apartment. Had something happened to Turner? No, if something had happened to him, it wouldn't have involved Park. It would have been someone from the detention center, and they would have called.

A few minutes later, the doorbell chimed. Kang swung open the gray steel door.

"What's going on, Detective? Do you want to come in?"

Park looked over Kang's shoulder and saw Kang's wife and daughter sitting in the living room. "No, here's fine."

"What's on your mind?"

"I thought it would be better if you heard this from me and not someone from your office."

Kang beetled his dark brows. "About what?"

"Moon's dead."

"What?"

Kang's outburst was loud enough for his wife to hear.

"Is everything okay?" In-sook said.

"Yes, darling." Kang motioned to Park to step outside into the hallway. Kang closed the door behind him. "What are you talking about?" Kang said, lowering his voice. "What do you mean, murdered?"

"He called me to say that he had new evidence that would exonerate Turner."

"What kind of evidence?"

"He didn't say, but I think it was about the man Turner claimed to have seen at the bar. Moon was going to tell me, but someone had followed him to his office."

A chill coursed through Kang's body. When Chun told him he would take care of Moon, he didn't think murdering him in his office was what he had in his mind.

"By the time I got to his office, it was too late. I found his body in a restroom. He had been strangled to death."

"Oh, my."

"Do you know what this means, don't you? We're going to have to reopen the Han murder case."

All Kang had to do was come out and tell Park that he knew who murdered Han, but that would make him an accessory to the murder of Moon and Han. He would go to prison, but worst of all, his family would be disgraced. In a Confucian society, that was a fate worse than death. People committed suicide to avoid bringing shame to their families. Recently, a politician under investigation for taking bribes threw himself off a mountain north of Seoul to avoid disgracing his family. Kang needed more time to figure out what to do, which meant reining in Chun before he caused any more problems.

"Could be just a coincidence." Kang fixed a cold gaze on Park.

"A coincidence? Do you even hear yourself? Turner's lawyer was murdered. So whatever he found out about Han's murder got him killed."

"Yes, of course. Thank you for bringing this to my attention. I'll follow this up in the morning. Have a good night, Detective."

"Wait a minute. That's it? You don't seem too worked up about this."

"What's your point, Park?"

"Turner probably told Moon about the guy he had seen at the Paradise Club. That's what probably got him killed. And don't think for a moment this is not going to blow back at us both. It's going to be like that murder case last year all over again. But this time, thanks to your press conference, the public is going to scream for our resignations."

Kang thought about what Park had said for a moment. Indeed, once the press found out and connected Moon and Han's murders, his career was as good as over, but not as bad if he was connected to Chun. Having to resign was the least of his worries.

"It's too bad Moon didn't tell you the man's name Turner claims to have seen at the bar."

"Yeah, too bad."

"Well then, that's it, I guess."

Park shot Kang a quizzical look. "No, it's not. I'm going to have to go back to the Paradise Club. Find out what I can from the owner. Maybe this time, she'll be more willing to talk. And in the meantime, we need to bring Turner into the station and have him look at some photos. And then we're going to have to release him."

Maybe the American wouldn't say anything, Kang thought. He could tell him that it had all been a mistake, that the woman from the Paradise Club broke down and admitted that there had been another man in the club that night. If the American went along with it—

"Kang, did you hear what I said?"

"Maybe we should not be too hasty until we have all the facts."

Park lifted an eyebrow. "What are you suggesting?"

"We hold back releasing Turner for now until we can investigate Moon's murder to see if his murder and Han's are connected."

"You're not serious, are you?"

"I'm just saying we keep the lid on this until—"

"Until what?" Park, with his hands on his hips, gazed at Kang, who shifted foot to foot under his scrutiny. "Why are you so intent on keeping Turner locked up? Obviously, whoever killed Moon didn't like him snooping around where he shouldn't."

"Until we can figure out how we can connect the two murders. As you said, we need to go back and talk to the owner of the Paradise Club."

"But in the meantime, we release Turner."

"Of course. I'll take care of it first thing in the morning."

Park slid Kang a guarded look. Maybe Kang's reluctance to release Turner was that he was worried about what the press would do when they found out. "I understand. Have a good night, Kang."

"Good night."

Kang waited until Park got into the elevator before going back inside the apartment. Then, he took down his black cashmere jacket and wool scarf from a coat tree in the foyer.

"Where are you going?"

Kang turned around, surprised to see his wife standing there.

"I'm going for a walk," he said.

"At this hour?"

"I just want to get some fresh air. I won't be gone too long."

"What was that all about?"

"Oh, just a case I've been working on."

"Is everything okay? You hardly touched your food at dinner." His wife said in a worried tone.

"Everything is fine. Why wouldn't it be?"

"You just don't seem yourself these days. Is there something you're not telling me?" His wife bit her lip the way she did when she was worried about something. "You're not seeing another woman, are you?"

Kang's eyes widened. "Of course not." He put his arms around his wife. "There's nothing for you to worry about, okay?"

His wife nodded and kissed him on the cheek.

———

AT THIS HOUR of the night, there was only one place Chun would be—a swank nightclub in the basement of the Tower Hotel on Namsan. On the drive over, Kang dreaded confronting his friend again, but Chun had gone too far this time. Han's death may have been an accident; Chun had said it had been self-defense, but this was spiraling out of control. Not that it lessened his culpability for her death, but with Moon, he had explicitly gone to his office to murder him. This had to stop now. If he wanted to threaten his wife with the photos of Sun-hee—let him. It was probably just a bluff, anyway. Chun needed him now more than ever. Right now, he was the only one who could protect his friend.

Chun had entertained him several times at the Tower and had no problem getting past security to Chun's private room at the end of a long hallway. When Kang entered the dimly lit room, he found Chun sitting on an L-shaped crushed red velvet sofa. On either side of him sat two women dressed in tight-fitting red silk dresses. The walls, covered with yellow wallpaper printed with a floral design, gave the room a pleasant feeling, even though the air reeked of stale cigarette smoke and perfume so sweet it made Kang gag. On a table in front of the sofa was a bottle of Scotch, several smaller bottles of tonic water, a metal bucket of ice, and a large platter of fruit, dried squid, and peanuts. An ashtray overflowed with cigarette butts.

"Well, look who we have here," Chun said. He wore a white shirt that was unbuttoned halfway down his chest. "Ladies, I would like to introduce you to my good friend, Kang Jae-min. Careful now, he's been known to bite."

The two women giggled, covering their mouths with thin, pale hands. One woman poured some Scotch into a glass for Chun and handed it to him with two hands. Kang stood silently, trembling with anger, clenching and unclenching his fists.

"Care for a drink?"

"No, thank you."

"What do I owe the pleasure of your visit?"

"I would like to talk in private."

"Oh, so you're here on business. Too bad." Chun put an arm around one woman and fondled her breasts. "And what, exactly, is the nature of your business?"

"You know goddamn what."

"I see. It's about that."

Chun took a drink and motioned to the two women with his head to leave. The one whose breasts he had fondled frowned. The two women, who were of the same height, stood and smoothed their dresses over their large hips before turning and slowly sashaying out of the room.

"If you'd like, I can fix you up with one of those ladies. I know it's not Sun-hee, but you'd be surprised what either of them can do."

"Knock it off, Chun."

"Doesn't hurt to ask." Chun motioned for Kang to sit, but Kang ignored the gesture.

"Do you know what you have done?" Kang narrowed his eyes and stared at Chun.

"Yes, I do. I took care of everything."

"By murdering Moon? Are you out of your mind?"

"He was snooping around where he shouldn't have. I told you to take care of this before it became our problem."

Kang felt his stomach tightening.

"Did you see what that son-of-a-bitch did?" Chun pointed to the scratch marks on his face and his swollen, red eye. "He tried to gouge my fucking eye out!"

"You bastard."

"Do you know he even stopped to see a retired cop?"

"Who?"

"This cop named Hwang. He tried for years to arrest me for one thing or another. After a while, he gave up." Chun poured himself a glass of Scotch. "How did you find out?"

"One of the detectives, Park Chong-hun, who investigated Han's murder, came by my apartment this evening. He discovered the body."

"Is that so?" Chun tossed back his drink. "What was he doing there?"

"Moon had called him. Said he had new evidence about the case."

"What new evidence?" Chun raised an eyebrow.

"Park didn't say. I guess Moon was going to tell him when he got to the office, but someone followed him to his office."

"Hmm, an interesting turn of events, wouldn't you say?"

"You bastard. You could have been seen."

"A thank you might be in order."

"Excuse me?"

"If I hadn't gone there, this conversation between you and me wouldn't be taking place. We'd probably be in jail right now. So, you can thank me anytime."

"Do you know what this means, don't you? The police are going to re-open the case."

"You need to relax. You're going to give yourself a heart attack."

"Right now, a heart attack would be the least of my worries."

"That's good. At least you still have your sense of humor."

"I don't think you understand the gravity of the situation."

"Then I suggest you make sure that Park finds nothing that

connects me to the murders. Which also means taking care of this American. Do I make myself clear?"

"When is this going to stop? I can't believe I allowed myself to get dragged into this."

"Like it or not, we're in this together. If I go down, you go down."

"No, I can't do this anymore. I won't do this anymore!" The veins on Kang's neck tightened. "I don't care about the photos you have of Sun-hee and me."

"No, I think I can find someone you care about more than Sun-hee. Someone closer to you."

Kang's eyes widened.

"I'd hate to see anything happen to that lovely wife and daughter of yours. That would be most unfortunate."

"You wouldn't."

"Fix this, or you'll find out. Do you understand?"

Kang was silent for a few seconds.

"Yes," Kang said in a weak voice.

"Good."

TWENTY-FOUR

DOWN THE CORRIDOR, I HEARD THE HEAVY STEEL DOOR unlocked and the sound of footsteps approaching my cell. Like Pavlov's dog salivating at the sound of a bell, my body tensed. When I looked up from my cot, the guard motioned me to get up and approach the cell door. Moon said he would have something soon for me, but I didn't think he would come through this fast. Although the guards showed little emotion when escorting prisoners to and from their cells, the guard standing in front of my cell expressed his dissatisfaction with this task, the way his thin lips curled into a snarl. Where were the other guards? Usually, two or three had escorted me from my cell.

I got up from my cot and walked outside the cell. The guard barked something in Korean, which I knew meant for me to hold out my hands while they were tied with rope. Instead of taking me to the conference room where I had met Moon two days ago, the guard brought me to a blue van outside. Where was Moon? Shouldn't he be here? Where the hell were they taking me?

I found out twenty minutes later when I was escorted into Kang's office and found both Kang and Park inside. But no Moon.

Neither Kang nor Park looked happy to see me. If anything, they looked worried.

Park said something to the two officers who had brought me to his office and pointed to my hands bound with rope and tied around my back. The next thing I knew, the ropes were removed.

"Moon's dead," Kang said in a cold, callous tone.

"What? What are you talking about?" I said, rubbing my wrists.

"Sit down, Turner," Park said.

Both Kang and Park looked worse for the wear. It didn't look like either had slept for some time. I thought back to the conversation that Moon and I had when he visited me in the detention center. Moon had stuck his neck out for me, which got him killed.

"What happened?"

"Apparently, Moon had gone to Itaewon to inquire about the man you claimed you saw at the club the night Han was murdered," Park said. "He called me late, the day before yesterday, and told me he had some information about your case. When I went to his office, I found him dead."

"Oh my God."

"What the hell did you tell him?" Park asked.

"I told him the same thing I told you about the man I had seen at the club. Maybe if you had acted faster, Moon would still be alive."

"Is that all?" Park said, glaring at me.

"Yes, that's all."

"Did you tell him anything else?" Kang asked.

"No, I didn't."

Kang and Park spoke to each other in Korean. I could tell that Park was upset with what Kang was telling him while he continued glaring at me. I didn't know where Park and Kang fit into the hierarchy of things—who was higher and had more power—but if I didn't know any better, Park had just given Kang a dressing down.

"It gets worse," Park said.

"How so?"

"The owner of the Paradise Club is missing." Park's expression hardened. "No one has seen her for two days, and the club is closed and shuttered."

"Oh, shit."

"Given the circumstances of Moon's death and the disappearance of the owner from the Paradise Club, we've been forced to reopen Han's murder case," Park said. "That means we'll have to let you go for now."

I took a long, deep breath and let it out slowly. "Wow."

"You're a lucky man," Park said.

"It's most unfortunate that two people are dead and another one missing, but at least you are free to go," Kang said.

I didn't expect Park to be gracious, but I thought Kang would have shown a little more emotion telling me I was a free man. After all, a few days ago, he threatened me with the death penalty. Instead, Kang didn't seem too pleased that he had to release me from custody.

"Just one big misunderstanding, right?" I said.

Park frowned. "Sarcasm, huh?"

"What do you think?" I said, turning to Park. "First, you don't believe me. Now, all of a sudden, after my lawyer is murdered, you're listening. Well, fuck you, too."

Park narrowed his eyes. "Shut your mouth."

"Gentlemen, please," Kang said, intervening before things got out of hand. "We just need you to sign a few documents, and then one of our staff will drive you back to your apartment," Kang said matter-of-factly. "Chamsil, right? Just down the street from Lotte World, I understand."

"Yeah, Chamsil."

"We're sorry again about the inconvenience, aren't we, Detective?"

Park huffed. "Yeah, sorry."

"See, no hard feelings," Kang said with a cheery disposition.

"Are we good here? Can I go now?"

"Just one thing, Turner," Park said.

"What?"

Park drew in a long breath and exhaled slowly. "Apparently, Moon was inquiring about a local hoodlum with ties to one of the city's crime bosses that controls the part of the city where the Paradise Club is located."

"Let's not jump to conclusions, Detective," Kang said, interrupting Park. "We don't know that for a fact."

"Excuse me?" Park scowled at Kang.

"I think we should let Mr. Turner rest. He's been through an ordeal the past couple of days," Kang said. "Of course, if we need you for anything, we'll be sure to contact you."

"Yeah, that's fine with me." I just wanted to get the hell out of here.

"I'm afraid you don't understand," Park said, casting Kang a cold sideways glance. "This local hoodlum could have been the man you saw at the Paradise. There was a reason the murderer went after Moon. If he thinks you can identify him, there's a good chance that he might come after you next."

"But he doesn't know where I live and work, right?"

"No, he doesn't. But if he could get to Moon, he can certainly get to you," Park said.

"What do you want me to do?"

"This man you saw at the club. If we showed you some photos, do you think you could identify him?"

"A little too late for that now, don't you think?" I said under my breath.

"Excuse me? Did you say something, Turner?" Park said.

"When?"

Park shot me a dirty look. He knew exactly what I had said. "The sooner, the better."

Before Park had an officer bring me home, he brought me to the police station to look through several books of mug shots. A few police officers who recognized me from the newspapers were surprised to see me in the station and not in handcuffs.

None of the men in the photos looked familiar to me until I got halfway through one of the books, and the hardened, icy stare of one man made me shudder. It was an older photograph, and the man was about ten, maybe fifteen years younger. Although the man did not have a scar on his cheek, there was no mistaking the man I had seen at the Paradise.

"There," I said, pointing to the photograph. "He's the one I saw at the club."

Park grabbed the book from my hands and gazed at the man I had identified.

"Chun Yong-chol. Oh, shit. I don't fucking believe it."

"What?"

"And you're sure this is the man you saw at the club."

I nodded.

"He's been a suspect in several murder cases, but we could never hold him."

"Why?"

"He has friends in high places."

———

FOR THE REST of the day, Kang stayed in his office. He didn't even bother having lunch. He wouldn't have been able to eat anyway, not with the whole world collapsing around him.

On his desk was Turner's file, which contained three thin sheets of paper describing the murder and the police investigation, his confession, and a document authorizing his release. Next to the file was a letter to his boss in a sealed envelope and a letter to his wife. There was only one way out for him now. In time, he hoped his wife would be able to forgive him.

Kang put on his coat and stuck the letter to his wife into an inside pocket. On his way out, the phone rang. He should have just left, but he returned to his desk and picked up the receiver. On the other end was his wife.

"Are you coming home soon?"

"Yes, I was just on my way out."

"Oh, good," his wife said. "Your friend is here waiting for you."

"Friend?"

"That's right. Yong-chol. He said that you were expecting him. He got here early. Is he going to stay for dinner?"

Kang's legs felt weak. He steadied himself against the back of his chair. "Put him on the phone, please."

"Of course."

"Jae-min, how are things with you?"

Kang gripped the phone. "If you harm my wife or daughter, I swear I'll—"

"Knock off the dramatics, Kang. You know why I'm here. I can see that you're not going to take care of our little problem, so let me make it easy for you. Where can I find him?"

Kang closed his eyes. He felt his stomach twisting into knots. "Find who?"

"You know who."

"You don't have to worry about him."

"Again, where can I find him? I understand that he's been released from the detention center."

"How did—?"

"I have my ways."

"He won't talk. He's too scared of what could happen to him if he does."

Chun was silent on the other end before he spoke again. "You never mentioned how beautiful and charming your wife was. If I had a wife as beautiful and charming as yours, I would do everything to ensure no harm would ever come her way."

Kang clenched his teeth.

"And your daughter—she looks just like her mother. It's a good thing for her she doesn't look like her father," Chun said, laughing.

"Maybe there's another way. Maybe—"

"Address. Now."

"Please don't hurt them."

"Give me the address, and I promise you no harm will come to your family."

"He lives in Chamsil. He works at ELS. It's a language school near Kangnam subway station."

"See, that wasn't so hard."

"Are we finished?"

"Yes, we're finished. By the way, your lovely wife asked me to stay for dinner, but I have a previous engagement. Maybe next time. See you around, Mr. Prosecutor."

Kang's wife came back on the phone. "Your friend is such a nice man. Very polite and gentlemanly. How come you never mentioned him before? He said he couldn't stay for dinner. Said he had some urgent business to take care of. We'll have to invite him back here soon."

Kang cringed, not knowing what to say. He felt as though he had just sold his soul to the devil.

TWENTY-FIVE

TWO HOURS LATER, WHEN I WALKED INTO MY APARTMENT, Keith and his girlfriend were on the sofa having sex. His girlfriend, who I had met the first night I arrived in Korea, shrieked, covered her breasts and pubic area as best she could with her clothes, and ran into Keith's bedroom.

"Bro! You got out!" Keith pulled up his underwear and slipped on a pair of sweatpants. Then he bounded across the room and gave me a big, sweaty bear hug. "Damn, it's good to see you!"

"Yeah, same here," I said, backing away from Keith.

"Want a beer?"

"Sure."

"Coming right up."

Keith grabbed two bottles of OB from the refrigerator and cracked them open with a bottle opener. He handed me a bottle, and we sat at the kitchen table.

"Welcome home," Keith said, holding up his beer bottle to clink with mine.

"Thanks, man."

We clinked our bottles and took a drink. The cold beer tasted good going down.

"Jesus, I couldn't believe what happened to you."

"You and me both, brother."

"When I went back to the club, you weren't there. At first, I thought you might have gone off with that girl you were sitting with. I waited for a while, but you never came back. But then I thought you were in the military and all, and you would find a way to get home. When you hadn't come home by Sunday night, I kind of figured something was wrong and called Gilbert. He freaked out when I told him what had happened but said it was too late to do anything. That was when the shit hit the fan. He told his boss, who in turn notified the president of the company. They all thought you were dead or something. Seoul is pretty safe, but Itaewon can get a little nasty. And then the next thing you know, we hear about some American charged with murder. You. Right there on the evening news and in the Korea Daily. Talk about the proverbial shit hitting the fan."

"You waited until Sunday night to call Gilbert?"

"Yeah, like I said. I thought you could handle yourself."

Thanks a lot, pal. I drank some of my beer. I was too tired to get into it with my roommate.

"And then Gilbert yells at me for taking you to Itaewon in the first place. His face got red, and the veins on his neck tightened. I thought he was going to have a stroke or something. I'm thinking, man, it's going to be like the same shit that happened to my buddy, Mike. He threatened to fire me right there on the spot, but the managing director likes me and told Gilbert to back down."

"Must have been rough for you, huh?"

Keith's eyes widened, but he grinned when he caught my sarcasm. "Oh yeah, right, man," he said apologetically. "You know what I'm trying to say, right?"

"No prob."

"What the hell happened, anyway?"

I told Keith how I had gone looking for him and ended up in the Paradise Club. I told him about Joo-hee and waking up next to her dead body in the morning. It should have been liberating and cathartic for me, opening up and talking about everything that I had gone through, but it also made me feel guilty, knowing that my actions that night ended up costing the lives of at least one person. I probably wouldn't have saved Joo-hee's life had I not met her that night, but I definitely would have saved Moon's life.

"Oh, man. That must have been awful for you."

"No matter what I told the police, they didn't believe me. One of them even took a cattle prod to me."

"No, shit, man. That's fucked up."

"Yeah, it sure was. Finally, I said fuck it. I told them what they wanted to hear so they would stop interrogating me." I drank the last of the beer and held up the empty bottle for Keith to see. "Got another one?"

"Sure, but would you like something stronger?"

"Beer is fine."

Keith got me another bottle from the refrigerator.

Keith was silent for a few seconds before he spoke again. "About that night—I'm really sorry for leaving you in that club all by yourself. If I hadn't gone off to pay that dude his money, you would have never wound up in jail."

"Do you think?"

Keith's jaw dropped. "I-I-I can explain—"

"Just fucking with you, man. We're good."

"Phew, that's a relief. Not that I don't deserve a good kick in the ass, mind you."

We were quiet for several seconds, not sure what else to say. After all, what could anyone say after having gone through the ordeal I had been through? Even having a beer with my roommate seemed surreal. I guess it really hadn't hit me yet; either that or I was doing a pretty good job of blocking it.

"By the way, your luggage finally came."

"It's about fucking time. I'm still wearing the same clothes I wore when I came here."

"Ah, there's just one thing."

I was about to take another swig of my beer but stopped. "What do you mean, there's just one thing?"

"You'll have to see for yourself."

That didn't sound good, but I didn't bother to press Keith for the details. I would find out soon enough. "By the way, how do I call the States?"

"You need to dial zero-zero-one followed by the country code, which is one, and then the number. You're not thinking about jumping ship, are you?"

I took another swig of the beer and shook my head. "I'd better call my mother. She's probably worried sick about me. I can only imagine what the embassy told her."

Keith's girlfriend walked out of his bedroom and into the kitchen. After having caught her and my roommate having sex, she avoided eye contact with me and walked to the door.

"I go now," his girlfriend said, glaring at Keith.

"Yeah, baby," Keith said, drinking some of his beer. "Take care. I'll call you later."

"Walk me to subway station."

"Can't you see I'm talking to my roommate?"

Keith's girlfriend gave him the finger. "Now, Keith!" She stamped her feet and glared at my roommate.

"Hey, it's okay. I'd better call my mother, anyway. She's probably sick with worry."

"Cool, man. We'll talk more when I get back."

AFTER KEITH and his girlfriend had left, I checked on my luggage, which Keith had put in my room. One bag was okay, but the other looked like a truck had run over it several times or had been dropped from the top of the 63 Building. The handle and zipper were broken, and both sides of the bag were torn and mangled. And then, for the pièce de résistance, someone had tried to duct tape the bag shut, but that didn't work. Various items of clothing were sticking out of the torn fabric.

"Fuck me."

I helped myself to another beer, and then I called my mother. I probably should have taken up Keith's offer for something stronger. By now, she was probably a nervous wreck, not having heard from me and piecing together whatever information my brother had conveyed to her. It was a little after ten in the evening back in Texas. If I was lucky, I would catch her before she went to bed.

She picked up on the seventh ring. Shit. She was already in bed.

"Hello?" Her voice was hoarse and cracked.

"Hello, Mom. It's me, Robert."

"Robert?"

She coughed, followed by the sound of her fumbling for something on the nightstand—either her glasses or cigarettes. A bottle or a glass fell over. The strike of a disposable lighter. She coughed again.

"Who?"

"Robert, your son."

"Robert? Is that you?"

"Yes, Mother."

"Oh, my God. It is you. When the embassy called me and told me you had been arrested and were in jail, I was sick with worry. I couldn't believe what they had told me. Charged with murder. You just got to Korea. It had to have been a mistake. Maybe they got you confused with another Robert, but the man on the phone said, No, ma'am. Robert Turner. LaSalle, Illinois. My God. What happened? Was it an accident? No, it wasn't an accident, he told me. This man who called from the embassy, he was very nice. Baxter, I think he said his name was. He told me the embassy was doing everything they could to help me, but it was complicated. And all the while, I'm thinking this can't be true. This can't be happening. How could my son be charged with murder? This Baxter, he was very nice, like I said."

Why the hell did Baxter call my mother? Stupid fuck. I specifically told him to call my brother, knowing this would happen. And what kind of shit was this, the embassy was doing everything it could to help me? "Mom, wait. Listen to me."

"I don't know why you had to go over there in the first place.

See, if you had listened to me, this would not have happened, but no, you have always got to do what Robert wants to do."

Whenever my mother was very angry or upset, she often addressed me in the third person.

"Mom, please."

"Baxter talked about hiring an attorney, but I told him I didn't have any money. You got yourself into this, you're going to—"

"Mother! Please be quiet and just listen!"

"That's no way to talk to me."

"I'm not in jail anymore."

"What are you talking about?"

"I'm not in jail. I got out today. I was innocent all along, but the police did not believe me. Someone else had murdered the woman."

I heard some bottles rattling, and then my mother drinking something. She coughed several times and dropped the receiver before she came back on.

"You didn't kill the woman?"

"Didn't you hear what I just said?"

"You're not in jail now."

"That's right. I got out today. A couple of hours ago, as a matter of fact."

"You could have called."

Getting into it with my mother was the last thing I wanted.

"They wouldn't let me."

"I had to hear it from the embassy."

"I'm sorry about that, too. I told them to call Randall first."

"Do you know the hell you put me through?"

"I said I was sorry."

"Your brother is all worked up about this, too. Do you want to talk to him?"

"What the hell is he doing there?"

"It's Christmas, remember? Randall! Your brother is on the phone!"

"Never mind." If I didn't get off the phone now, my mother and I would go round and round and end up right where we were at now. "I just called to say that I'm okay and there's nothing to worry about. I'll call back later."

"Are you coming home?"

"No, I'm not coming home."

"I would think you would want to come home after what you've been through."

"I'm not coming home, okay?"

My mother was quiet for a few seconds. Then I heard her light another cigarette.

"I'm sorry about everything again, Mom. I just don't want you to worry. Everything's all right now. Talk to you again soon. I love you."

———

THE FOLLOWING DAY, when Keith and I went into school, I had a meeting with Gilbert and the director of the school, Choi Yong-hwan. Choi's office was on the first floor, just off to the right of the information desk, where several prospective students waited to register for classes. As soon as I walked in with Keith, all eyes were upon me. News traveled fast that one of the new teachers had gotten arrested.

"You're famous, Bro," Keith said, clapping me on the back.

I certainly didn't think so.

"Good luck in there." Keith gestured with his head to the director's office. "Remember, try to bow at about a forty-five-degree angle when you bow. Keep your hands to your sides and hold the bow for a few seconds. And whatever you do, don't look Choi in the eyes. The trick is to be sincere. Shit like that goes a long way in Korea."

"Got it. Thanks."

"One more thing."

"What's that?"

"Kick some ass."

I grinned and knocked on the door to Choi's office.

"Come in," a voice said from inside.

I thought for sure I was going to be fired when I walked into Choi's office. Gilbert, who was standing to the side of Choi's desk, was seething. I thought his head was going to explode. Remembering what Keith had told me, I bowed deeply and held it for several seconds.

"Do you have any idea how much trouble you caused us? What were you thinking?" Gilbert said in a dry, grating voice. "In your contract, there's a provision that states any violation of Korean law will result in the immediate termination of your contract and dismissal."

The fine print. Actually, I skimmed over that part of the contract.

"It's bad enough that you had to get arrested, but now we've got to worry about immigration fining the school and who knows what else. You're lucky that after the police were finished with you, they didn't deport you!"

I stood there and took it. I hadn't been reamed out this bad since the military when I wore a Three Stooges t-shirt to basic training. Of course, that was my fault, not to mention my misfortune.

Choi stared at me from behind an enormous mahogany desk that was too big for him and occasionally nodded as Gilbert made several more points about how foolish and careless I had been. He was a short, round-faced man with wispy black hair combed across his head to cover a bald spot. His name, in Korean and Chinese, was etched into a black mother-of-pearl inlaid nameplate that covered the front edge of his desk. He let Gilbert rant and rave before he finally spoke.

"Most unfortunate. Most unfortunate. By the way, we are sorry. Although your roommate should have exercised better judgment taking you to Itaewon, that doesn't change the fact that what happened to you was terrible in so many ways. As unfortunate as it was for you, we still have our reputation to consider. Mr. Gilbert is right. We can't have our English teachers setting a poor example that could harm our school."

Oh, boy. Here it comes. I'm going to be sacked, and I haven't even started to teach.

"By the way, given the circumstances, that you were in the wrong place at the wrong time and that you were not at fault, we will not terminate your contract."

I took a deep breath. Wow. That was close. I bowed deeply again.

"Thank you. I'm sorry for what happened and the inconvenience I might have caused you, the school, and the staff."

"You're welcome. We just want you to know that we're terribly sorry that we got caught up in all of this and that we're here for you."

"I came here to teach, and that's what I intend to do," I said. "I just want to put all of this behind me."

"Good," Choi said, standing. He held out his hand for me to shake.

———

THIRTY MINUTES AWAY IN BOGWANG-DONG, Captain Park and his partner, following up on their investigation of Chun, met with his boss, Kwon Yong-ho.

"What can I do for you, officers?" Kwon asked, looking at the name card Park had given him. "You're not here about my donation to the policeman's benevolent association, are you? I hope there's no problem. I told one of my associates to take care of it personally."

Not sure what Kwon meant, Park looked at his partner and shrugged. "We're not here about that. We're here inquiring about one of your associates, Chun Yong-chol."

"What about him?"

"We were hoping you could shed light on his whereabouts."

Kwon didn't bat an eye. Instead, he answered Park, all cool and calm. "He's not in trouble, I hope."

"We would just like to ask him a few questions."

Kwon picked up the pair of green metal Chinese Baoding balls and rotated them in the palm of his hand. "May I ask what this is in regards to?"

"Just routine." Park wanted to be careful not to tip his hand about the true nature of their investigation. "His name came up in an investigation, and we're just following up on it."

"I see." Kwon cast a doubtful look at Park. "Sorry to disappoint you, officers, but I haven't seen him in weeks."

"Would you happen to have an address where we could find him?"

"No, I don't. He moves around a lot. It's sometimes hard to keep up with him."

Park smiled. "I see. What about some of the places that Chun has been known to frequent?"

"Sorry, I can't help you with that either. Chun is a private person and what he does when he's not working with me is his own business."

"And what exactly does he do for you?"

"He oversees my import operations."

"Okay then. I guess that'll do it for now. Thank you for your time, Mr. Kwon."

"My pleasure." Kwon set the Baoding balls back in their case and picked up Park's name card. "The next time I see him, Captain Park, I'll be sure to mention that you want to talk to him."

"Thank you." Park saluted and walked out of the office with Shin.

Outside and out of earshot from Kwon's office, Shin turned to his partner.

"Not too talkative, was he?"

Park nodded. "Let's park an officer down the street to keep an eye out on the building just in case Chun shows up after all."

TWENTY-SIX

Despite having been detained for over a week, I had only missed two days of classes. Gilbert thought it might be good for me to do administrative tasks until the next term to give me time to recover, but I just wanted to teach. I just wanted to put everything behind me. It didn't take long for me to get acclimated. Keith and another teacher, Sheila, a tall blonde from London who would have been my mentor had I not spent my first week in jail, showed me around the staff room.

"Just holler if you need any help," Keith said as we walked up the stairs to our classrooms. In an effort to create an English environment conducive to learning English, the school had named the classrooms after US States, though not in any geographical relevance. My classroom was Texas, and Keith's classroom was New York, right next door.

From my classroom window, I could look across the narrow street behind our school and into another building opposite our language institute. On one of the upper floors of the building, I could see another foreigner teaching a similar, I presumed, English class. The teacher, a bald man with a beard, looked out his classroom window toward where I was standing and waved. I waved back.

My first class didn't go so well. Thankfully, none of the students recognized me from the newspapers or television, except one male student sitting in the back of the class who spent most of the two-hour class staring at me. Because another teacher had filled in for me the first two classes, the students spent most of the class asking me questions to get to know me.

"Where are you from?"

"How old are you?"

"Can you use chopsticks?"

"Are you married?"

"Can you eat spicy food?"

"What do you think of Korean women?"

The last question got to me. The image of Joo-hee's lifeless body on the bed popped into my mind, and I shuddered. I blinked my eyes, and the image disappeared, but not the goosebumps that ran up and down my arms. When I looked up, all the students were staring at me, waiting for me to say something.

"Teacher, you okay?" a student nearest me asked.

I nodded, but I wasn't okay.

"Let's take a ten-minute break."

I hurried upstairs to the roof and smoked a cigarette to calm my nerves. I thought about what Gilbert had said about taking some time off before I started teaching. Maybe he was right.

The rest of the class and the day went without further incident. I felt better after Keith and I had lunch at a Korean restaurant down the street from our school.

"How did it go?" Keith said. He ordered us two bowls of bubbling tofu stew.

"It was a little rough at first."

"You'll do just fine. The worst is behind you."

In the afternoon, I had to go to the immigration office with one of the office staff to register. The immigration officer did several double-takes at me while scrutinizing my passport and documents. Perhaps he had seen my photograph plastered across newspaper headlines or on television. Nonetheless, everything checked out. He stamped my passport. I was good to go. In two weeks, I would have my little blue alien residence booklet.

Then, it was back to school for two classes in the evening. Both went much smoother than my morning class.

"A couple of us are going to celebrate Sally's birthday tonight. Do you want to come?" Keith said at the end of the night while we were putting away our books and attendance folders in the staffroom.

"Sure. That sounds like fun. But no Itaewon this time."

Keith laughed. "Don't worry. We're going somewhere better."

"Where's that?"

"The Airport."

"What? Kimpo?"

Keith laughed again. "No, man. It's this bar called The Airport. It's close to here. Just across the street."

"Yeah, sure. Count me in."

The Airport, as it was appropriately called, had a section of a 707 Korean Air fuselage in the center of the room. The seats had been replaced with tables and chairs, and that's where Keith and I found Sally and several other teachers from school waiting for us. Several pitchers of beer had already been ordered, along with plates of nuts, strips of dried squid, and rectangle sheets of seaweed. In the center of one table was a white cake garnished with fruit.

It might have been Sally's birthday, but I was the center of attention. Although I had already met most of the teachers at school, when Keith showed me around, everyone wanted to hear about what had happened to me.

"They didn't beat you, did they?" Sheila said.

"One of the officers knocked me off a chair and kicked me in the ribs several times."

"Oh, you poor thing." Sheila touched my arm.

"I heard about the police torturing prisoners," Eoghan, a teacher from Ireland, said, pouring himself a glass of beer.

"One of them had a cattle prod," I said.

Sheila gasped and put a hand over her mouth.

"It must have been awful," Sally said, her big brown eyes wide with horror.

"Yeah, it was horrible." I cringed, remembering the interrogation. "They kept asking me the same questions over and over about why I murdered the woman. And every time I told them I didn't remember what happened, they got angrier with me."

Even though I left out some of the more graphic details, I felt my insides twisting into a knot.

"Why didn't they believe you?" Sally asked.

"They refused to believe I had just passed out and didn't remember anything."

"How did you end up in that bar in the first place?" Sheila asked.

"That would be me," Keith said with a sheepish look.

"I don't know about you guys, but I definitely would have broken after the first hour." Mike, a bald, portly teacher from Canada, said. "I can't even keep a secret from my roommate."

Everyone around the table laughed, which was replaced by an awkward silence until Keith raised his beer glass, sensing that it was time to change the subject. "Here's to Sally on her birthday. Happy Birthday!"

"Happy Birthday, Sally!"

We clinked our beer glasses around the table.

After drinking the contents of my glass, I leaned close to Keith. "Thanks for saving me."

Keith smiled. "I figured you needed a break from all the questions."

"Yeah, thanks."

Keith grabbed a pitcher of beer and filled my glass. "Let's hope you never have to go through anything like that again."

"Amen, Bro." I clinked my glass against his and was ready to take a drink when I froze. In the back of the room, standing halfway in the shadows, near a hallway, I thought I saw the man I had identified in the photos at the police station.

"What's wrong?" Keith asked.

Several customers at the next table got up to leave, blocking my view of the man. When they left, the man I thought I had recognized turned out to be someone else.

Quit acting so paranoid.

"Nothing," I said, but just to be sure, I looked again. But the man had left.

I think all the excitement of my ordeal and my first full day of teaching caught up with me because, after a few beers, I could hardly keep my eyes open and decided to call it a night. I wished Sally a Happy Birthday again and said goodnight to everyone.

"You know how to get to the subway station from here, don't you?" Keith said.

"Yeah, I should be able to find it."

"See you back at the apartment."

I walked out into the frosty night air, which hummed and crackled with the buzz of lit-up signage along the busy sidewalk toward the Kangnam subway station. Although it was only eleven-thirty, many clubs, bars, and restaurants were already letting out for the evening. With an impending war in Iraq about to break out any week, I read in the newspaper that the Korean government had recently instituted a mandatory curfew for bars and restaurants, fearing that any war with Iraq would disrupt the flow of Middle East oil to the country. It wasn't so much the bars, clubs, and restaurants having to close early to have people off the streets as it was to have them turn off all the neon signage to save energy.

When I got to the subway station, it was crowded, with everyone trying to catch one of the last trains home. I fell in behind the crowd of commuters descending to the bowels of the station. No sooner had I reached the bottom than a shrill chime announcing an arriving train, followed by a Korean announcement. Then, somewhere down the tracks, a horn sounded, followed by a sudden rush of warm air as the train pulled into the station.

As I moved to the edge of the platform, I felt someone come up behind me and touch me on the back. My body tensed. What if I was right, and the man I had seen at the restaurant was the man who killed Joo-hee and Moon? Or maybe it was someone else. All he would have to do is push me in front of—

The train screeched to a stop; the doors opened, and the sea of people on the platform surged forward into the waiting cars. Bodies pressed against bodies. The warm, stuffy air reeked of perfume and alcohol. With no place to sit, I stood holding onto a brown overhead strap wedged between other commuters. It was only five stops to Shinchon, my subway stop, about a ten-minute ride.

A buzzer sounded. The doors closed, and the train lurched forward. The air was full of electrical charge as the train started moving down the tracks. I gazed at the reflection of the subway riders in the window, hypnotized by the gentle rocking of the subway car. Some of them stared at me—something I had been warned about in the information I had received about teaching in South Korea, about how many Koreans often stared at foreigners on trains and buses—but thought nothing of it.

After a few seconds, in my peripheral vision, I caught a glimpse of someone standing at the back of the subway car, looking in my direction. Although the person was partially hidden by several commuters gripping the overhead plastic straps, I sensed whoever this person was, they were intent on watching me. When I returned the person's stare, the person's dark iron-hard eyes locked with mine. A shudder coursed through my body. Maybe it was the person I had seen at the bar earlier, and they had followed me onto the subway. I couldn't be sure. Perhaps I was just being paranoid again. My heart hammered in my chest. If it was the same person, should I get off at the next stop or stay on the train until I got home?

The subway slowed as it neared the next station. Overhead, an announcement was made in Korean, followed by English. The next stop is Yoksam. The exit doors are on your right. Although I was standing close to one of the exit doors, if I made my move too soon, the person would have time to follow me off the train. But, on the other hand, if I waited too long, the person and I would still be on the train together, and I wouldn't have time to step off. It was like that scene in The French Connection, when Gene Hackman's character, Popeye Doyle, was following one of the French villains onto a New York subway. Hackman, who didn't want the villain to know he was being tailed, stepped off and on the train one too many times, not fooling the villain, who got away.

When the subway screeched to a stop, I and the other riders who were standing lurched forward. The doors opened, and around a dozen people exited the car. I decided to take my chances and stay on the subway. It was the right thing to do. When I glanced back to where the person had been standing, whoever it had been had gotten off.

Sollung. Samseong. Sports Complex. At my destination, Shinchon Station, only a few riders, including myself, exited the car. One bumped into me, knocking my Eastpak book bag off my shoulder. When I bent down to pick it up, I saw a man, who was wearing a leather jacket, bound up the steps.

A warm wind swept around me as the subway left the station. The platform was eerily quiet as I walked toward the steps leading to the exit above. Across the tracks, on the opposite platform, several people waited for the subway.

Nearing the stairs to the upper level, footsteps echoed behind me. I turned to see if anyone was following me, but no one was on the platform. Then, the shrill, metallic ringing sound of the electronic bell signaling a subway approaching in the opposite direction, followed by a horn blaring down the tracks as the train neared the station, startled me. I looked one last time behind me, but seeing I was the only one on the platform, I hurried up the steps.

The upper level of the subway station was deserted except for a subway worker sleeping inside the ticket booth. I inserted my yellow subway pass inside the waist-high steel tripod subway turnstile, pushed through the three stainless steel revolving arms, and turned left up the stairs to the subway entrance. At the top of the steps, I stopped and looked down the steps.

No one.

From the subway station to my apartment took only fifteen

minutes. Unfortunately, since the time I had taken the subway home, it had started to rain. I pulled my jacket over my head and hastened down the sidewalk past the tiny newspaper kiosk where I bought my cigarettes and through the gate leading to my apartment complex. I got about fifty yards inside the complex when footfalls echoed off the wet pavement. If anyone was following me, there were plenty of places to lose them between the rows of buildings and side streets which crisscrossed the complex.

My heart pounded and my muscles tensed.

The footfalls grew louder. Whoever was behind me was close. I quickened my pace and looked for a place to run. I could hear the person's breathing and smell soju on their breath. Whoever it was, was right on my ass. I felt the hairs on the back of my neck stand on end. If I took off running down the street, I might be able to outrun whoever was behind me.

Before I could react, the person behind me, a young man, passed me and entered an apartment building on the right.

"Jesus H. Christ!" I jumped back several steps, watched the man disappear into the building, and then bent forward, putting my hands on my knees and taking a deep breath.

I continued down the street for another hundred yards and then zig-zagged through the complex until I came out in a parking lot in front of my apartment building. I got about halfway across the parking lot when a silver sedan careened around the corner and drove up behind me, forcing me to jump out of the way.

The driver rolled down the window.

It was Park.

"Get in! Now!"

TWENTY-SEVEN

I GAZED AT PARK AND THEN LOOKED AROUND THE PARKING LOT nervously. It was weird how he just showed up, as I'd been thinking that someone had been following me. I heard, from the end of the parking lot, the sound of a car starting. I saw headlights flash on. My heart did a backflip. The car sped out of the parking lot, squealing its tires. It pulled out onto the busy street, almost hitting an oncoming car.

"What's going on, Park?"

"There's no time for that."

"What? Is my life in danger or something?"

"Just get in the car!"

Park's serious and excited tone were all the convincing I needed. I climbed into the car, and Park sped away. We came out on a side street, and the next thing I knew, we were zipping along the Olympic Expressway, heading past Olympic Stadium.

"Do you mind telling me what the hell is going on?"

"About two hours ago, the body of a police officer was found in an alley close to your school. His throat had been cut."

"Oh, shit."

"For your protection, we had an officer watching you in case

Chun came after you. I'm sorry for scaring you like I did, but we need to get you somewhere safe until we catch this guy." Park looked into the rearview mirror and swerved to change lanes. "It gets worse. The owner of the Paradise Club—her body was found in a dumpster this afternoon, and another one of the bar girls, Miss Han's roommate, hasn't been seen for several days."

"Oh, my God." I stared out the window and shook my head. As much as I felt vindicated, I was also worried for my own life. "If you had listened to me from the beginning. None of this shit would have happened."

Park turned and glared at me. "Don't you think I know that? But don't worry, we're going to catch this son-of-bitch."

"Yeah, right. Better late than never, huh?"

Park muttered something in Korean, which probably wasn't good, but fuck him. He was as much to blame as it was the guy who was after me. Do you know how you have those critical moments in your life when faced with some life-changing, life-altering experience and how you think in five or ten years; when you look back on that time, you'll see everything with more meaning and clarity? I don't think this wasn't going to be one of those times.

Then, I had a terrible thought.

"We've got to go back."

"What are you talking about?"

"My roommate. If he's after me, my roommate could be in danger, too."

"Is your roommate home now?"

"No, he's not. After work, we went out for drinks, but I came home early."

Park darted his eyes to the rearview mirror and frowned. "Shit."

"What?"

"A car has been tailing us since we left your apartment complex. I thought I had lost him when I pulled onto the expressway, but he's still behind us."

"What are you going to do?" There was no place for us to pull off as far as I could see. We passed a sign that said Banpo Bridge.

"Whoever it is, I think I can lose them."

Park stepped on the gas and passed several cars. Then, when he was sure that he had put enough distance between us and whoever was following, he veered across multiple lanes of traffic and shot up an off-ramp, barreling through a red light and swerving onto Banpo Bridge. There was not a lot of traffic on the bridge at this hour, but several irate drivers, who Park had cut off, sounded their horns and flashed their lights.

Park looked in the rearview mirror again and breathed a sigh of relief.

"Lost him."

"What about my roommate?"

"Your roommate?" Park changed lanes again. "Oh, yeah. As soon as we get to where we're going, I'll call."

As we crossed the bridge, light snow fell—tiny crystals hardly visible in the streetlights that lined the bridge. Rising in the distance was the ever-ubiquitous presence of Seoul Tower.

"Where's that?"

"There's a place outside the city. It's not far from here. A farmhouse where we'll stay until this blows over."

"What do you mean?"

"Someone knew that I had one of our officers follow you. But, at this point, I don't know who to trust."

And the hits kept on coming.

"Right now, you're the only person who can link this man to the murders of Han and Moon. We're going to catch him."

"Yes, you've said that already."

"Don't worry."

"That's easy for you to say." I still couldn't help but think if the police had listened to me from the beginning, they might already have this guy in custody. Instead, they jerked me around until they had no choice but to release me after Moon was murdered. Now, they had two more murders on their hands.

I looked out the passenger window again and tried to keep up with the different shops rushing by the car. Some shops, I figured, were restaurants or mini-markets. A few looked like pharmacies. Besides, at this hour, everything was shuttered for the evening. No one was on the sidewalks. Above the darkened neighborhoods, a few brightly glowing red crosses, like the ones I had asked my roommate about the night we went to Itaewon, hovered in the snowy night.

Soon, there were fewer buildings and streetlights. I could tell that we were nearing the outskirts of the city. Park slowed down. Ahead was some kind of checkpoint.

"What's happening?"

"Military checkpoint," Park said. "They're looking for North Korean infiltrators."

I'd learned about stuff like this when I read up on South Korea after being hired to teach. Although the Korean War had ended in 1953, there had been no formal peace treaty between the two Koreas; as such, the two countries were still technically at war.

Two South Korean soldiers carrying automatic weapons approached our vehicle. The one closest to the car saluted Park, who had already rolled down the window. Park handed his police identification card to the soldier, who looked at the card. Park said something in Korean to the soldier, who handed back the card and saluted again. The soldiers moved out of the way as we drove through the checkpoint.

"What did you tell them?"

"I told them to be on the lookout for a man with a scar on his face who's wanted in connection with several murders."

"Do you really think Chun will follow us here?"

"Anything is possible."

I didn't like the sound of that. "This place where you're taking me—is it safe?"

"You'll be fine."

"I hope so."

<h1 style="text-align:center">TWENTY-EIGHT</h1>

CHUN THOUGHT HE HAD LOST THE RUSTED SILVER SONATA HE had been following since Chamsil. The car had cut across several lanes of traffic and nearly sideswiped another vehicle when it turned onto the Banpo Bridge off-ramp. Chun waited until the last possible second to turn off the same off-ramp. However, halfway across the bridge, he spotted the same vehicle several car lengths ahead.

The driver was most likely a cop, the way he kept on switching lanes to see if anyone was tailing him, but the question was, where was this cop taking Turner?

Chun was angry at himself for allowing things to get out of hand the way they had. But, at the same time, he was of the opinion that if you wanted something done right and on time, you usually had to do it yourself. He should have known better than to rely on Kang to take care of the American. Kang had served him faithfully in the past, but he would probably have to take care of him when all of this was over.

Leave no loose ends.

Lee was no longer a loose end. With the American released from custody, it would only be a matter of time before the police went back to the Paradise Club and talked to her. She had been a nervous wreck the first time he asked her to lie about the night of Han's murder. Could she do it again? He couldn't take the chance. Suffocated her by placing a pillow over her face while she slept.

The bodies were stacking up.

The girl from the club, Han's roommate, was smart. She got out of town. He couldn't be sure what she knew or didn't know, but she knew better than to go to the police.

That left Turner the only person who could place him in the Paradise Club.

While waiting for Turner outside the language school, he'd noticed a man across the street from the school who looked like a police officer. When this man looked in his direction and did a double-take, Chun knew he had been recognized.

It was easy luring him down an alley and slitting his throat, but in the meantime, Turner had left the school. No problem, thanks to Kang, he knew where the American lived. He was familiar with the neighborhood. He had an acquaintance, one of Kwon's associates, a businessman, who lived in an apartment across the street from the sprawling Lotte World entertainment and shopping complex. When this businessman couldn't pay back the money he had borrowed from Kwon, Chun had to make a house call. He'd broken the businessman's hand by slamming it inside the car door of his Mercedes.

However, by the time Chun caught up with Turner near his apartment in Chamsil, Turner had gotten into the car he was following now. Someone had tipped either the police or Turner off, and he had a pretty good idea who. Chun would take care of him later.

Before reaching Kupabal, Chun went through the same military checkpoint Park had gone through earlier. One of the soldiers approached his vehicle, saluted, and asked for his identification card. The soldier shone his flashlight onto the card and stared at Chun's face. Either the soldier was too cold and tired or did not recognize him as the man Park had warned him about, but the soldier handed the identification card back to Chun without saying anything. Finally, the soldier saluted again and waved Chun through the checkpoint.

Chun thought he had lost Park, but a mile down the road, he saw a vehicle slowing and turning off the main highway. This was going to be a lot easier than he thought. Out here, in the middle of a snowstorm, no one would be left to stand in his way when this night was over.

TWENTY-NINE

The snow, which had started falling after midnight, would continue to fall through the night. More than six inches would fall by morning, paralyzing the city and making travel treacherous. Kimpo Airport was closed, and train service between Seoul and Pusan was interrupted. An intra-city express bus traveling from the eastern coastal town of Sokcho to Seoul lost control coming over a mountain pass and slid off the highway, killing three and injuring ten. A twenty-car pile-up on the Kyongbu Expressway from Seoul to Pusan resulted in several casualties. Later, it would be reported that it was the worst snowstorm in twenty-five years.

Only someone crazy would want to be out on a night like this.

Park had driven for about twenty minutes after turning off the highway along a narrow road. The headlights, the only light in the all-encompassing darkness, cut an eerie swath through the falling snow, illuminating nothing but rice paddies on either side of the road and long, narrow cylindrical-shaped greenhouses. The wet, heavy snow fell faster than the windshield wipers could sweep it away. Park leaned forward over the steering wheel and strained to see the snow-covered lane ahead.

If this snow kept on coming down like this, there would be no way whoever had been following us would be able to find us out here. Park was right. I would be safe wherever he was taking us.

The headlights picked out a one-story structure surrounded by a stone fence about fifty yards ahead. Park slowed his vehicle, eventually stopping in front of the fence. In the beam from the headlights, the structure appeared to be constructed from concrete blocks and topped with an orange tile roof. A smaller building, probably a tool or storage shed, was off to the right.

"We're here."

"Where?"

"We're north of Kupabal, on the outskirts of the city. This used to be my uncle's house."

I couldn't tell if Park was trying to be friendly to me to make up for being such an asshole before, but I'd give him the benefit of the doubt. I was in no position to question his attempt at being friendly. After all, he was the one saving my ass. But I still wouldn't have minded taking a swing at him for being such an asshole.

Once inside, Park located the light switch and flipped it on, revealing a large, sparsely furnished room. On the right was the kitchen with a kitchen table, chairs, and refrigerator; on the left was the living room and, in the back, wooden doors leading to two more rooms. On one of the walls was a large black-and-white painting of a mountain in winter, similar to the one my roommate had. On another wall was a black-and-white photograph of an elderly couple wearing traditional Korean clothes, which I took for Park's uncle and aunt. In the center of the room was a kerosene heater. Park checked to see if there was any fuel inside before he pressed and released the ignition switch. The heater sputtered and hissed to life, and soon the room was warm and cozy.

"Let's see if there's anything to eat," Park said, looking through the cupboards. He found a box of crackers and instant ramen. "Take your pick."

I pointed to the box of crackers. Park tossed me the box.

"You said this used to be your uncle's place," I said, examining the box of crackers with the brand name, "Digestive Crackers, the Original British Biscuit," written on the front. I checked for an expiration date but could not find one. They were probably okay to eat.

"That's right." Park found a brass kettle and filled it with water and barley tea that he had also found in the cupboard. "He had a stroke three months ago."

"I'm sorry to hear that."

He set the brass kettle on top of the kerosene heater. "It was too much for him to live here alone after his wife died, so he moved in with my wife and me. I spent a lot of time here when I was growing up. It's not too far from Pukhansan."

"Pukhansan?"

"It's a mountain range north of Seoul. The name means 'mountain north of the Han.' In ancient times, it was once referred to as the guardian of the city. My uncle's property borders Pukhansan National Park to the east."

Park's attempt to be friendly did not set my mind at ease. There was a madman on the loose. "What do we do in the meantime?"

"We just sit tight and wait until this storm blows over. My partner will relieve me in the morning."

"Shin."

Park nodded. "By the way, he's sorry about everything."

"I bet he is."

"Listen, Turner. You were our only suspect. We had to do what we did."

"Whatever."

"Hopefully, we won't have to stay here too long."

Gilbert was going to go through the ceiling when I didn't show up for work tomorrow, but at this point, I could give a rat's ass what Gilbert did. After all the shit I had been through, maybe it was time to think about heading home. I still had my former boss's contact information. Perhaps I could get my old job back. And if I was lucky, Christine, my old girlfriend, would take me back.

"And then what?"

"We've got the building where Chun's boss has an import and

export business under surveillance. So if he shows up there, we'll nab him."

"And if he doesn't."

"Then we'll just have to sit tight here and think of something else."

Park made it all sound so easy. But, again, if he had only believed me from the beginning, I wouldn't be in this predicament. Remembering that I wanted to call Keith when we arrived, I spotted a black telephone on a table.

"Do I have to dial anything to call Chamsil?" I said, walking over to the phone and picking up the receiver.

"No. Just dial the number."

I nodded, but I heard no dial tone when I put the receiver to my ear. "Shit."

"What?"

"No dial tone." I tapped the telephone hook several times, but there was still nothing.

"The storm must have knocked out the phone service. Sorry, Turner."

"What do we do now? My roommate's life could be in danger."

"You said you and your roommate went out drinking after work?"

"That's right. He was still in the bar when I left."

"Then, he should be okay. Besides, Chun is not going to come after your roommate. He wants you." Park handed me a cup of tea. "Here, drink this. It'll make you feel better."

I didn't think so, but I had had nothing to drink since leaving the bar I had been at earlier in the evening. I could use a stiff drink, but this would have to do. I held the cup of tea up to my nose and inhaled the rich, warm aroma.

"Why did you come to Korea?" Park poured himself a cup of the barley tea and pulled up a chair next to mine.

"I told you already to teach English."

"I know, but couldn't you find a job back in your country?"

"I had a job, but I wanted something different." Park still unnerved and annoyed me. "You sound like my mother."

"How's that?"

"My mother also wanted to know why I wanted to come to Korea. She couldn't understand how I could give up a good job to travel here to teach English."

"What kind of job."

"A copy editor."

"You should have listened to your mother."

"In hindsight, I guess I should have. This wasn't the adventure I imagined."

The tea tasted good, and the warmth radiating from the kerosene heater made me feel drowsy. Park walked over to a window and kept a lookout. If someone in his department had tipped Chun off, we would be sitting ducks out here. He might have been a prick before, but he had gone to great lengths to protect me. Besides, his ass was probably on the line, too.

I closed my eyes and must have fallen asleep because when I opened them, it was morning, and sunlight was streaming in through one window. I looked around nervously for Park, but he was gone.

"Park? Are you here?"

No answer.

"Park?"

I got up from the chair and walked to one of the rooms in the back. I opened the door to a small room. Inside was a black mother-of-pearl wardrobe and some bedding folded up on the floor, but Park wasn't inside. I checked the other room. Park wasn't in it, either. Where the hell did you go? I walked over to a window and looked outside. Park's car was also gone. What the hell? Did he just leave me here? Well, shit, this was no good. Maybe he went into town to get us something to eat.

When I turned around, Joo-hee stood in the middle of the room.

She was wearing the same red dress she had on the night she was murdered. Blood was running down the side of her face.

"Why did you let him kill me?"

I tried to open my mouth to say something, but I couldn't move.

"Didn't you hear me yelling for you?"

A tear rolled down her pale cheek.

"Why didn't you stop him? You could have saved me."

I wanted to say something, but the words got stuck in the back of my throat.

She grabbed my jacket.

"He's going to come for you now. You have to run. Now!"

The next thing I knew, Park was shaking me.

"W-W-What's going on?" I said, looking up at Park.

"You were having a bad dream."

I rubbed my eyes. "How long was I out?"

"Not too long. It's going to be light soon."

I stood and walked over to the window and looked outside. Snow continued to fall in large, wet flakes. Since we arrived at the farmhouse, it must have snowed five to six inches. I was about to turn around and walk back to the chair when a pair of headlights shining through the falling snow froze me.

"Are you expecting anyone?"

"What do you mean?"

"There's a car coming down the lane."

Park walked over to where I was standing and looked out the window.

"Who is it?"

Park unholstered his revolver and watched the car pull up alongside his car.

"I don't know."

"Shin?"

"It's not Shin. He's not supposed to come here until later."

The driver had still not gotten out of the car, which was still running. Through the intermittent sweep of the windshield wipers, one person, the driver of the vehicle, could be seen inside.

"Why doesn't the person get out?" I said.

"Quiet."

Another minute passed before the driver turned off the engine and the headlights and got out.

"It's Kang." Park heaved a sigh of relief.

"Kang? Was he supposed to come here?"

"No, he wasn't," Park said, holstering his revolver. "Something must be up."

The door opened, and Kang entered the farmhouse. He brushed the snow from his black cashmere jacket, stamped his feet, and said something in Korean to Park.

Although I couldn't understand what he was talking about, judging from Kang's tone, something was up, and it didn't sound good. No way was I going to be left out of this conversation.

"Speak English!" I said.

"Boy, it's a mess out there," Kang said. "I thought I would never make it."

"What the hell are you doing here?" Park glared at Kang. "How did you find out about this farmhouse?"

"Shin told me. You were not at home, so I called the station. Shin filled me in on everything."

"You still haven't explained why you drove out here."

"I tried to call you, but I couldn't get through."

"The lines are probably down on account of the storm."

Kang walked over to one of the windows. He parted the curtains and gazed out the window. "If we leave now, we still might be able to make it."

"What are you talking about?" Park said. "Go where?"

Kang turned and stared at Park and me. The color had drained from Kang's face, and he started to shake. "It's all my fault. I should have stopped him when I had the chance or told you."

"You're not making any sense. Stop who?"

"Chun Yong-chol."

"What are you talking about, Kang?" Park's eyes had turned cold, and his expression hardened.

"I knew everything. The drugs and Han's murder. He said it was an accident. He had only gone to her apartment to scare her. I knew you were innocent, but I did nothing about it." Kang gave me a shamefaced glance. "He was trafficking methamphetamine. Han knew about it, and he killed her."

"You fucking son-of-a-bitch," Park said. "How the hell did you get mixed up with Chun?"

"We met in an orphanage after the war. Later, when I became a prosecutor, I helped him out from time to time."

"Are you fucking serious?" Park's nostrils flared. "You worked for a Korean hoodlum?"

And the hits kept on coming.

"No one was supposed to get hurt. I took care of things for him. I tipped him off when there was going to be a raid or crackdown. If he had any enemies, I made sure they went away to prison for a long time."

Park grabbed Kang by his jacket. "And all this time, you knew about Chun and what he could do."

"That's why I came out here to warn you. I know what I did was wrong."

Park slammed Kang against the wall hard enough to make Kang wince. "A little late for that, don't you think? Thanks to you, one of my men is dead."

"What?"

"One of my men that I had watching Turner was murdered last night."

"I had no idea. I tried calling you, like I said, but you had already left."

I'd been speechless with amazement and fury, but I found my voice. "You slime!"

"I had no choice, Turner," Kang turned to me. He looked a lot different than he had several days ago before when I'd been brought to his office and charged with murder. His face wore a solemn expression of deep concern. "You have to believe me. He threatened my family."

Well, if this didn't beat all. The same guy who had been all apologetic the other day for putting me through this ordeal in the first place was about to serve me up to the same man who had put me behind bars in the first place. Un-fucking-believable.

Up to this point, Park had shown a lot a restraint. I had to hand it to him. But I had a feeling that was about to change.

"You told him where I lived and worked, didn't you?" I moved toward Kang.

"Not now, Turner."

"He threatened my family."

"And now, he probably followed us here, thanks to you."

"I'm sorry."

"You bastard. I ought to—"

"Turner, that's enough." Park glared at Kang before he released his grip and backed away.

Except I wasn't through. "And then you have a change of heart, which is supposed to make everything okay again? How do we know you're not still working for him?"

"I swear I'm telling you the truth. If I was still working for him, do you think I would tell you everything I have?"

"What do we do? We can't just sit here and wait," I said, staring at Park.

"Quiet. I need time to think." Park said. "Turn off that light."

I switched off the overhead light while Park walked to the window closest to the door and peered out through a crack in the curtains.

"Can you see anything?" I asked.

Park shook his head. "I wouldn't be surprised if he's already out there watching us right now to see what we will do."

"What do you have in mind?" I said.

"I don't know. I'll think of something." Park removed his .45 revolver from its holster again. "Stay away from the windows and keep trying to get an outside line."

Park opened the door and stepped outside.

THIRTY

Despite the heavy, wet snow that continued to fall, in the early morning light, Park had a good view of the road leading to the farmhouse and the rice paddies on either side. If Chun was out there, he had most likely parked his car somewhere down the road and used the treeline as cover to get nearer to the farmhouse.

Park looked to his left at the tool shed and woodpile next to it. That's where I would hide, he thought. Chun had two choices to get inside the farmhouse. Either he entered through the front door or circled around to the back of the farmhouse and entered through the back door—Chun would have to rely on the element of surprise if he were to get inside. The tool shed would provide cover for him to do, either. He assumed that Chun would have some kind of weapon, most likely a knife or an iron pipe—weapons of choice for a Korean hoodlum—which meant he would have to get close enough to use them. But, of course, Chun would have already thought about this and was simply waiting to make his move.

Where the hell are you?

Park moved cautiously to the right corner of the farmhouse.

Holding his revolver in front of his body, his eyes darted left to right, looking for any movement. He searched the snowy ground for footprints, but there were none. So far, so good. Walking toward the back of the shed, which would give him the best hiding spot to ambush Chun, a pair of footprints leading to the back of the shed froze him in his tracks. Fear coursed through his body. He turned and crept toward the footprints, which, judging by the freshly fallen snow, had just been made.

Park took several footsteps and stopped. He heard a creaking sound coming from somewhere behind the tool shed. Having spent a lot of time on his uncle's farm, he knew that his uncle had built a wooden overhang on the side of the tool shed. Underneath, his uncle had stored a garden tiller, and other farming implements hung from the wooden rafters.

Where are you, Chun? Come on out, you bastard.

A security light mounted on a utility light pole next to the tool shed cast eerie, jagged shadows on the freshly fallen snow. Park saw movement out of the corner of his right eye and had started to turn when Chun whacked him on the back of the head with a shovel. The force of the blow knocked Park to the ground and the revolver from his hand. Chun raised the shovel again before swinging it downward with all his might. Park rolled desperately out of the shovel's path, causing Chun to hit his shadow.

"Neo jwo pae beo-ril geo-ya," Chun said. I'm going to kick your fucking ass.

Park frantically groped for his revolver in the snow, but Chun swung the shovel against the side of Park's head, knocking him back into the snow. Although he was in excruciating pain, Park still had some fight left in him. Before Chun could finish him off, Park brought his right leg up and kicked Chun in the balls. Chun howled in pain and dropped the shovel.

Park found his revolver and got to his feet, but not fast enough to stop Chun, who charged at him, tackling him to the ground. The two men struggled to gain control of the weapon until an explosion ripped through the cold air, startling both men. Park pushed Chun off his body, gazing at him with an expression of horror on his face. Pain coursed through Park's body. He lifted his head and looked down at his lower stomach. Blood had immediately drenched his shirt.

Still holding the revolver, Chun staggered to his feet and walked to the front of the farmhouse.

THIRTY-ONE

"What was that?" I peered outside through a crack in the curtains. "Gunshot?"

"That's what it sounded like to me," Kang said, holding the telephone receiver to his right ear. "Park must have got him."

I saw a figure moving outside and froze.

"What's wrong?" Kang asked.

The door flew open, and in the doorway stood Chun, holding Park's revolver. Kang and I stepped back. Chun gazed at us with eyes swollen with rage, then pointed his revolver at Kang and started talking in Korean. I didn't understand the words, but he spoke with a certain resigned tone, and my guess was the essence of it was, "You're next."

What he said clearly frightened Kang, who, oddly, looked less frightened than determined—to do what, I did not yet know, but I noticed that while he and Chun talked, he had set the phone down and was inching closer to the kerosene heater.

Chun turned and stared at me with hooded eyes. "So you're Turner. Nice to meet you again, though we've never been properly introduced to each other. Tell me, was Han worth it?"

As Chun turned the revolver toward me, Kang grabbed the

brass tea kettle from the top of the heater and flung it at Chun. "Now, Turner!"

Chun screamed in pain when the hot tea splashed on his face and upper body. Momentarily blinded, Chun stumbled backward. Then, seizing upon Chun's incapacitated state, Kang charged at Chun, knocking him to the floor.

"Run, Turner!" Kang said, trying to wrestle the revolver from Chun.

Unable to run out the front door, which was blocked by Kang and Chun while they grappled and fought for control of the revolver, I ran to the back of the farmhouse and tried the back door. It was nailed shut.

"Dammit!"

I shouldered the door, but it would not budge. My only recourse was to escape through one of the rear windows, which were also nailed shut. I looked around for something to break the window. Seeing a wooden chair off to the side of the windows, I grabbed it from the back and smashed it against one of the windows. I kicked the remaining glass away from the frame and dove through the busted window.

Once outside, I sprang to my feet, ran to the property's edge in the back of the farmhouse, and—briefly remembering basic training—scaled a five-foot concrete wall. On the other side were snow-covered rice paddies and several long, narrow greenhouses like the ones I had seen earlier. A shot rang out from inside the house, and I ran between two of these structures. When I got to the end, I stopped and ducked around the corner. From here, crouched behind the greenhouse, I could see the back of the farmhouse through the plastic covering stretched over the steel ribs.

Chun emerged from the farmhouse a few seconds later, climbing through the broken window. I watched him walk to the same wall I had climbed over. He looked over the top of the wall and gazed in my direction for several seconds until something caught his eye. My footprints!

My heart pounded as I sized up the situation. Out here, I was a sitting duck. I had to somehow throw Chun off my path. But how? As far as I could see, there was nowhere to run. If I ran to my left or right and crossed either rice paddy, I was as good as dead. How many bullets did he have left? I did the math. He had already fired two rounds—one for Park and one for Kang. That left him with four bullets, more than enough for what he intended to do to me unless he had gone through Park's pockets and found more bullets.

And then I saw my escape route.

Visible through a grove of birch and pine trees behind me was a road and what appeared to be the entrance to the park, the one that Park had mentioned earlier. But, more importantly, it was a road that led somewhere and perhaps my way out of here.

You can do this, Turner.

I could see the top of Chun's head as he hurried along the concrete wall until he found the gate. It was now or never. I slowly stood from my crouched position and took off running toward the grove of trees. The snow, which came up to my calves, slowed me down. The only way I could increase my speed through the snow was by taking short, fast steps with high knees. I found myself skipping more than bounding through the snow, using my entire body, which also took more effort.

I kept my head low and ran for my life. Fifteen, maybe twenty yards until I reached the end of the field. Ten yards. Five yards. The icy air whistled around my ears, causing my skin to tingle. When I reached the grove, I zig-zagged through the trees, watching the road ahead. It was eerily quiet inside the grove of trees; the only sounds were my heavy breathing and pine branches creaking from the weight of snow on them. The smell of the damp pine trees made the air feel fresh and clean. I felt a sense of serenity inside this grove for a brief moment. Then, behind me, a branch snapped! It must have snapped from the weight of the snow; either that or Chun was much closer than I thought.

I didn't want to turn to find out.

The terrain became hilly and, in the snow, harder for me to run. Hopefully, it would also slow down Chun. Rising in front of me through the pine trees were the jagged granite snow-covered peaks of Pukhansan that Park had told me about last night. In the gray light and falling snow, the majestic peaks were ominous and breathtaking.

I came to a road that led up a foothill to a stone and wooden structure that looked like some fortress or castle with a tunnel running through the center, stone walls on either side, and topped with a gray tiled roof. I hurried up the road toward the fortress-looking structure. Inside the tunnel, I stopped to catch my breath and blow on my hands to warm them. Then, I looked down the hill and down the road leading to the fortress and could see a dark figure emerging from the grove of trees I had hurried through moments earlier.

"Dammit!"

I ran through the tunnel, which was only about twenty feet long, and came upon several buildings, shops, and residences. It didn't look like anyone was living in them or up at this hour. I stopped at one of the smaller buildings, which looked like a grocery store, and tried the door, but it was locked. I peered through the window—between a faded poster of a buxom Korean woman in a green bikini holding a green bottle of rice wine and another poster advertising OB beer—thinking that I saw a light on in the back.

"Please help me!" I pounded on the door.

I hoped whoever was in the back had heard me and would come to my rescue. I looked through the window again. Yes, a light was definitely on in the back, but I could see no movement.

Please, Dear God, if anyone is inside, please let them hear me and open the door.

Peering harder through the grimy window, I thought I saw a shadow move across the floor.

I banged on the door again. "Help me!"

But no one came.

There was not enough time to try another place. By now, Chun had reached the mountain fortress and would soon be here. I hurried back onto the road and followed it down a gradual slope, careful not to slip. On my left was a valley strewn with immense boulders, some the size of compact cars; to my right, pine and birch trees towered overhead. Either way, I was road-bound for the time being.

The snow came down hard and fast, with heavy wet flakes. I could barely see more than a few yards in front of me. The only good thing about this heavy snow was that if it slowed my progress, it also slowed down Chun. However, he could easily follow my tracks in the snow, so unless I could put enough distance between him and me and find a way to get off this road, I was fucked.

I looked over my shoulder to see if Chun had gained on me and didn't see that the road had dipped. I lost my balance, sliding down the incline several yards before crashing into a metal guardrail. I grimaced from the pain and tried not to scream. I lay there for several seconds, angry at myself for not being more careful, before getting back on my feet and trudging ahead.

I came to a bend, and several yards ahead, barely distinguishable in the falling snow, I saw a dark figure standing on the side of the road. I was saved! However, as I approached this figure, I could not understand why this person had not seen me or been alerted to my presence. When I got right in front of the figure, I saw it wasn't a person. It was a Buddhist statue.

A hollow, rhythmic wooden sound broke the silence. It started out low and sounded like someone tapping two pieces of wood together, which was eerie and peaceful. The sound increased in tempo and volume and appeared to be coming from somewhere around the bend. Following the sound, I hastened up the road until what appeared to be a Buddhist temple, built on the side of a hill, suddenly materialize out of the falling snow. Coming from inside one of the buildings was the source of the tapping sound I heard — someone inside who might be able to help me.

I hurried under an intricately designed and vibrantly pink, green, and blue-colored wooden gate — set on top of two stone pillars interwoven with dragons — and up a stone staircase which led to several wooden buildings. Overhead, metal wind chimes, suspended from wooden eaves painted with colorful geometric patterns, gently tinkled in the swirling snow. I entered the largest building, equally designed and brightly colored, as was the gate — embellished with the wooden heads of two dragons on the front and a row of painted Buddha images along the top — through a blue, four-paneled wooden lattice door. Inside the chilly, dimly candle-lit room, I found an elderly Buddhist monk, dressed in a padded gray robe, standing in front of an altar and a golden Buddhist statue, tapping a wooden bell — carved to resemble a fish — with a wooden stick. Pink and green lotus-shaped lanterns hung from the dark wooden rafters. The warm, woody odor of incense hung heavy in the cold air, mingled with the musty smells of old books and the sweet fragrance of freshly cut chrysanthemums.

Startled by my presence, the monk stopped tapping and stared at me with a confused expression on his weathered, ruddy face.

"Help me!" I said, hoping that my frantic attempt to communicate with him would alert him to the danger I was in. "There's a man after me. He's already murdered several people."

The monk drew his thick brows together and cocked his bald head.

"Please! Help me." I pointed to the door I had just entered. "He's not far behind!"

Alarmed by my second outburst, the monk set the wooden bell and stick down on the altar and moved toward the door I had entered.

"No, No, No! You don't understand. This man, he's after—"

A shot rang out.

The next thing I knew, the monk, who had been standing in front of the entrance, fell back, clutching his chest. I dove to the floor and took cover inside the entrance, not far from where the monk lay. A dark red stain spread across the front of his robe. He drew in several labored breaths, his chest slowly rising and falling before he died.

I stared at the body of the monk on the floor. Another person dead because of me. If I hadn't come here, the monk would still be alive. But then I'd probably be dead or not too far from it. Right now, I had to figure a way out of here. There was a side door, which was open. Maybe I could somehow get around to the back and find a way out. But to get to it, I had to first cross in front of the entrance where the monk lay. I closed my eyes and took a deep breath. I did a silent count, one, two, three, and then sprinted to the open door.

Another shot rang out, but the aim was wide to the right. The round hit a vase of white chrysanthemums, just missing me by inches, in an explosion of white petals and shards of green celadon. Once outside, I ran to the back of the building, which had been built against a rugged outcropping, part of which had been hollowed out by natural forces creating a grotto filled with tiny Buddha figures and a metal altar—more importantly, though, a way out of here. Next to this grotto were steps leading up the hill behind the temple. I had maybe a minute or two before Chun realized I was no longer inside and had escaped around the back.

I scrambled up the snow-covered steps and came to the top of the hill, which had been leveled, and a Buddhist altar erected. In the center stood a tall, grayish-white stone Buddha statue surrounded by stone lotus flowers. There was no other way up or down this hill.

Dammit. A dead end.

Or so I thought.

Through the darkened snow-covered boughs behind the statue, I saw what appeared to be rough-cut stone blocks poking through the snowdrifts along the top of the ridgeline. Yes! It was the fortress wall I had seen earlier! If I could follow the wall back to the gate I had passed through earlier, I could find my way back to the farmhouse and get the hell out of here.

But I wasn't out of the woods yet.

Even if I made it back to the farmhouse, I still had to get back to the city. If I were lucky, I might be able to take Kang's or Park's car. But where would I go once I got there? Who would I talk to? And who was going to believe me? I thought about the military checkpoint Park and I had passed through last night. That would be the best bet. But then what? I could see myself back in another police station, going through the same interrogation process again.

To reach the ridgeline and the fortress wall, I had to climb down the side of a ravine. Once on the bottom, I stumbled along a dry stream bed, slipping over snow-covered boulders and stones of various sizes. I looked over my shoulder once, but there was no sign of Chun. Either he couldn't keep up with me, or he had already figured out what I had intended to do and was going to flank me. The only way I would find out was once I reached the ridgeline.

Once I started back up the hill on the other side of the stream bed had crossed, it took me several minutes to climb to the ridgeline and the fortress wall. In the distance, I could barely make out the fortress gate in the falling snow. I caught my breath and hurried down the ridgeline toward the fortress gate. The thick snow muffled all sounds except my heavy, labored breathing. The ridgeline dipped and rose in several spots, forcing me to hold onto the wall to avoid losing my balance. Just below the path I walked along, jagged rocky outcrops presented a formidable danger if I were to fall.

I looked over my shoulder once to see if Chun had indeed followed me to the back of the temple, but there was no sign of him. Thankfully, the rocky spine I traversed along the fortress wall evened out after a while and did not slow me down despite the deep snow.

Unfortunately, I didn't see part of the wall that had crumbled until it was too late. My right foot got stuck between two stone blocks, causing me to lose balance. I saw the ground flash past my face as my legs flipped up in the air, then all I could see was white. For a moment, I couldn't tell up or down and where I was in relation to anything else. And then my full weight came crashing to the ground, the momentum pitching me down the slope. The snow offered little cushion. In a frantic attempt to stop my slide, I tried to grab onto something, flailing with my arms until I grabbed hold of a bush sticking out of the snow. Clinging to the bush, I lay there for several seconds catching my breath and holding onto that bush for dear life. Tired, cold, wet, and scared, how much more would I have to endure before this nightmare was over? I expected Chun to show up anytime and end it right here for me.

You've got this, Turner.

I reached deep inside myself for the last trickle of energy and pulled myself up, praying to God that the little bush would support my weight until I found a foothold. Then, I clawed my way to the top.

With no time to rejoice in my small victory, I pushed on, close to collapsing from exhaustion, hoping that I hadn't lost any valuable time.

THIRTY-TWO

CHUN GREW ANGRIER AND ANGRIER BY THE MINUTE AS HE trudged through the deep, wet snow. This wasn't a soldier he was chasing. It was a damn English teacher. He was angry at himself for missing the opportunity to take care of him back in Seoul. And then, when he followed Park and Turner all the way out here, Kang had a backbone after all and a conscience to match, showing up at the farmhouse and complicating, at least for the moment, everything. It was his own damn fault for being soft and not getting rid of Kang earlier.

Even though Kang and Park were dead, he was out here, running around in the foothills of Pukhan Mountain and freezing his ass off while chasing down the American. One thing was for certain, he looked forward to putting a bullet in him and ending this once and for all.

If the American somehow eluded him, which was a very big if, there would be nothing he could do to stop him from going to the police. And once he did, every cop on this side of the Han River would be after him for killing Park. There was no way he was going to let that happen.

On the other hand, if he could kill Turner and put the gun in his hand, maybe the police would think Turner committed the murders.

Chun stopped to catch his breath. Six people dead already. One more, and it would be seven. Lucky seven. He chuckled at the morbid thought. Of course, it was all that bitch's fault. If she hadn't stumbled upon him in the back room of the Paradise Club, he would be in bed all nice and cozy, perhaps with one or two of the hostesses from the club at the Tower Hotel.

Of course, there was Kwon. Even though Kwon had been like a father to him, there was no way he would give him a pass for the heat that killing Park and Kang would bring—even if he didn't learn about the drugs. Killing Kang, maybe, given that Kang had enough dirt on him and Kwon to bury them both. But, Park? No fucking way. Given the alternative, he would rather have the police catch him than Kwon.

Nonetheless, it was time he made his move against his boss. It wasn't exactly how he had envisioned it happening, but with everything that had transpired over the past several days, he had no choice. Kwon might have been old and weak, but he still had a lot of muscle in the city. Not that Chun was afraid of the other men Kwon had working for him, but when he made a move against his boss, he had to do it right.

He felt terrible about the monk, though. When he saw the American run into the temple, he didn't expect the monk to emerge first. That was just bad luck for the monk and lousy karma for him. But there was no time for karma now. That was a debt for another day.

After the American had slipped away by running out the back of the temple, Chun figured he would try to make it back to the farmhouse or the park entrance. It was pointless to try to follow him along the ridgeline. Besides, there was only one way out of here. His best bet now was to backtrack to Daeseomun Gate, the entrance to the fortress, and wait there. Once he had taken care of the American, there would be no loose ends. Of course, he still had a mess to clean up back at the farmhouse, but that was the least of his worries right now.

The snow continued to come down hard, slowing down his progress. He could barely see more than a few meters ahead. But rest assured, if the weather was slowing him down, it was also slowing down the American. It was a good thing the weather was as bad as it was. Usually, the park and trails would be swarming with early morning hikers. It was the perfect cover for the ghastly deed he had to do.

When this was all over, and it would be over soon enough, he would visit one of his favorite bathhouses for a hot soak and a massage. Then, he would call on Kwon and take care of him and anyone else who got in his way.

When he reached the fortress gate several minutes later, he climbed up to the top and waited underneath the tiled roof. From here, he could see anyone approaching the gate from the road, the ridgeline, or the valley below. All he had to do was get close enough to the American.

Damn, it was cold. He pulled up the collar on his overcoat and stamped his feet, but that did little to alleviate the shivers which rushed through his body. At least he was out of the blowing snow.

Come on, where the hell are you?

Chun had felt cold like this once before; not long after he ran away from the orphanage and came to Seoul. Before he started working for Kwon. It was the dead of winter, and he ended up living in the ruins of an office building destroyed during the war. Two kids died from exposure that winter. One of the kids, Pyong-ho, who had become Chun's best friend, died in his sleep. In the morning, he took Pyong-ho's jacket off his dead body. The sleeves were too short, but Chun didn't mind. At least he was warm.

Thinking about Pyong-ho after all these years made him sad. He recalled that South Korean soldiers had killed his friend's parents, suspecting them of being Communist sympathizers. There was a lot of that going on back then. They just got caught in the middle and died for it. Besides Kang, who lay dead back at the farmhouse, Pyong-ho was the only other real friend he had.

Chun got Pyong-ho's image out of his mind and gripped the revolver he had shoved into his coat pocket. The American would be here soon.

He would not have to wait long.

THIRTY-THREE

THROUGH THE FALLING SNOW, I COULD SEE THE OUTLINE OF the fortress gate ahead. Just another fifty yards. So far, so good. I just might make it out of here after all. But I was overcome with fatigue. Each step through the deep snow took all the energy I had left, as if my feet were weighed down with lead weights.

Fifty more yards and I would be home free.

I got about ten yards from the fortress gate when a figure stepped out from behind the columns supporting the tiled roof.

Chun.

He pointed the revolver at me. There was nowhere for me to run, even if I could.

"Now it's just you and me." He was out of breath, his eyes wild with anger.

After everything I had been through, it came down to this. There was not a damn thing I could do. I closed my eyes.

Our Father, who art in Heaven, hallowed be Thy name....

An eerie silence settled around me in the falling, swirling snow, but the ear-slapping explosion I expected from the revolver in Chun's hand did not come. Instead, the silence was broken by a loud, bone-crunching thwock. When I opened my eyes and stared at Chun, his face was frozen in fear. Chun opened his mouth as if to scream, but whatever sound he tried to make was stuck in the back of his throat. The revolver slipped out of his hand and fell to the ground. His eyes rolled back into his head. His knees buckled, and his body went limp before crumpling to the snowy ground.

Behind him stood a Korean man in a gray down jacket holding a pickax handle. The smooth, light brown handle was stained with Chun's blood and a clump of hair.

To my left, two figures materialized from out of the falling snow and walked up to the man holding the pickax handle and Chun's body. One of these men, an older man in a long, dark overcoat, grabbed the pickax handle from the first man's hand and brought it down on Chun's back. He chopped left and chopped right. Chun turned his body and raised his arms to fend off the blows but could not. Down, the pickax handle came again. Left and right. The sickening sound of bones cracking and breaking filled the air, intermingled with Chun whimpering for the older man to stop. Left and right again.

When the older man was finished, he handed the bloody pickax handle to the first man and located the revolver in the snow. He checked to see if there were any remaining rounds in the chamber. Chun continued to whimper for several seconds before the older man stood over Chun and fired the remaining round into Chun's head.

I turned and vomited.

"Are you hurt?" the older man asked, standing. He handed the revolver to one of the men standing behind him.

I stared at Chun's body on the ground. The snow around his body had turned a deep red.

"Are you injured?"

I looked up at the man and shook my head. I wiped off my mouth with the back of my left hand.

"My name is Kwon Yong-ho," the man said. He took off his gloves and held out his hand.

I reluctantly shook his hand, still stunned by what had

happened, and then dropped my hand to my side. "I don't understand."

"Chun used to be in my employment. He had become a vulnerability and a liability." Kwon went through the pockets of Chun's jacket and pants. He removed Chun's wallet, a Rolex wristwatch, and a diamond-encrusted ring and shoved them into a pocket on his overcoat. When Kwon was finished, his two men rolled Chun's body off the top of the fortress and down to the rocky ravine below.

I stared at Chun's broken, battered body, which had landed crookedly on a large boulder at the bottom of the ravine. Anger coursed through my veins. Thoughts flooded my mind in a kaleidoscope of images: Joo-hee's lifeless body on her bed, Shin zapping me with the cattle prod, and Park's interrogation methods. Kang threatening me with the death penalty. And Moon, poor Moon. The only person who believed me ended up dead trying to help me.

"We have to go now," Kwon said, taking me by the arm. "The park will be swarming with police soon."

Still in shock, I silently gazed at the man who had murdered Chun. Who was this Kwon, and where was he taking me? What kind of work did he do to employ someone like Chun? Then I remembered something Kang had said that Chun was involved with some crime boss. I couldn't understand why Kwon was helping me. If he had been worried about Chun being a liability, I was just as much a liability. I just watched the man brutally beat Chun to death.

On the other hand, what choice did I have? I watched one of Kwon's men clean the bloody pickax handle in the snow.

"Please, Mr. Turner. We go now."

How did he know my name? How did he know where to find me?

"Yes, yes. I understand. We have to leave now."

We walked to the fortress gate and climbed down. Soon, we were walking down the road I had hurried up earlier. It had finally stopped snowing, and the sun poked through the dark gray clouds.

Along the way, we passed several middle-aged Korean men and women dressed in brightly colored hiking outfits walking up the road in single file.

Kwon and I were silent for a few seconds until this group was out of earshot.

"How did you know—"

"Where to find you?"

I nodded.

Kwon filled me in on how he suspected Chun had been responsible for the murder of Joo-hee. He also knew about Chun and Kang working together and the drugs. However, it wasn't until he heard about me in the news, followed by the death of Moon, that those suspicions were confirmed.

"We followed him here, but it was too late by the time my men and I got to the farmhouse. We found a police officer outside. He was shot up badly."

"Park."

"Who?"

"Detective Park Chong-hun."

Kwon nodded. "One of my men attended to him."

News that Park was still alive surprised me. "He wasn't dead?"

"No."

"There was another man. Kang."

Kwon shook his head. "He didn't make it."

Although Kang had been ready to ask for the death penalty, not to mention ready to serve me up to Chun, I actually felt bad that he ended up dead. After all, if he hadn't warned Park and me, both of us would lie dead back at the farmhouse. And shit, the guy had a family and all.

"When we couldn't find you or Chun, we figured you had tried to escape, and Chun chased after you. We were right."

"Lucky me."

One of Kwon's men had gone ahead and gotten Kwon's black sedan and was waiting for his boss when we came to the main road. His driver got out of the vehicle and opened the back door.

"Is there anywhere I can take you?"

"Chamsil."

"Good. Get in."

I climbed into the backseat with Kwon, and the car slowly started down the road. Kwon and I were quiet for several minutes. I looked out at the snow-covered countryside, my first real glimpse of Korea. The sun broke through grayish-white clouds, punctuated by patches of powder-blue sky. Snow glistened like diamonds on the roofs of stone and wooden farmhouses. With boughs weighed down with snow, the tips of evergreen trees touched the ground, forming tiny, lacy green and white igloos. Lost in thought, when the car came to an intersection, two police cars and two ambulances with their lights flashing and sirens wailing passed in front of us, shaking me from my reverie. I could only imagine the shit that would hit the fan again.

"Here, drink this. It will make you feel better." Kwon said, taking out a flask from the inside pocket of his jacket and handing it to me.

I took a small, exploratory sip of the pale amber liquid inside the flask. It had a medicinal taste, something like some syrupy stuff I had been forced to swallow as a little kid. I grimaced as the liquid burned its way down my throat. I took another drink, which went down smoother than the first, and soon felt the warmth of the liquid spreading through my body. It also did wonders for my nerves and helped to calm me.

"The police will most likely question you. What you want to tell them is up to you," Kwon said. "But being you and I have no business together in what has happened here today, I trust you will say the right thing."

Sitting in the backseat of the black sedan with a man who I had just seen put a bullet into the skull of his employee—I was in no position to argue. Of course, the police would want to question me about Park and Kang. I would have to get my story straight. Again.

There was no way Keith or anyone else, for that matter, who was going to believe what had happened. I wasn't even sure if I believed it myself. I could only imagine the meeting I would most likely have with Gilbert and the Director. Not even forty-eight hours after our first meeting, I'd be back sitting in the Director's office telling him how sorry I was for fucking up again. Not that any of this was my doing, but as Gilbert and the Director said in our first meeting, the school had a reputation to maintain. One of the school's teachers involved in a shootout with an organized crime member, which also involved a police officer and prosecutor, would do wonders for that reputation. I'd be lucky if I wasn't fired on that spot.

I thought about Chun's battered body lying at the bottom of the ravine and how close I came to ending up at the bottom of that same ravine. I shuddered and took another drink from the flask before handing it back to Kwon.

And then I thought about Joo-hee. That's how this all started. Funny how fate controls our lives. Had I not gone looking for Keith that night, how much of what happened would not have been set into motion? Chun would still have gone to the club that night to confront Joo-hee. She still might have been murdered by Chun that night, or maybe another night. Moon would still be alive, as would Chun and Kang, and the monk back at the temple.

Kwon took out a thin, gold case about the size of a pack of cigarettes from an inside pocket in his jacket. He opened it and handed me his business card. On one side, the information was in Hangul, but the flip side was in English: Kwon Yong-ho – Exports. Itaewon, Seoul.

"If you ever need anything, like a custom-made suit or a mother-of-pearl jewelry box, I can fix you right up," Kwon said. "No charge."

"I'll keep that in mind."

"And if you ever have any problems while you're here, I have a lot of friends in high places."

"What was that?" I said.

"If you need anything else while you're here, Mr. Turner, you may call."

"Oh, yeah. Of course. Thanks."

I gazed out the window as we neared the outskirts of Seoul.

Everything looked the same but different this morning. In the distance of the clear morning sky, I could see the tops of some of the taller buildings in the heart of the city. Seoul Tower rose to greet me again.

After multiple near-death experiences and a nation of people wanting me to die, you'd probably think I'd want to get on the first plane back to the States. But there was nothing there for me other than what I was supposed to do—find a girl, a job, a place to rent. All of those things are far more interesting here. For better or worse, this was now my home. It was now up to me to make the most of it. No matter where I am, no one can promise me tomorrow. I'm never going to give away today again.

ACKNOWLEDGMENTS

I would like to thank my family for all their love and support while working on this novel. It would be an understatement to say I couldn't have done it without their support. They are my rock and my pillar of strength.

ADDITIONAL BOOKS BY JEFFREY MILLER

War Remains

Damaged Goods

Ice Cream Headache

When a Hard Rain Falls

I'll Be Home For Christmas

The Panama Affair

The Roads We Must Travel

Bureau 39

The Day the Earth Swallowed Louis

The Hatchet Man

ABOUT THE AUTHOR

Jeffrey Miller has spent over three decades in Asia as a university lecturer and writer, including six years as a feature writer for *The Korea Times*, South Korea's oldest English-language newspaper. Originally from LaSalle, Illinois, he relocated to South Korea in 1990, where he nurtured a love for spicy Korean food, Buddhist temples, and East Asian History. He is the author of eight novels and two collections of short stories. His first novel, *War Remains*, won first prize in literary fiction from the Military Writers Society of America in 2011. Other works include *Ice Cream Headache*, *Bureau 39*, *The Day the Earth Swallowed Louis*, and *The Hatchet Man*.